THE GOD WALKS . . .

A deep and dreadful twilight had fallen over Borea. Eastward, the clouds boiled down, like an inverted ocean hurled by a volcano of the upper air.

Suddenly the clouds raced away, roaring with thunder voices, hastening one another with lashes of lightning. And finally de Marigny saw why they fled in such chaotic panic . . .

For now He came, striding down from vaults of space as a giant descends an invisible stairway, falling out of the sky on great webbed feet, glaring down on the white waste through huge carmine stars that burned as the fires of hell themselves in His darkly daemonic head. ITHAQUA THE WIND-WALKER WAS BACK ON BOREA!

IN THE MOONS OF BOREA

BRIAN LUMLEY

A JOVE/HBJ BOOK

Jove/HBJ books are published by Jove Publications, Inc.
(Harcourt Brace Jovanovich), 757 Third Avenue, New York,
N.Y. 10017

For the "Old Folks" at No. 25.

Contents

PART ONE: *BOREA*

Chapter One

Paths of Fate

THEY SKIRTED the forest on foot, the Titan bears shambling along behind on all fours, their packs piled high so that there was no room for the men to ride. Only three of the animals went unburdened, and these were hardly bears for riding. A stranger party could scarce be imagined. Here were bronze Indians straight out of Earth's Old West, squat, powerful Eskimos from the Motherworld's perpetually frozen north, great white bears half as big again as those of the Arctic Circle, and a tall, ruggedly handsome, leather-clad white man whose open, short-sleeved jacket showed a broad, deep chest and arms that forewarned of massive strength.

To the oddly polyglot party that followed Hank Silberhutte, their Warlord seemed utterly enigmatic. He was a strange, strange man: the toast of the entire plateau and master of all its might, mate to Armandra the Priestess and father of her man-child, destroyer of Ithaqua's armies and crippler—however briefly—of Ithaqua himself. And yet he mingled with his minions like a common man and led them out upon peaceful pursuits as surely as he led them in battle. Yes, a strange man indeed, and Ithaqua must surely rue the day he brought him to Borea.

Silberhutte the Texan had been Warlord for three years now, since the time he deposed Northan in a savage fight to win Armandra. He had won her, and with her the total command of the plateau's army. That had been before the War of the Winds, when the plateau's might had prevailed

11

over the bludgeoning assault of Ithaqua's tribes, when Ithaqua himself had been sorely wounded by this man from the Motherworld.

Mighty wrestler, fighter who could knock even a strong man senseless with a blow of his huge fist, weapons' master whose skill had quickly surpassed that of his instructors, telepath (though the plateau's simpler folk could not truly understand the concept) who could throw—had thrown—mental insults at Ithaqua, the Wind-Walker, and yet walk away unscathed: Silberhutte was all of these things. He was as gentle as his strength and size would allow; he instinctively understood the needs of his people; when lesser men approached him in awe, he greeted them as friends, equals; he respected the Elders and was guided by their counseling, and his fairness was already as much a legend as his great strength.

When he could by right have slain Northan, his hated, bullying Warlord predecessor—when nine-tenths of the plateau's peoples had *wanted* Northan dead—Hank Silberhutte had let him live, had given him his life. Later, when Northan turned traitor, siding with Ithaqua and his icepriests to help them wage war against the plateau, Kota'na the Keeper of the Bears had taken that life, had taken Northan's head too; and even though he was wounded in the fighting, Kota'na would not give up his grisly trophy to any man but his Lord Silberhutte.

And it was Kota'na who came now at an easy lope through the long grass toward where Silberhutte stood, Kota'na, whose proud Indian head was lifted high, eyes alert as those of any creature of the wild. He had scouted out the ground ahead, as two other braves even now scouted it to the rear; for though they were well clear of the territories of the Wind-Walker's tribes, still they were wary of skulking war parties. The Children of the Winds did not usually wander far afield when Ithaqua left them to go striding among the star-voids, but one could never be sure. That was why three of the bears were not in harness; they were fighters, white monsters whose loyalty to their masters was matched only by their ferocity when confronted with their enemies. Now they were nervous, and Hank Silberhutte had noted their anxious snufflings and growlings.

He noted too Kota'na's uneasiness as the handsome

brave approached him. The Indian kept glancing toward the dark green shadows of the forest, his eyes narrowing as they sought to penetrate the darker patches of shade. Borea had no "night" as such, only a permanent half-light, whereby shaded places were invariably very gloomy.

"What's bothering you, bear-brother?" Hank asked, his keen eyes searching the other's face.

"The same thing that bothers the bears, Lord Sil-ber-hut-te," the Indian answered. "Perhaps it is just that Itha-qua's time draws nearer, when he returns to Borea . . . ," he shrugged. "Or perhaps something else. There is a stillness in the air, a hush over the forest."

"Huh!" the Texan grunted, half in agreement. "Well, here we camp, danger or none. The forest goes on for twenty miles or more yet, Kota'na, so if we're being shadowed, we won't lose our tail until we're beyond the woods. We'll keep five men awake at all times; that should be sufficient. Six hours' sleep, a meal, and then we press on as fast as we can go. Fifty miles beyond the forest belt we'll be back in the snows, and we'll find our sleighs where we left them. The going will be faster then. Fifty miles beyond that, across the hills, we'll sight the moons of Borea where they hang over the rim. Then—"

"Then, Lord, we will be almost within sight of the plateau!"

"Where a pretty squaw called Oontawa waits for her brave, eh?" the white giant laughed.

"Aye, Lord," Kota'na soberly answered, "and where the Woman of the Winds will doubtless loose great lightnings to greet the father of her child. Ah, but I am ready for the soft comforts of my lodge. If we were fighting, that would be one thing—but this dreary wandering . . ." He paused and frowned, then: "Lord, there is a question I would ask."

"Ask away, bear-brother."

"Why do we leave the plateau to wander in the woods? Surely it is not simply to seek out strange spices, skins, and tusks? There are skins enough in the white wastes and more than enough food in and about the plateau."

"Just give me a moment, friend, and we'll talk," Silber-hutte told him. He spoke briefly to the men about him, giving instructions, issuing orders. Then, while rough tents

13

were quickly erected and a list for watch duties drawn up, he took Kota'na to one side.

"You're right, bear-brother, I don't come out under the skies of Borea just to hunt for pale wild honey and the ivory of mammoths. Listen and I'll tell you:

"In the Motherworld I was a free man and went wherever I wanted to go, whenever I wanted to go there. There are great roads in the Motherworld and greater cities, man-made plateaus that make Borea's plateau look like a pebble. Now listen: you've seen Armandra fly—the way she walks on the wind—a true child of her father? Well, in the Motherworld all men can fly. They soar through the skies inside huge mechanical birds, like that machine that lies broken on the white waste between the plateau and Ithaqua's totem temple. He snatched us out of the sky in that machine and brought us here. . . ."

He paused, beginning to doubt Kota'na's perception. "Do you understand what I'm trying to say?"

"I think so, Lord," the Indian gravely answered. "The Motherworld sounds a fine and wonderful place—but Borea is not the Motherworld."

"No, my friend, that's true—but it could be like the Motherworld one day. I'm willing to bet that hundreds of miles to the south there are warm seas and beautiful islands, maybe even a sun that we never see up here in the north. Yes, and I can't help wondering if Ithaqua is confined to this world's northernmost regions just as he is during his brief Earthly incursions. It's an interesting thought. . . .

"As to why I come out here, exploring the woods and the lands to the south: surely you must have seen me making lines on the fine skins I carry? They are maps, bear-brother, maps of all the places we visit. The lakes and forests and hills—all of them that we've seen are shown on my maps. One day I want to be able to go abroad in Borea just as I used to on Earth."

He slammed fist into palm, lending his words emphasis, then grinned and slapped the other's shoulder. "But come now, we've been on the move for well over ten hours. I, for one, am tired. Let's get some sleep, and then we'll be on our way again." He glanced at the gray sky to the north and his face quickly formed a frown. "The last thing I want is to be caught out in the open when Ithaqua comes walking down the winds to Borea again. No, for he surely has a score to settle with the People of the Plateau—especially with me!"

In no great hurry to find Elysia (Titus Crow had warned him that the going would not be easy, that no royal road existed into the place of the Elder Gods), Henri de Marigny allowed the time-clock to wander at will through the mighty spaces between the stars. In the case of the time-clock, however, "wander" did not mean to progress slowly and aimlessly from place to place, far from it. For de Marigny's incredible machine was linked to all times and places, and its velocity—if "velocity" could ever adequately describe the *motion* of the clock—was such that it simply defied all of the recognized laws of Earthly science as it cruised down the lightyears.

And already de Marigny had faced dangers which only the master of such a weird vessel might ever be expected to face: dangers such as the immemorially evil Hounds of Tindalos!

Twice he had piloted the time-clock through time itself; once as an experiment in the handling of the clock, the second time out of sheer curiosity. On the first occasion, as he left the solar system behind, he had paused to reverse the clock's temporal progression to a degree sufficient to freeze the planets in their eternal swing around the sun, until the worlds of Sol had stood still in the night of space and the sun's flaring, searing breath had appeared as a still photograph in his vessel's scanners. The second time had been different.

Finding a vast cinder in space orbiting a dying orange sun, de Marigny had felt the urge to trace its history, had journeyed into the burned-out planet's past to its beginnings. He had watched it blossom from a young world with a bright atmosphere and dazzling oceans into a mature planet where races not unlike Man had grown up and built magnificent if alien cities . . . and he had watched its decline, too. De Marigny had recognized the pattern well enough: the early wars, each greater (or more devastating) than the last, building to the final confrontation. And the science of these beings was much like the science of Man.

They had vehicles on the land, in the air, and on the water, and they had weapons as awesome as any ever devised on Earth.

. . . Weapons which they used!

Sickened to find that another Manlike race had discovered the means of self-destruction—and that in this instance they had used it to burn their world to a useless crisp—de Marigny would have returned at once to his own time and picked up his amazing voyage once more. But that was when he was called upon to face his first real threat since leaving Earth's dreamworld, and in so doing, he went astray from the known universe.

It was strange, really, and oddly paradoxical; for while Titus Crow had warned him about the Hounds of Tindalos, he had also stated that time's corridors were mainly free of their influence. Crow had believed that the Hounds were drawn to travelers in the fourth dimension much like moths to a flame (except that flames kill moths!) and that a man might unconsciously attract them by his presence alone. They would scent the id of a man as sharks might scent his blood, and it would send them into just such a frenzy!

Thus, as de Marigny flew his vessel forward along the timestream, he nervously recalled what Crow had told him of the Hounds—how time was their domain and that they hid in time's darkest "angles"—and in this way he may well have attracted them. Indeed he found himself subconsciously repeating lines remembered from the old days as he had seen them scribbled in a book of Crow's jottings, an acrostic poem written by an eccentric friend of Crow's who had "dreamed" all manner of weird things in connection with the Cthulhu Cycle Deities, or the "CCD," and similarly fabled beings of legendary times and places. It had gone like this:

Time's angles, mages tell, conceal a place
Incredible, beyond the mundane mind:
Night shrouded and *outside* the seas of space,
Dread Tindalos blows on the ageless wind.
And where the black and corkscrew towers climb,
Lost and athirst the ragged pack abides,
Old as the aeons, trapped in tombs of time,
Sailing the tortuous temporal tides . . .

And even as he realized his error and tore his thoughts from their morbid ramblings—as mental warning bells clamored suddenly and jarringly in the back of his mind—de Marigny saw them in the clock's scanners . . . the Hounds of Tindalos!

He saw them, and Crow's own description of the monstrous vampiric creatures came back to him word for word:

"They were like ragged shadows, Henri, distant tatters that flapped almost aimlessly in the void of time. But as they drew closer, their movements took on more purpose! I saw that they had shape and size and even something approaching solidarity, but that still there was nothing about them even remotely resembling what we know of life. They were Death itself—they were the Tind'losi Hounds—and once recognized, they can never be forgotten!"

He remembered, too, Crow's advice: not to attempt to run from them once they found you, neither that nor even to use the clock's weapon against them. "Any such attempt would be a waste of time. They can dodge the beam, avoid it, even outdistance it as easily as they outdistance the clock itself. The fourth dimension is their element, and they are the ultimate masters of time travel. Forward in time, backward—no matter your vessel's marvelous maneuverability or its incredible acceleration—once the Hounds have you, there is only one way to escape them: by reverting instantly to the three commonplace dimensions of space and matter. . . ."

De Marigny knew now how to do this and would ordinarily have managed the trick easily enough, but with the Tind'losi Hounds fluttering like torn, sentient kites about his hurtling vessel, their batlike voices chittering evilly and their nameless substance already beginning to eat through the clock's exterior shell to where his defenseless id crouched and shuddered . . .

And so he made his second mistake—an all-too-human error, a simple miscalculation—which instantly took him out of his own timestream, his own plane of existence, leaving him dizzy and breathless with the shock of it. For he had not regained the three-dimensional universe measured and governed by Earthly laws but had sidestepped into one which lay alongside, a parallel universe of marvels and mys-

17

teries. One moment (if such a cliché is acceptable in this case) the Hounds of Tindalos were clustered about the time-clock, and the next—

—They were gone, and where they had been, an undreamed-of vista opened to de Marigny's astounded eyes! This was in no way the void of interstellar space as he had come to know it, no. Instead he found himself racing through a tenuous, faintly glowing gray-green mist distantly rippled with banners of pearly and golden light that moved like Earth's aurora borealis, sprinkled here and there with the silver gleam of strange stars and the pastel glow of planets large and small.

And since his own senses were partly linked with those of his hybrid vessel, he also detected the eddies of an ether wind that caught at the clock to blow it ever faster on an oddly winding course between and around these alien spheres. A wind that keened in de Marigny's mind, conjuring visions of ice and snow and great white plains lying frozen fast beneath moons that bloated on a distant horizon. The moons of Borea . . .

Chapter Two

Paths Cross

"LORD SIL-BER-HUT-TE! Hank! Wake up, Lord!"
Kota'na's urgency, emphasized by his use of the Warlord's
first name, brought Hank Silberhutte to his feet within his
central tent. A moment later he stepped out into the open,
shaking sleep from his mind, gazing skyward and following
Kota'na's pointing finger. All eyes in the camp were turned
to the sky, where something moved across the heavens with
measured pace to fall down behind the horizon of forest
treetops.

The Warlord had almost missed the thing, had witnessed
its flight for two or three seconds only; but in that short
time his heart, which he believed had almost stopped in the
suspense of the moment, had started to beat again, and the
short hairs at the back of his neck had lain down flat once
more. Borea was no world in which to be out in the open
when there were strange dark things at large in the sky!

But no, the aerial phenomenon had not been Ithauua, not
the Wind-Walker. If it were, then without a doubt Silberhutte's party had been doomed. It had certainly been a
strange and alien thing, yes, and one that aught surely not
to fly in any world. But it had not been the Lord of the
Snows.

"A clock!" Silberhutte gasped. "A great-grandfather
clock! Now what in the—" And his voice suddenly tapered
off as memory brought back to him snatches of a conversation which had taken place (how many years ago?) in the
home of a London-based colleague during the Wilmarth

Foundation's war on the CCD, the "Cthulhu Cycle Deities," in Great Britain. At that time Silberhutte had not long been a member of the foundation, but his singular telepathic talent had long since appraised him of the presence of the CCD.

Titus Crow had been a prime British mover in that phase of the secret confrontation, and at the home of the learned leonine occultist Silberhutte had been shown just such a clock as had recently disappeared over the treetops. A weirdly hieroglyphed, oddly ticking monstrosity whose four hands had moved in sequences utterly removed from horological systems of Earthly origin. By far the most striking thing about that clock had been its shape—like a coffin a foot taller than a tall man—that and the fact that there seemed to be no access to the thing's innards, no way into its working parts. It was then that Titus Crow had told Silberhutte:

"I'm taking a chance that you'll perhaps think me a madman, my friend—certainly it will be a test of your credulity—but in any case I'll tell you what I think the clock really is. It is a gateway on all space and time, a vessel capable of journeying to the very corners of existence and beyond. That's my belief. One day I'll learn all there is to know about the thing. When I do . . ." And Crow had paused to shrug and smile, adding: "But that is all in the future. At the moment I may rightly compare myself to an ape attempting to fathom the splitting of the atom!"

Yes, Crow had called the clock a gateway on all space and time, a bridge between worlds—between universes!

Silberhutte stared out across the forest roof where the clock had disappeared, and suddenly he was taut as a bowstring, incredible hope springing up in him, flaring bright where he had believed hope to have all but faded away. Could that thing in the sky—that coffin-shape so briefly glimpsed—could it possibly . . . ?

"What is it, Lord?" Kota'na asked, his voice low, hushed. The Keeper of the Bears was worried. He had never seen the Warlord stirred by such emotions before. Silberhutte's gaze burned—like a great hound straining at the leash, he seemed to lean toward the forest—and his fists had tightened into huge knots which he held half-raised before him.

Again Kota'na spoke: "Was it some terrible toy of the Wind-Walker, Lord?"

"No, I don't think so." And the great white Warlord suddenly relaxed, took a deep breath, turned to grasp Kota'na's shoulders. "Bear-brother, I want you to come with me, you and two others and a bear. Quick as you can, choose the other men now. We get under way at once. The rest can break camp and head for home with all speed."

"But—where are we going, Lord?"

"Into the forest," Silberhutte answered at once. "Where else? If that flying thing is what I think it is—by *God!*—bear-brother, if only it is!" He gave a great cry and threw his arms wide.

"Yes, Lord?" prompted Kota'na. "What then?"

"Then?" and Silberhutte's eyes were deep as the spaces between stars. "Then, Kota'na, the Motherworld may not be as far away as I thought."

De Marigny set the clock down in a glade beside a pool. There was a curious absence of vegetation about that pool, and if he had been more observant, he might have noticed, as his vessel slowly descended and came to rest, a peculiar bluish *withdrawal* of something or things into the water. Before leaving the safety of the clock, he scanned the forest around him: no slightest thing moved, no birds called. That, too, might have warned him—did in fact caution him to a degree—but what could there possibly be to fear? He would only leave the clock for a few moments, and it would never be more than a pace or two away.

His reasons for coming down here, at a fair distance from the encampment of primitives he had viewed from on high, were threefold. One: he wanted the humanoid natives of this world to have time to think about what they had seen, to assimilate the fact that the clock had done them no harm, before taking a closer look at them or trying to contact them. Two: following what felt like a thousand attempts to leave this alien time dimension into which he had erroneously entered, he was feeling fatigued. All of his efforts to leave had failed miserably, highlighting his inadequate beginner's grasp of the clock's refinements; now he wanted to rest both mind and body before trying yet again. And three: the pool had looked inviting and refreshing, the glade peaceful and quiet, and the forest itself had seemed to offer green walls of protection, looking for all the world like the familiar forests of Earth.

Only now, stepping out through the clock's open frontal panel, did de Marigny become aware of the odd texture of the soil in the glade, its unnatural feel, crumbly and lifeless. A dozen or so paces took him to the water's edge where he went down on one knee, failing to note as he did so that the glade seemed to grow quieter still. Not a ripple disturbed the surface of that pool, and yet it failed to mirror the man who kneeled at its rim. He paused—his hand poised ready to dip, inches above the surface of water which carried an odd bluish tinge—and the quiet deepened tangibly. Now he felt it: the tension in the air, the sensation of a trap ready to spring shut!

He threw himself back and away from the pool, sprawling in the crumbling soil, scrambling frantically away from water which was suddenly alive with awful activity. The surface frothed and parted and lumpish blue shapes slithered over de Marigny's booted feet, fastening to his legs through the thin material of his trousers. Half-lizard, half-leech, eight inches long and shaped like flatworms or bloated tadpoles, there were thousands of the blue-veined creatures.

The water boiled with them, these *things* whose appetites had stripped the glade of life. De Marigny tore them bloodily from lacerated limbs, kicked frantically back from the pool toward the clock where it stood behind him, gasped for air as shock and horror gripped him. The farther he struggled from the pool, the less certainly they slithered after him; but their lidless red eyes regarded him evilly and their razor mouths gaped hungrily. Finally he stripped the last of them from his legs, scrabbled upright, and turned to the clock—only to stumble into the arms of an apparition out of his wildest nightmares!

Wolf-headed and terrible the figure stood, arms encircling him, staring from wild wolf eyes into his own fear-taut features. Now he saw that the figure was human and only dressed in the trappings of an animal, and that others similarly adorned surrounded the clock and gazed impassively at him. They were like Red Indians out of old Earth, and the eyes that stared from wolf heads were anything but friendly.

De Marigny mustered his strength to twist under and out of the bronze vise that held him and made a dive for the clock's open, greenly lit panel—only to be met in midair by the flat of a tomahawk that hurled him into a black pit of oblivion. . . .

De Marigny's return to consciousness was slow and painful. His eyes felt full of ground glass behind closed and swollen lids. He barely stifled a cry of anguish when he tried to open them, then abandoned the attempt for the time being and concentrated instead on regaining a measure of orientation. This was far from easy for there was a roaring in his ears that came and went in regular pulses, bringing red-peaked waves of pain and surging nausea. As his mind began to clear, he tried to think, to remember where he was and what had happened, but even that small effort seemed to splash acid around inside his skull.

Very slowly the red burning died away, was replaced by an awareness of a sickly chill creeping into muscles and bones already cramped and stiff. He forced back the bile that rose suddenly in his throat and tried to lick parched lips, but his tongue met only sand, dry and tasteless. His teeth were full of the stuff; he gagged on it. Rolling his head weakly, dizzily to one side and freeing his mouth, he spat out grit and blood and what felt like a tooth, then fought to fill his lungs with air. One nostril was full of sand, the other sticky and warm with blood.

Anger surged up in de Marigny—at the stupidity of this dazed, slothful body which would not obey his commands—at his dull mind because it refused to answer his questions. Where the hell was he? What had happened to him? He seemed to be lying facedown in coarse-grained sand or loose soil—

Then, in a series of vivid mental pictures, memory flooded back. Scenes flashed before his mind's eye: of the glade in the forest and the pool of leech-things; of the barbaric, wolf-headed warriors standing in a ring about the time-clock.

The time-clock!

If anything had happened to—

He gritted his teeth, lifted his head to shake it free of sand, then bit his lip and fought off the fresh waves of pain his actions brought. He blinked and was glad of the stinging tears that welled up to wash his eyes, even though he was blinded by the light that they admitted. It had a weak light, this strange world, true, but painful for all that and filled with a thousand bilious fireball flashes.

Nausea returned immediately, forcing him to close his eyes again. The scene he had so briefly gazed out upon—of a greenly shaded background above a sandy expanse—faded quickly from his tortured retinas, was replaced by a dull red throbbing that brought a groan of pain and despair from battered lips. Plainly he had suffered a brutal beating and kicking even after being knocked unconscious.

He wondered if there were something wrong with his limbs; while they gave him no great pain, still he could not move them. Could it be his attackers had crippled him? Again he tried to move and finally discovered the truth: his wrists were bound behind his back, and his feet were tied at the ankles. His neck, too, must be in a noose of some sort; he had felt it tighten when he shook his head. Grimly he considered his position. Having tired of their sport with his unconscious body, his tormentors had obviously staked him out—but for what purpose?

Then de Marigny thought again of the hideous pool-things and the way the slimy coloring of their internal juices had given the pool its unnatural bluish tinge, and suddenly he found himself wondering if—

He forced his eyes open again, slowly this time, to let them grow accustomed to the light, and gradually the scene before him took shape. He lay in something of a shallow depression with his chin buried in coarse sand, the soil of the silent forest glade. Beyond his immediate horizon was a more distant one of shaded greens, the forest wall at the far side of the pool. De Marigny shuddered, and not at all because of the cramped chill steadily creeping into his bones.

Turning his head carefully to the left, he saw a stretched leather thong that reached out from his neck to where it was tied to a peg driven deep into the soil. He was similarly tied down to the right. Since he could not move his legs at the knees, they too must be tethered. He struggled briefly, uselessly, then slowly and methodically began cursing himself for a fool. To have been so utterly careless, so criminally stupid as to get himself into a mess like this. It was unthinkable!

Disgusted with himself and with his predicament, he nevertheless attempted to analyze his desperate mistake. He believed he knew how it had come about.

His adventures in Earth's dreamworld—the terrible threats and dangers he had faced and conquered there, until it had seemed he must be almost indestructible—had lulled him into a state of false security. How *could* he have come through so much only to fall prey in the end to the primitives of some nameless planet on the rim of reality?

What angered the Earthman more than anything else was the fact that he was wearing the cloak brought back by Titus Crow from Elysia, an antigravity device which allowed the wearer to soar aloft as effortlessly as any bird. He was sure that in the dreamworld his reactions would have been instinctive: to reach for and activate the buttons in his harness that would have lifted him instantly to safety. But here in this strange new world . . . things had simply seemed to move too fast for him.

If only he might free one hand and reach the controls of his cloak, he had no doubt that—

Any further thoughts of escape were aborted, driven from his mind the instant that he caught sight of a pulsating, blue-veined leech-thing that suddenly came slithering over the rim of the hollow in which he lay. It saw him at once, tiny red eyes fixing upon him hungrily, jellyish body throbbing as the creature slid and slithered down the slight declivity toward his face.

Frozen in horror, de Marigny could only think: "My face—*my eyes!*" But even as the pulsating leech reared up in front of him, inches away, and even as a dozen or so more of the awful things appeared almost simultaneously over the lip of the hollow, still he could not avert his gaze. Hypnotized and immobilized by his unthinkable situation, by the fate about to descend upon him, de Marigny could only watch and wait for it to happen, and—

—The earth shuddered beneath him as a leather-booted foot came down on top of the menacing leech-thing in the moment that it made to strike for his face. Its juices splashed him as it was ground into the moistureless soil.

A second later and the silver blade of a wicked picklike weapon flashed down once, twice, and the thongs that tethered de Marigny's neck were severed. He felt cold metal touch his wrists and his hands were free, his legs too. Another second and—amazing sight!—a snarling, coughing mountain of white fur, a bear almost eleven feet tall, shambled swiftly into view, stomping the now retreating leech-things and shaking the ground with its massive weight.

Then, before the astounded Earthman could even muster his thoughts to consider these miraculous developments, he was hauled gently but irresistibly to his feet. Left to stand on his own, weak and bloody as he was, de Marigny might well have fallen, but steely arms supported him and keenly intelligent eyes stared into his own first in concern, then in recognition.

He stared back—stared even harder—then gasped and shook his head in dizzy disbelief. Finally he managed to mumble: "Hank? Hank Silberhutte? I don't—"

"Neither do I, Henri," the Texan interrupted, "but I'm glad to see you anyway."

"The feeling," de Marigny wholeheartedly, bone wearily agreed, "is mutual, Hank, to say the very least!"

He gazed then at Silberhutte's brawny companions—two bronze-skinned Indians and an olive Eskimo—and at the monster bear which stamped and roared now at the edge of the pool. "But where in all the corners of space and time are we?"

Knowing that the newcomer to Borea was suffering from shock, Silberhutte carefully released him, nodding in satisfaction as de Marigny staggered a little but somehow managed to stay on his feet. "We're on Borea, Henri, one of the worlds of an alien universe. I've been here some time now, since Ithaqua brought me here. And you . . . well, I saw your arrival. So Crow was right about that old clock of his, eh?" The effect of Silberhutte's words on the other man was immediate and electric.

"The clock?" de Marigny's jaw dropped and the color drained from his face. "The time-clock!" He whirled about, staggering wildly, his eyes frantically searching the glade for his fantastic machine.

In the sand he saw a deep indentation where the clock had stood; leading from it, twin tracks cut deep grooves in the gritty soil, terminating where they entered the abrupt shade of the forest. Beyond, a trail of crushed leaves and grasses led away into the undergrowth. Again de Marigny whirled, once more facing Silberhutte and his polyglot companions.

"No, no!" he cried, shaking his head in denial. "I've *got* to get the clock back. I—"

But finally he had exerted his already overtaxed body and mind beyond their limits. Bright lights flashed inside his head as, with unspoken protests still whispering on his lips, he reeled and toppled. Already unconscious, he was not to know how easily Silberhutte caught him up in massive arms to bear him out of the glade and away from the pool of the leech-things.

Chapter Three

The Pursuit

DE MARIGNY DREAMED of ice stars and planets, all frozen in galactic glaciers that flowed out of deepest infinities of lost dimensions. The Hounds of Tindalos chased him along corridors of ice between razor-sharp cliffs that reached blue-rimmed needles high overhead. Without warning an avalanche of huge, jagged ice splinters crashed down upon him, cracking the time-clock open like a nutshell and spilling him out onto the ice. The Hounds were on him at once, black rags of death whose lusting, ethereal feelers found and held him fast. He fought madly to escape them, but—

—He threw his arms wide and awakened with a cry of horror, only to find himself held down by Silberhutte's huge, strangely cold hands. The Texan held him until his body relaxed, only then allowing him to fall back into a deep warm bank of furs. De Marigny felt the furs move against him and saw that his head rested against a forepaw as big as a real pillow. The warmth he felt was the body heat of Silberhutte's vast bear! He instinctively drew away from the creature where it reclined beside him on the forest's floor.

"You were cold," Silberhutte explained from where he kneeled beside him. "Morda was the only one who could warm you. Kota'na has rubbed you with the body grease he uses. Morda won't harm you—he thinks you're the bear keeper's little brother!" The grin quickly faded from the

28

Texan's face as he asked: "How do you feel now, Henri? The wolf-warriors gave you a pretty rough time."

"Wolf-warriors? Yes, they certainly did," the other slowly answered, "but I feel better now." He licked his lips and frowned at an unfamiliar but not unpleasant taste.

"Kota'na got a little soup down you and some of his tea," Silberhutte explained. "The tea is good; it would straighten out a corkscrew!"

"My head still feels a bit loose," de Marigny answered, "but apart from that . . . I expect I'll live." He stood up unaided and the great bear's paw closed possessively around him. He carefully extricated himself as Kota'na approached and ordered the bear up onto its feet.

"Morda," Silberhutte informed, "is not normally very gentle with anyone. He's trained for the fight. It seems you've found a firm friend there, Henri."

Staring after the towering creature as Kota'na led it away, de Marigny answered, "I would hate to be his enemy!"

He took hold of the Texan's arm. "Hank, I have to get after the time-clock. It's my one way out of here. All explanations, everything I would like to know—questions you must surely be wanting to ask me—will have to wait. The time-clock is—"

"—All important, Henri?" Silberhutte finished it for him. "Yes, I know. To me, too. I'm as much a prisoner here on Borea as you are, and I've been here that much longer."

"Then I'll be on my way now, at once."

"Now? On your own?" Without malice Silberhutte laughed. "You don't seem to understand, Henri. There isn't any way you can get the clock back on your own. Even if you could, they'll be miles away by now."

"Do you think so? Dragging the time-clock behind them? Why, the thing must weigh a ton, Hank! They'd need to be superhuman."

"You didn't see their wolves, then?"

"I saw their wolf masks—but behind them they were only men."

"Oh, yes, the wolf-warriors are men, Henri. Ithaqua's people, the Children of the Wind. But I was talking about their wolves: creatures big as ponies—bred as mounts, as

29

beasts of burden—and some bred to kill! We found the party's tracks, and there were wolves with them, big brutes, too. They'd easily pull that clock of yours. Yes, and there are other reasons why we can't simply go chasing after them. Ithaqua is due back on Borea at any time now, and when he returns we must all be safely back in the plateau."

"Hank," de Marigny answered, "I accept all you say, though I don't understand half of it as yet, but . . ." he paused. "Look, I've no time to explain, so I'll simply show you. You see, Titus Crow used the time-clock to journey to Elysia, and when he returned, he brought back something with him. He brought this." He opened his cloak wide.

"Your cloak? I don't see what—"

"Do you see now?" De Marigny touched the large studs that looked merely decorative where they were set in the leather of the cloak's harness. He rose slowly at first, then shot skyward through the branches of the surrounding trees.

Now it was Hank Silberhutte's turn to stare in amazement. He knew only too well that Ithaqua could walk on the wind, as could his daughter Armandra. But this was Henri-Laurent de Marigny, a common man of Mother Earth. And yet here he soared aloft on the wind as surely as any hawk!

"All right, Henri," he called out to the man who glided now above the treetops, performing intricate aerial maneuvers. "You've convinced me. Come on down."

De Marigny alighted a moment later to find Silberhutte standing on his own. His three companions kept well back, coming forward only when they were sure that the man in the cloak intended no more immediately foreseeable flights, and they now regarded him with something akin to awe. Morda stood behind them, padding from one gigantic hind foot to the other in seeming agitation. The bear, too, had witnessed de Marigny's flight.

"I'm convinced," Silberhutte repeated. "Convinced that you stand a slight chance . . ." He reached out to touch the deceptively strong fabric of the cloak. "What kind of weight can this thing carry?"

"The weight of two men," de Marigny answered at once. "It's speed is reduced by extra weight, of course, but even so—" He paused, stared hard at Silberhutte, then said,

"Whatever it is you're thinking, forget it, Hank. You've done enough already."

"I've done nothing, old friend. And listen: I've as much interest in the time-clock as you yourself. What's more, I know something of Borea, and a whole lot more about the Children of the Winds. You'll stand a far better chance of getting the clock back with me along. Yes, and while we're on the trail of the clock, I guess we've a lot to talk about. We both have tales to tell."

For a moment, considering Silberhutte's suggestion, de Marigny made no answer. He looked into the eager, honest eyes of this white giant, a man tall as Titus Crow himself but broader yet. Without question Silberhutte must be formidably strong. And did not his companions treat him with the utmost respect, and they themselves men obviously well versed in the arts of combat?

Finally he said, "All right, Hank, and glad to have you along. But first we'll have to make you a seat or sling of some sort that we can suspend from the cloak's harness. There's just a bit too much of you for me to carry like a babe in arms for any great length of time."

An hour later, after a meal of smoked meat, bread, and wild honey washed down with richly spiced tea, the two were ready to take their departure. While they had eaten, Umchak the Eskimo had worked with leather barely mature, fashioning a seat which, attached to the cloak's harness, would hang immediately beneath de Marigny where he himself floated in the spread of the cloak's canopy.

First they tested the cloak's strength. In ascending, it was very slow, and descent was deceptive in that the "brakes" had to be applied that much sooner, but in level flight the loss of speed was not so great as de Marigny had feared. Maneuverability, however, was an almost total loss. Carrying two men, the contraption was simply too cumbersome to perform any but the most rudimentary routines of flight.

Eventually de Marigny was satisfied that he could handle the cloak adequately under the circumstances, and then they descended to say their farewells to the three who breathlessly waited below. De Marigny wrapped himself in a warm fur from Kota'na's pack while Silberhutte delivered his final instructions to his retainers. Moments later, as de

Marigny hovered only a few feet above the forest's floor, Silberhutte again climbed into his own makeshift harness and they were off.

As they rose up through the forest, Kota'na called: "And if we get back to the plateau before you, Lord, how shall I tell the Woman of the Winds what you are about?"

"Tell your mistress what you know," Silberhutte shouted down.

"She may well be displeased, Lord, that I return without you."

"Then tell her that you keep only the bears, Kota'na—that the Lord Silberhutte is his own man. Now begone—and all speed to you, bear-brother . . ."

And with that they were away, climbing above the tree-tops to circle once, twice, before setting a course that followed the way the wolf-warriors had taken.

At first they flew close to the treetops, descending occasionally to ensure that they still followed the course of the twin ruts in the forest floor that told of the clock's passing. But soon they were able to climb a little higher as the trees below thinned out and the trail became that much easier to follow. By then it was apparent that they followed a course which circled to the east, back toward the territories of It-haqua's tribes, those lands bordering on the great white plain which lay south of the impregnable plateau.

The miles were quickly eaten up beneath them, and as they went, their elevation offered a view of great beauty and mystery. To the north the peaks of a low range showed white heads above belts of gray cloud, behind which the moons of Borea were hidden except for their uppermost rims. To the south the green forest extended unbroken until hidden by distance and a wall of mist that rose until it merged with the far gray sky. Flying over rivers and lakes, they told of the adventures each had known since last he saw the other.

De Marigny related the fantastic story of how he had gone to the assistance of Titus Crow and Tiania the girl-goddess in Earth's dreamworld; Silberhutte in turn told of all that had transpired since Ithaqua bore him away from Earth's icy northern mountains to Borea; and so they grew to know one another. They had been merely distant col-leagues in the old days, meeting on no more than two or three occasions. That had been at a time when the ancient but increasingly imminent threat of the CCD had drawn so many fine men together, though there had been little enough time to spare for the founding of firm friendships.

And as time passed and they talked—or rather, as they half-shouted at each other, for they had to make themselves understood above the hum of the wind in their ears—so the terrain below changed. The trees thinned out until only the occasional pine stood up from banks of coarse grass and weeds, and finally even the last of these lone trees faded away into the distance behind them.

By then they were heading in a mainly northerly direction, still following the twin ruts where they left their mark in grasses and soil below them, and de Marigny had noticed a degree of tension creeping into Silberhutte's voice, a tautness about him where he hung in his harness directly below the cloak and its flier.

When the big Texan stopped talking altogether and began to pay even more attention to the ground only ten to twelve feet beneath him, de Marigny was prompted to ask: "Is something wrong, Hank?"

"Yes," the Texan answered. "They must have joined forces with a second party along the way. There are more wolves now and about nine men. That will make things more difficult for us. Also we've been flying for at least two hours. Given that we're traveling at four or five times their speed, or very nearly so, and taking into account that the woods back there must have slowed the wolf-warriors down considerably, they can't be all that far ahead. See up front there, that narrow belt of shrubs at the foot of the hills? It's my bet that—"

He paused for a split second and froze in his harness, then cried: "Henri, get us up—*get us out of here!*"

Chapter Four

Ambush!

TOO LATE de Marigny saw what Silberhutte had seen: a pair of wolf-warriors rising from behind covering clumps of grass. Between them, shaking off loose grasses and twigs which had been strewn over it to give it camouflage, a great wolf suddenly sprang erect. Not even in his wildest dreams had de Marigny ever imagined the existence of such a beast!

With the eyes of a wolf, yellow and gleaming, and the same lolling tongue, the thing stood as tall as a pony but yet had the low-slung frame of a wolf. Indeed it was a wolf—but its head was the size of a horse's head!

The cloak was on a course which would take the fliers immediately over the heads of the ambushers. Seeing this, de Marigny began slowly to climb, banking to one side as the cloak strained to gain height. He heard Silberhutte yell some incoherent instruction or warning, and at the same time saw the stroboscopic flash and glitter of tomahawks already twirling through the air. He saw, too, the tensing of shaggy-furred muscles as the great lean monster on the ground prepared itself to spring.

One of the razor-honed tomahawks barely grazed de Marigny's ankle as it whistled harmlessly by. The other was inches lower, slicing something that twanged, sagged momentarily, and then snapped. De Marigny had only sufficient time to realize that both weapons had been aimed at him, not Silberhutte, before all balance was gone and the cloak began to yaw wildly. At the same time a massive

34

snarling fury launched itself with all the force of steel-spring legs, clawing at Hank Silberhutte where he swung now in only half a harness, and in another moment the cloak and its passengers were dragged swiftly down out of the air.

Then—a kaleidoscope of action. De Marigny was privileged to witness Silberhutte's awesome speed and ferocity. He had been right about the Texan's great strength, but he would never have guessed that so large a man might be endowed with such lightning reflexes.

For even as he struck the ground with the wolf's great paws about his shoulders, Silberhutte had sunk his wicked picklike ax into the beast's shoulder, causing it to leap back away from him with a howl of pain. One of the two Indians, rushing upon them with a spear aimed at de Marigny's middle, found the shaft of his weapon trapped in a giant's fist, wrenched from his hands, driven hiltfirst into his naked belly so that he doubled over in agony. That blow itself, crushing the bronze heathen's organs, must certainly have crippled or even killed him. But to be doubly sure, as he bent forward and his screaming face came down, Silberhutte's leather-clad knee smashed upward to cut the scream short. Face bones, neck, and spine all broke in unison and the rag-thing that had been a man flopped awkwardly over onto its back.

Desperate as he was to get into the fight and go to the Texan's assistance, de Marigny was already fighting his own battle. In fact as he struggled to make the cloak manageable, he was actually obstructing his companion's action, for one leather strap still fastened Silberhutte to the cloak's harness. At last de Marigny regained control of the cloak and commenced a laborious ascent—only to be knocked sideways by a badly aimed swipe from the partly crippled leg of the now limping wolf. Then the thing was astride him, jaws slavering, terrible fangs bared as the fetid muzzle lowered toward his face.

Silberhutte's weapon was a steely blur as he cut himself free of the restraining harness. He bounded onto the wolf's back, hooked the fingers of his free hand into its nostrils, smashed down once with the spine of his terrible weapon. The needlepoint of that picklike tool drove through skull

35

and into brain and the wolf collapsed atop de Marigny with a final, hideous death spasm.

"Get up into the air, Henri!" Silberhutte roared, leaping from the motionless carcass. "It's our one chance. You can try to help me later—but not if it means risking your own life. And don't worry, they won't kill me. They'll be wanting to keep me for Ithaqua. He has one hell of a score to settle with me! Now go on, man—*fly!*"

Fighting free of the dead wolf, de Marigny saw the Texan brandishing his bloody weapon—from which the second of the two redskins shrank back—saw him turn until he faced squarely in the direction of the scrubby bushes at the foot of the hills. Racing from that quarter and no more than two dozen or so flying paces away came a pair of wolves with riders on their backs and a third man clinging between them.

And de Marigny knew that Silberhutte was right. So far the wolf-warriors had not attempted to kill the plateau's Warlord out of hand; he would provide the Wind-Walker with a great deal of pleasure. Any ordinary death he might suffer at the hands of the Children of the Wind would only anger Ithaqua—but certainly they had tried to kill de Marigny! Well, he had no intention of dying just yet.

Now, with mere moments to spare, his fingers touched the control studs and the man in the cloak sprang aloft. Looking down, he was in time to see Silberhutte bowled over by the wolves, spread-eagled by the riders of those beasts as they fell on him in a concerted tangle of thrashing bodies and bore him to the ground. . . .

For what must have been all of eighteen hours (he could only guess at the passage of time in this strange world where night appeared never to fall and the light was little better than that of an early, misty dawn), de Marigny followed the wolf-warrior party, flying above them and to their rear, well out of range of their spears and tomahawks. Unlike the Indians of the Motherworld they did not carry bows; Silberhutte had explained that slender bows broke too easily when Ithaqua was close by, that the drastic fall in temperature his presence invariably occasioned made wood brittle as chalk. Also, in a world where both Armandra and her dread sire—aye, and certain of his ice-priests,

36

too—controlled the winds so marvelously, light and slender missiles such as arrows could all too easily be turned back upon those who dispatched them!

In its entirety the party consisted of four wolves and seven Indians. Between two of the wolves the clock was secured to a travois affair of stout poles with several layers of tough hide stretched between them; Silberhutte was strapped face-down to the shaggy back of one of the other beasts. He had been unconscious for three-quarters of the time, knocked down by the flat of a tomahawk that had all but caved in his skull when the wolf-warriors overran him, and de Marigny had at first feared him dead. When at last he had seen the Texan move, then Silberhutte's aerial colleague had been both vastly relieved and delighted, particularly when the prisoner had turned his head on one side to gaze skyward, nodding his awareness when he saw the cloak belling out like a great kite on high.

De Marigny marveled at the strength of the wolf-warriors that they could go so long without resting. Four rode upon the backs of the wolves while the others half-ran, were half-dragged along beside the animals, their fists knotted in the shaggy hair of the huge beasts' flanks. Periodically they would take turns about riding, but even though they obviously relished this occasional respite, still they seemed singularly tireless. But while the stamina of the redskins was not in question, de Marigny himself was beginning to feel very tired, cold, and hungry. Time and again he thought to bless Kota'na, whose fur he wore so gladly.

Twice he had let the party move well ahead before descending to solid ground and giving himself a little exercise, rubbing the numbness from stiff limbs and shaking the weariness out of a head that still ached abominably. On both occasions he had caught up with the wolf-warrior party easily enough afterward, but now his fatigue was such that he began to despair. Surely they must rest soon, when he too might be able to snatch a little sleep?

But it was not until several more miles had been covered that the party made camp. Silberhutte was bundled down from the wolf's back and given food—the sight of which, whatever it was that the Texan was offered, made de Marigny's mouth water—following which the Warlord's hands were tied again, and he was put into the close care of three guards. The other four Indians immediately settled down on the naked ground and went to sleep, as did the wolves.

De Marigny was amazed at the apparent invulnerability of these men to the cold (even in this more or less temperate zone the temperature was well down), until he remembered what Silberhutte had told him about the Wind-Walker's effect upon those who came too close to him: the permanent alterations his presence wrought in human tissues and body temperatures. This was why the Warlord's hands always seemed so cold while he himself suffered no discomfort in the most bitter conditions. As for de Marigny: he was growing colder by the minute. His one consoling thought was that however bad his plight might seem to be, Hank Silberhutte's was so much more desperate.

As soon as he was sure that the party was settled in for a few hours at least, de Marigny flew off to one flank and sought a place to hide, shelter, and rest. He found it some miles away in a small cave whose entrance was all but covered by scrub, and there he rested down, pulling Kota'na's fur close about him. . . .

When he awakened, de Marigny guessed that he had slept overlong. His limbs were stiff and he was colder than ever. Beating his arms across his chest to get the circulation going, he left his cave and came into the open. Then, with his fur wrapped about him to its best advantage, he took once more to the sky.

To the north the sky was overcast, bearing the merest threat of a storm. When de Marigny had arrived on Borea, he had flown high over the plateau, remembering it now as a grimly foreboding jut of gray rock standing massively up from a vast plain of snow. He knew that it could not be long before he flew back into that region, and that then indeed he would be hard put to survive in such low temperatures. Moreover Silberhutte had told him that was where the Children of the Wind were most densely concentrated, where they worshiped Ithaqua at his totem temple. If the Texan's captors got him that far, then there would be no further hope of rescuing him.

He returned to the now forsaken wolf-warrior campsite, passed it over without pause, and flew on, ever northward, scanning ahead and following the ruts made by the travois's runners. Flying as fast as he could, another twenty minutes saw him entering a region where the terrain began to climb. Up ahead he spied ragged-crested hills and knew that the going must now be that much rougher for the wolf-warriors.

As the hills rose up, their sides grew steeper, filled with gullies and crevasses. Great boulders stuck up here and there on the slopes, with loose shale collected about their bases. Many of the crevasses were deep with jagged sides, their floors deep-shadowed and boulder strewn. The hills were desolate and dangerous.

Then he saw the wolf-warriors. They were ahead of him and higher, their attention fixed upon the problem of getting the time-clock up onto the final ridge. All of them were there, engaged in the same task, and as yet they had not seen him. He alighted, crouched down behind a boulder, and took a longer, closer look at their problem.

Normally they would find little difficulty in scaling these heights—indeed, beyong this final rise they would begin to descend, and it would be that much easier—but they had reckoned without the weight of de Marigny's clock. The thing was incredibly heavy. Once when Titus Crow was studying the weird hieroglyphs on its four-handed dial, it had taken four strong men to move it for him.

Right now three wolves crouched at the top of the ridge. They were roped to the travois, straining to haul it up after them. Strapped to its frame in folds of hide lay the clock, refusing to budge up the rocky incline. Below, levering away at the stubborn device, five of the Indians cursed and shouted and fought to maintain their balance on the difficult surface. A sixth wolf-warrior goaded on the wolves at the top of the ridge, thumping their sides with his naked fists. The seventh and last, the leader of the party, sat on the back of the fourth wolf immediately behind Hank Silberhutte. He sat there level with the travois but on a firmer piece of ground, shouting instructions at the men who labored to do his bidding. Silberhutte, apparently bored by the whole thing, sat silently, his hands tied behind him.

De Marigny saw his chance: a heaven-sent opportunity to fly at the back of the leader of the party and unseat him, then to pick up Silberhutte as best he could and carry him over the ridge to safety. And perhaps if Silberhutte had known that de Marigny was close and that he had a plan in mind, then all might have gone according to that plan. He did not know, however, and the Warlord had his own ideas.

Uppermost in Silberhutte's mind was a determination to make as much trouble for his captors as he possibly could, if only to slow them down until de Marigny could catch up. As a last resort he knew he could call on his woman, Armandra, the Priestress of the Plateau, but not until no other option remained. Armandra was not immortal—a tomahawk or spear could kill her just as easily as they could any other mortal—and quite apart from purely physical dangers, Ithaqua himself was due back on Borea at any time. Thus the Texan kept his mind locked tight, telepathically blank, and prayed that Kota'na and the others would not get back to the plateau before he had somehow managed to escape. If they did, and if Armandra took the notion into her head that he was in trouble, then nothing on Borea would prevent her from coming out after him.

Just as de Marigny was about to make his move, the big Texan half-turned where he sat, drove his elbow viciously into his captor's belly, and toppled him from the wolf's back. Then, somehow, he got to his feet, balanced for a moment on the beast's shoulders, launched himself head-long at the five redskins where they levered at the travois and its burden.

A second later saw complete tumult, with Indians flying everywhere, the two wolves on top of the ridge scrabbling frantically to maintain their positions as suddenly they were obliged to take the full weight of the clock, the leader of the party yelling and screaming where he had fallen to the stony slope, and Silberhutte himself, completely off-balance, hands still tied behind him, slipping and sliding diagonally down the steep incline away from the havoc he had created.

To add to the confusion, with a snapping of thongs and a rending of hide, the clock suddenly broke free. It toppled over and stood for a moment on its head, then crashed down and outward, end over end, in a series of leaps and bounds back the way it had come. Fearing that it would dislodge his sheltering boulder which would then crush him, de Marigny immediately ascended out of the clock's path. This in turn made him visible to the frantic wolf-warriors.

They saw him—and at once the air rang with their savage cries of fury and outrage. He got the impression that they half-blamed him for their present problems.

Quickly rising higher still, de Marigny took in the scene below at a glance. The clock had finally come to rest face-up where its base had jammed against a huge boulder. Already three of the Indians were scrambling down the slope after it. Two more were picking their way toward a wide crevasse. But where was Silberhutte?

De Marigny's heart almost leaped into his mouth when he saw his friend's predicament. For the Texan was stretched out full-length on the perilous slope, facedown and motionless, his head and shoulders already hanging over the lip of the crevasse—and that crevasse yawned at least a hundred feet deep! The toes of the Texan's boots were dug into loose shale which threatened at every moment to slide him headfirst into space, and there was nothing he could do—no move he could make—without precipitating his own death.

De Marigny glanced longingly once more at the time-clock, glared at the Indians picking their way down to it, then turned his attention back to Silberhutte. The shale was beginning to slip. . . .

Suddenly the Texan felt the whole unstable surface moving beneath him. He held his breath, gazed straight down into the abyss, willed himself to remain perfectly still where he had fallen, and offered up a silent prayer to those lucky stars which had ever guided and protected him. The movement beneath him subsided, but not before he had moved out another inch or two over the lip of the crevasse.

He could hear the wolf-warriors cautiously approaching him from the rear but dared not turn his head to look back. If they took him a second time, then in all likelihood he'd end up in Ithaqua's clutches anyway. The pit was greatly preferable to that . . . but the fire of life burned bright in Hank Silberhutte, and it was not a spark easily extinguished.

Now he could feel fingers fumbling at his booted feet, could hear the hoarse breathing of the heathens where they crouched fearfully behind him, precariously perched on the shale. Then—impossible, miraculous sound—he heard a cry from close at hand:

"Hang on, Hank! Just another second!"

De Marigny? *De Marigny!* . . .

Yet even as hope surged up in the Texan, in the same moment he felt the shale move again, and this time there was no stopping it. He slid forward, heard the frenzied shrieks of the redmen as they also began to slide, cursed his useless hands that were bound behind him, finally plummeted into air filled with falling shale fragments.

Only at that very last second did the Warlord close his eyes—for no man likes to see death hurtling upon him—but in the next moment he opened them again as his chin sank into fur and jarred against solid flesh beneath.

Slimly muscular legs wrapped about his waist like a vise as, almost in his ear, that same triumphant voice shouted: "Got you, Hank!"

And de Marigny did indeed have him! The Texan's descent, barely begun, was checked as the cloak took the strain and hovered back away from the sheer face. And not a moment too soon.

Whirling, screaming bronze figures shot past in a thrashing of arms and legs. Then, slow but sure, the cloak bore the two Earthmen up, up into air dark with the pent-up fury of the storm, bitterly cold air that already seemed to carry a faint tang of ozone. A single tomahawk whirled harmlessly by as they sailed up and over the top of the ridge.

Before them lay a valley and beyond that a low mountain range. Already feeling the strain on his legs where they gripped the Texan's waist, de Marigny picked an open area in the valley and headed for it. It shouldn't take too long to fashion some sort of sling or seat for the extra passenger, then they would get on their way again.

For somehow de Marigny knew that time was now of the essence, that any attempt to retrieve the clock must for the moment be aborted, that hideous danger loomed above Borea's lowering sky, and only the plateau could offer any certain refuge. With one supporting arm about Silberhutte's neck he used his free hand to manipulate the studs that controlled the cloak's flight, urging as much speed as possible from that garment of the Elder Gods as it dropped down like a great bird into the valley. . . .

Chapter Five

The Coming of Ithaqua

ARMANDRA, the Priestess of the Plateau, stood high above the white waste and stared down from the plateau with troubled eyes. She saw, tiny with distance, Ithaqua's pyramid throne and the circle of totems that ringed it. Her great green eyes surveyed Borea's bleakest region, the snow plain which not so very long ago had been a battleground in the War of the Winds, but her mind was elsewhere.

In her present mood she was not fit company, and so she had sent her handmaiden, Oontawa, away. Even Tracy, the Warlord's sister, with all her assurances that her brother would come to no harm, had not been able to comfort her; neither Tracy nor her man, James Graywing Franklin, the modern Indian come from the Motherworld with Hank Silberhutte and his party. For the Woman of the Winds was filled with premonition, and the golden medallion she wore at her throat seemed to grow more chill against her milky skin with each passing moment—which was a strange sensation for a woman to whom even the most frigid temperatures made for no slightest measure of discomfort.

The trouble was that Hank Silberhutte was away from the plateau; that and the fact that Ithaqua, Armandra's alien father, was due to return shortly to this wintry world. Aye, and knowing that the Wind-Walker must soon come, still the plateau's Warlord saw fit to keep his mind closed to her. Anger flared momentarily in Armandra's breast, and the small gusts of wind that came into this lofty aerie to play with the fringes of her fur jacket stood off, grew still, as the merest tinge of carmine flecked her great eyes.

But what use to be angry about the Warlord, this man from the Motherworld who ruled her heart as surely as she ruled the plateau? What use even to love him, when all he could think of in Ithaqua's absence was to be out and exploring the woods and lands beyond the mountains? A fine father for their child, this man, whose willful nature was already apparent in his offspring.

Then she softened. Ah, but the boy would have Hank's strength, too, and perhaps something of his mother's powers. Not too much of the last, Armandra secretly hoped, for powers such as these must eventually bring him into conflict with his monstrous grandsire, that hellish Old One who even now walked the winds between the worlds as he returned to Borea from undreamed-of wanderings.

She stood on a natural balcony of rock high on the plateau's face. Behind her a smoothly hewn corridor ran around the inside of the plateau's rocky perimeter. In the one direction it led to the mazy, multilevel tunnels, caves, dwellings, and stairways of the plateau's honeycombed interior, in the other to her own and the Warlord's private and luxurious chambers. Armandra stared out between thick bars which alone separated her from a vertiginous drop to the foot of the plateau. The bars were set wide apart, allowing the winds free entry, which was as well for they loved her and were her subjects.

Yet now, with a raised finger, she instantly hushed their humming and wailing to cock her head on one side in an attitude of listening.

Nothing. . . .

Still she cautioned the winds in their play, clenching her fist tight about the medallion where she wore it, searching in its sensitive alloys for those dread vibrations which were ever precursory of Ithaqua's coming. And again . . . nothing. But in her heart Armandra knew that he must return very soon, and that before then the Warlord must be back in her arms.

And where *was* the Warlord? He had not opened his mind to her since finding the newcomer from the Motherworld staked out by the leech pool in the forest. Armandra frowned when she thought of that newcomer—of him, and

45

of the strange vehicle which had brought him to Borea. In the Warlord's mind when he spoke to her, she had detected a hidden interest in that strange device, that "time-clock" . . .

Armandra was no fool. She knew well enough that if one man could use such a machine to enter Borea, then that another might surely use it to leave this World of the Winds if he so desired. "A gateway between all the worlds of space and time"—that was how her man had described de Marigny's machine: "A vehicle of the Elder Gods."

And again she frowned. . . .

She wondered who this stranger was, this Henri-Laurent de Marigny, of whom it seemed the Warlord had knowledge in the Motherworld. And did all men of Earth have such long, strange-sounding names? Suspicion and panic rose up in Armandra like a tide. What if he had come to Borea to take Hank away in his flying machine? What if they were already gone, away from Borea and out into the ether currents that wash between the worlds?

She trembled where she stood. No—she could not believe that—it wasn't so. But then where was he? Again she sent her thoughts out across the bleak white waste, threatening thoughts which she well knew she could never action:

"You—Warlord—father of my child. Do you not know my pain? Are you so heartless that my concern for you, which wounds me, means nothing? Explain yourself, husband, or I swear I'll send a wind to blow you off Borea forever!"

"Eh? What's this?" the answer came back immediately, like joyous laughter in Armandra's mind. *"Do you greet me with lightnings, Armandra?"*

"I greet you with—with my entire self, great fool! Oh, Hank—where have you been? What have you been doing, and why has your mind been closed to me for so long? Yes, and where are you now—and how long before you return?"

Armandra sent a host of mental questions surging out to him, demanding to know everything. And then, before he could put his own thoughts in order, she continued with yet more questions: *"And where is the newcomer's 'time-clock' now? Do the wolf-warriors have it still? I hope so, for only*

46

*one person has ever had the power to walk on the wind in
Borea. I am that person, and I am jealous of my power."*

"Oh?" the Warlord's thoughts finally found their way
through her telepathic barrage. *"Is that so, wife? And what
of your father's kite-men?—and what of Ithaqua himself?"*

"The kites are crude," she answered, *"and could not fly
without my father's breath in their sails. As for the Wind-
Walker: I was talking about people, human beings. Would
you call Ithaqua a human being?"*

"No," Silberhutte agreed, *"never that—he's totally inhuman. But in any case you're mistaken, Armandra. For you
see, Henri also walks on the wind, and this flying cloak
which bears him up is no clumsy kite!"* And he opened up
his mind to let the Priestess of the Plateau see through his
eyes where he soared along, high over the white waste,
seated on a huge knot of leather at the end of hastily
plaited thongs that were fastened to de Marigny's harness
where he flew the cloak above him.

*"Do you see, Armandra? You're not the only one who
can fly. De Marigny flies, too. Yes, and so do I!"* Without
malice, with love, Silberhutte's thoughts laughed in Armandra's mind.

For a moment she was dumbfounded by the vision his
mind had opened for her. It was not the time-clock she had
seen but some other device—a flying cloak. First a flying
coffin, now a flying cloak! And how many more surprises
did this man from the Motherworld, this de Marigny, have
in store? Armandra stood high in the plateau's wall and
searched the horizon minutely for the peculiar flying shape
which she knew must soon come into view, for the visitor
in his flying cloak, who now bore her own man safely back
to her.

"As for your other questions," the Warlord continued,
*"I'll try to answer them now. I went off with Henri—the
two of us flying the cloak—to track down the wolf-warriors
and get the time-clock back. Well, things went wrong and
they caught me. Henri rescued me, saved my life. As to
why I closed my mind to you: as long as there was any
danger or the chance of danger I wouldn't let you see what
was happening. I didn't want you leaving the plateau for
my sake at a time when Ithaqua's return is imminent.
And—"*

"Ithaqua!" she cut him off, her own thoroughly alarmed thoughts turning his aside. *"Oh, no—NO!"* And high on her rock-cut balcony she clutched at the medallion cradled in the hollow of her neck where it had begun to vibrate in sympathy with the Wind-Walker's approach.

"What is it, Armandra?" the Warlord anxiously questioned, half-knowing the answer even before she dared express it in thought. *"Is he—?"*

"Yes, Hank," she cried, her thoughts awash with waves of fear—fear for her man out above the white waste, flying over Ithaqua's own territory at this very moment—*"he's coming back! Oh, Hank, hurry! My father comes, striding down the winds to Borea even now!"*

Now she could actually see the fliers, a double dot in the sky over Ithaqua's temple, growing larger by the second. Silberhutte had closed his mind to her yet again—perhaps to urge more speed from the man who flew the cloak, more likely to isolate himself from Armandra's mind should her dread father appear on the scene too soon, when the Warlord's thoughts would probably be the last he would ever think—and so the Priestess of the Plateau scanned the far, misted horizon for a larger, darker shape.

Then her eyes detected a movement on the plain southwest of the plateau: the shape of a snow-ship sent out earlier to patrol the far western edge of the white waste and keep a lookout for Silberhutte's party as that band returned. Since the warriors who manned the ship would not return empty-handed, Armandra knew that Kota'na and the rest of her husband's chosen men must be aboard.

She shuddered. So now there would be two targets for Ithaqua when he came: the snow-ship and the flying cloak. Wasting no more time in useless fretting, ignoring the now insistent throbbing and humming of the medallion about her neck, Armandra closed her eyes and lifted up her bare arms until they were horizontal, pointing with her index fingers out over the white waste.

Slowly, eerily, her long red hair floated up over her head, drifting lazily, weightlessly above her. Her face became suffused with a carmine tinge that brightened steadily as it burned out from beneath closed lids. The bones of her skull began to show through her flesh like an X-ray picture, and twin carmine stars blazed where her great eyes had been. Now she herself drifted up from the rocky floor, long legged, straight-backed, regal as a materpiece of some fantastic macabre sculptor, her hair and head ablaze with an inner light.

A moment later, coming suddenly upon her from the corridor at her rear, an Eskimo watchkeeper from the roof of the plateau stopped dead in his tracks at the fearful sight of his sovereign in the act of commanding the winds. Seeing that Armandra was already aware of all that transpired, without daring to disturb her in any way, he bowed himself out backward and hurried back the way he had come.

His skin crawled with the sensation of unseen energies, powers of air and space that concentrated now about Armandra, held as yet in check by her, ready to leap in obedience of her slightest command. . . .

"Henri, we're in big trouble," Silberhutte shouted up to the man who flew above him. De Marigny barely heard the other's words before they were snatched away by squalling winds which seemed to howl now from every corner of the sky. He held the cloak on course as steadily as he could and glanced down to see the Texan twisting this way and that where he hung suspended, scanning the sky and shaking his whipping hair out of his eyes.

"Is it Ithaqua?" de Marigny shouted back.

"Yes, and any time now. Look at the sky—there, to the east!"

De Marigny looked as bidden—and saw a fantastic, freakish thing. The sky itself seemed acrawl with sentient, *deliberate* motion.

The clouds, white and gray and a mixture of both— heavy nimbostratus and wispy cumulus alike, from all strata of Borea's atmosphere—were being drawn, sucked toward some central point. It seemed to de Marigny that he gazed upon a huge whirlpool in the sky, a cauldron of boiling clouds. More strongly yet the winds howled and rushed, threatening now to drag the cloak and its passengers, too, toward that portentous and awe-inspiring aerial phenomenon.

In a matter of seconds the sky became still darker and angry, until it was as if a deep and dreadful twilight had

49

fallen over Borea. Now the clouds jostled and careened above, blue-black and laced with brightly flickering traceries of electrical fire; while eastward, at the center of the tumult, there seemed to be a great, continuous explosion taking place in the upper atmosphere. The clouds boiled down and outward from that point, like an inverted ocean hurled back by the emergence of a volcano of the upper air, except that where the cone should be, only an area of clear sky now showed.

The clear patch rapidly enlarged as, suddenly, the clouds took flight. They raced away from that spot, writhing and roaring their terror with thunder voices across Borea's tortured heavens, hastening one another with lashes of lightning. And finally de Marigny and his passenger saw *why* the clouds fled in such chaotic panic. . . .

For now he came, striding down from vaults of space as a giant descends an invisible stairway, falling out of the sky on great webbed feet, glaring down on the white waste through huge carmine stars that burned as the fires of hell themselves in his darkly demonic head.

Ithaqua the Wind-Walker was back on Borea!

Chapter Six

Traitor Winds

"HENRI, can you get us out of here?" Silberhutte's shout fought the shrieking wind, reaching up to the man who piloted the cloak.

"I can get closer to the ground," de Marigny yelled back. "Try to stay close to whatever cover there is. But there's no way we can make more headway. Perhaps he won't see us."

"Not much hope of that. He doesn't miss a thing. But look over there—the snow-ship. That'll be Kota'na and the rest of my men." The Warlord paused to let the shrieking of the wind die down a little, then continued: "That ought to give Ithaqua a tiny problem: which target to pick off first!" Unwittingly he had echoed Armandra's own thoughts.

Now the Old One's temple stood to the rear, and as the cloak dropped toward the white waste, so snow and ice crystals came up in stinging flurries to greet it. The temperature had dropped alarmingly, and de Marigny was sure that he must already be suffering from exposure. He could barely feel his fingers where they worked at the control studs, and his beard, hair, and eyebrows were rimed with frost.

With only three or four miles to go now to the plateau, still that looming refuge of rock seemed a thousand light-years away. De Marigny's exhaustion was reaching a critical stage, and he could barely keep his eyes open in the blast of ice crystals that rushed and eddied over the surface of the white waste. Occasionally, through breaks in the flurries, he would catch a glimpse of a great wedge-shaped ship that sailed on three massive skis across the icy surface half a mile to his left, but it was becoming too much of an effort to do anything other than control the cloak as it was rocked and buffeted by gust after gust of frigid air, snow, and diamond-hard particles of ice.

Then Ithaqua's shadow fell over them as they flew, and looking up, de Marigny was spurred to greater effort as he stared into the gigantic face of that living doom called the Wind-Walker. What did the old Eskimo legends of Earth say? That to gaze into Ithaqua's eyes was to be damned forever? Well then, de Marigny knew he was damned, and moreover that the threatened doom would not be too long in coming.

Hideously anthropomorphic, the Old One stood in a sky from which all clouds were totally fled now. He stood there, impossibly still, on a half-mile-high pedestal of thin air, peering down through eyes which had narrowed to the merest carmine slits.

"My God," de Marigny thought to himself. *"He's seen us!"*

But no, three-quarters obscured by snow flurries as they flew low over the surface, the Wind-Walker had not seen them . . . yet. But he had seen the snow-ship and knew it to be of the plateau. The flaring, bottomless pits which were his eyes opened up wide, and his monstrous black blot of a head rocked back in an attitude of crazed laughter. His whole body shook with silent, lunatic glee—but in the next moment he was still and cold once more.

Slowly the vastly bloated figure reached a taloned hand into the sky where clouds were already forming, materializing even as he moved. His hand reached into the new-formed cloud bank, withdrew holding a huge ball of ice! Lower the Wind-Walker stepped, down an invisible staircase of frozen air, and his eyes glared more hellishly yet as his arm went back, almost leisurely, in preparation for a throw.

"Get us up, Henri," Silberhutte yelled. "Up, man, where he can see us!"

But de Marigny had already anticipated the other's scheme, had indeed undertaken a rapid ascent on his own initiative; and up above the flurries rode the cloak, up into the view of Ithaqua where he stood poised in midair, a gigantic statue of black ice imbued with monstrous life. And the ploy—however dangerous, however reckless—worked, at least for the time being.

With the plateau no more than a mile distant, making what speed they could against the rushing wind and howling snow devils, the snow-ship and cloak with its two passengers battled their way across the white waste beneath the gaze of the Wind-Walker. And the carmine orbs of his eyes went from ship to cloak as he paused in alien approximation of consternation.

Lower still he stepped, glowing eyes huge and flecked now with sparks of gold, down toward the plain beneath. The snow-ship he finally dismissed with one last searching glance; the cloak—ah!—that was where his real interest was centered.

Ithaqua could hardly credit his good fortune. Unless he was mistaken, the flying device that fled across the snow beneath his burning gaze bore two of his worst enemies, enemies of all the Great Old Ones. Men of Earth, one brought here in great error by himself and the other . . . now *that* was most interesting. Could it be that yet a third male human being—the most hated of all human beings—could it be that he, too, was on Borea? For how else could this earthbound worm beneath, the pilot of the flying cloak, have reached Borea other than in the time-clock of Titus Crow, nemesis of the CCD?

Well then, if Titus Crow were close at hand, there was danger—even for Ithaqua of the Snows, great danger—in the shape of the weapon that Kthanid the Elder God had built into the time-clock, whose ray was as a rapier against the flesh of the CCD. Even now Crow might be rushing to the rescue of the two who rode the cloak. Ithaqua's eyes became carmine slits once more as he thought of Crow. His hand closed into a giant's fist, crushing the ice ball he carried into blue shards that flew in all directions like an aerial bomb burst.

Then his hand opened and reached down; taloned doom that closed on the fleeting pair as an eagle falls to its prey. Utterly impotent to avoid its approach, Silberhutte and de Marigny watched the descent of that vast demon claw, that

53

hand open and reaching to snatch them out of the icy air, to crush them into raw red pulp. And knowing that this must be the end, still the Texan thought to open his mind and send one last blast of telepathic hate in Ithaqua's direction:

"Do your worst, Hell-Thing—for it's what I would do to you given half a chance!"

A great black shadow blotted out the sky as Ithaqua's hand came down upon them, fingers closing. Then—

From nowhere, at the last moment, a whirling snow devil enveloped the cloak, thrust it furiously toward the plateau's now looming rock face. The Wind-Walker's hand closed on thin air, and astounded and enraged, he hurled his arms wide to the skies and screamed silent threats at his minion elementals one of which, obviously in error, had whisked his enemies from his grasp. Again he reached for the pair, more in anger than eagerness this time, but once more they were rushed from his frustrated, bloating fingers by—*by traitor winds!*

The first time might have been a mistake, however stupid a mistake, but not the second. Not twice. Not after his warning. No, this was outside interference. This was . . . Armandra!

Armandra, the Woman of the Winds, Ithaqua's wayward daughter who would not accompany him on his enforced interstellar wanderings. Armandra, the Priestess of the Plateau, who had stepped out through the wide bars of her high balcony to command the winds in defiance of her alien father. And now she too spoke to him with her mind, using that telepathic power she shared with Hank Silberhutte alone, defying Ithaqua as she had ever defied him from where she stood white and wondrous on a pedestal of air in front of the plateau, her arms flung wide to the white waste:

"See, monstrous father mine, how even the small winds turn against you! And you would have me walk beside you on the great winds that roar between the worlds? No, I will stay here on Borea and command the little winds and lightnings when you are away, for while the elementals of air and space and the storm fear you, they have only love for me. Aye, and I for them; but I loathe their master as surely as they do, as surely as I am his daughter!

And now, together with the snow-ship, the men who flew the cloak were also forgotten as Ithaqua gazed upon Armandra. She was within easy reach, facing him squarely, her own eyes as carmine in their starry intensity as were his, and she stood away from the plateau's face by at least a hundred feet. One fast grab with bloated, greedy fist . . . she would be his!

Flesh of his flesh, blood of his blood. If he could only take her—carry her away from Borea and show her the wonder of distant worlds, the great ice planets on the rims of star systems whose suns were mere dying embers—then she would know the glory and the power that were his, and perhaps she would want to share them with him. Aye, and there was her child, too, a man-child. A grandson for Ithaqua, who in his turn would walk the winds between the worlds and work for the release of Great Cthulhu.

While these thoughts and others flashed through the mind of the Great Old One, both snow-ship and cloak slipped in through the gates of one of the plateau's keeps. The ship slowed to a halt as ice anchors were thrown out; men and bears hastily disembarked and were hustled by eager helpers into the plateau's familiar maze of tunnels and caves. The men in the cloak alighted, and they, too, took shelter in the mouth of a major tunnel. From there, heart in mouth, Silberhutte gazed up at the aerial confrontation taking place above.

He gazed—cried out!—as Ithaqua's hand swept forward and his fingers began to close on Armandra . . . then cried out again, this time in exultation as the Wind-Walker drew back empty-handed, throwing up taloned hands before eyes which were suddenly fearful and flinching. Like a scalded dog the Snow-Thing stood off from the plateau, and Silberhutte felt the acid blast of telepathic loathing and fear that radiated from him.

Briefly the Warlord felt these things, momentarily, and something more. Bright in his mind's eye he saw a symbol—one which was now almost as painful to him as it was to Ithaqua and all others of the CCD—the symbol of a five-pointed star ablaze with searing flames!

"Tracy!" the Texan shouted his joy as Armandra slipped back in through the bars of her aerie to safety. "Tracy, you're a wonder!"

For he knew that somewhere on the plateau's face, even now his sister leaned out over the white waste and held up one of the star-stones of ancient Mnar to ward off the Wind-Walker, and he knew also that for the moment Ithaqua was impotent to harm any of those he held dear.

"It was Tracy, Henri," he cried, turning to de Marigny. "Tracy, with one of her blessed—one of her damned—star-stones. Thanks to Tracy, and to Armandra, we've all come through it!"

De Marigny managed a weak nod of understanding, but he was too far gone to find the strength to smile. His eyes were glazed slits; he was covered with rime and frostbitten from head to toe; his legs, which he could hardly feel, would not hold him up straight, and so he leaned against the tunnel's wall. Silberhutte saw his dangerous condition at a glance, picked him up, and ran with him into the tunnel toward the light of distant flambeaux. As he ran, he called for assistance, for the plateau's best physicians. . . .

. . . And well away from the plateau where the power of the star-stones could not touch him, Ithaqua silently raged and blustered and bloated up more gigantic yet as he called forth the fiendish elementals of the Great Storm, the malevolence of interstellar spirits, the wrath and fury of thunder and lightning to hurl against the plateau.

But the plateau, impervious as ever, paid not the slightest heed.

Chapter Seven

Marooned

SLOWLY but surely de Marigny recovered from his sustained ordeal of privation. In the Motherworld he might well have died, but here on Borea, where temperatures outside the plateau could fluctuate wildly—especially under the influence of Ithaqua or certain of his ice-priests—medicine in the fields of frostbite, exposure, hypothermia, and allied ailments was far advanced. For even in an environment where the great majority of members of the various levels of "society" were immune to all but the extreme lower levels of temperature, still the inhabitants of the plateau were human beings. Layers of human skin will crack; frigid air will shred the delicate webs of agonized human lungs, and human blood itself will freeze without a great deal of persuasion. In the plateau, as anywhere else, Necessity had been the Mother of Invention—especially of the medicines of snow and ice. . . .

So the Earthman recovered, and within twenty days Earthtime he was mobile again and already exploring the plateau's mazy interior network of caverns and tunnels on all their many levels. He found his way to the gymnasiums, arenas, and great meetinghalls; to the cavern lakes of the lower regions where the Eskimo fishermen cast their nets by the light of flaring flambeaux; to the stables, storehouses, and trading centers; eventually to the roof itself, where guardsmen kept vigilant watch over the white waste and the movements of Ithaqua's acolytes and worshipers at the totem temple.

Of Ithaqua: de Marigny was told that when the wolf-warrior party with the stolen time-clock finally arrived at the Wind-Walker's temple and dragged their prize to the foot of his ice-pyramid throne, he had shown little real or immediate interest in de Marigny's space-time vehicle. He had continued to spend the greater part of his time glowering at the distant plateau from under half-lowered lids, the carmine of his eyes as smokily pensive as lava bubbling in the throat of a massively threatening but momentarily passive volcano.

Gradually, however, as the time grew closer to his departure, when once more he must forsake Borea to go out on his endless wanderings between the dimensional spheres, Ithaqua's interest in the time-clock increased. Often he would pause in his scowling where he crouched atop his pile of heterogeneous artifacts from the Motherworld frozen into a pyramid of steel-hard ice, pause to lift up the time-clock in a massive fist and stare at it with eyes that flared murkily.

At other times he would assume the size and proportions of a man and call his ice-priests to him to converse with them (by whichever means he used), for they understood the ways of men better than he, and obviously he hatched some plot against the men of the plateau—particularly the Warlord and the newcomer from the Motherworld. Often, too, he would take a woman of one of his tribes in icy hand and stride off with her on the wings of the wind into unknown regions to the east. Those women he took did not go willingly for they were common women and not worth sparing once Ithaqua had done with them, and always he returned alone. In Armandra's own words: "Insatiable as Space and almost old as Time, my father is as lustful—and bestial—as ever he was!"

When de Marigny was nearly mended, he was given an audience with Armandra in her own sumptuous apartments. There she questioned him minutely in all aspects of his adventures with Titus Crow, adventures of which Hank Silberhutte had already appraised her but which she seemed to find both thrilling and enthralling when retold by de Marigny. And right from the start it was perfectly obvious to the Woman of the Winds that never before had she met a man like this one. Even in the Motherworld he had been something of an anachronism—the perfect gentle-man in a world where morals and all standards of common courtesy were continually falling, even in the highest strata of society—but here on Borea his like was unknown.

For while he treated her like the queen she was and be-haved as the very gentlest of gentlemen in her presence, and while she quickly warmed to him who had saved the life of her beloved Warlord, still she sensed that he would be equally gallant with any lady of quality. Nor did it re-quire much effort on the handsome Earthman's part to convince her that his presence on Borea was purely acci-dental, that he had not deliberately sought out Hank Silber-hutte to perform some fantastic interplanetary, hyperdi-mensional rescue! He was on his way to Elysia, home of the Elder Gods, and only the tides of fate had washed him up on Borea's chilly strand.

As for the esteem in which he held her, which amounted to something very much akin to awe, de Marigny hardly needed to fake it. He was after all of French descent, and she was one of the most beautiful women he had ever seen. As gorgeous in her beauty as Titus Crow's own Tiania, Ar-mandra was a young but fully mature, indeed a regal per-son, and it was more her great beauty that held de Marig-ny's appreciative attention than the fantastic powers he knew she commanded.

Shortly after his audience with the Priestess of the Pla-teau, because the Warlord thought it would be good ther-apy for his rapidly recuperating body, de Marigny found himself given over into the none-too-gentle hands of the plateau's weapon masters. And Silberhutte had been right. For as time passed, the newcomer became so engrossed in his studies that he soon mastered all the elementary tech-niques of the plateau's weaponry and went on to develop a flair and panache quite unique in one previously unaccus-tomed to such arts.

Therapeutically then, his daily sessions in the gymna-siums and arenas worked wonders for the stranded Earth-man, but his main reason for giving himself up so com-pletely to his tutors was not the perfecting of physical efficiency or the mastery of murderous weapons of war. He did it to keep his mind off the fact that he was marooned here on Borea, lost on an alien world in a strange parallel dimension. For Elysia seemed farther than ever from his grasp, and the wonders Titus Crow had so graphically described were fading in his mind's eye with each passing hour.

De Marigny's living quarters on the perimeter wall of the plateau where they overlooked the white waste through a number of small windows cut deep and square through solid rock, were spacious, sumptuous, and warm. They were heated by the same oil fires that kept the plateau's precipitous face free from the layers of ice which must otherwise soon close up all entries and exits alike and deprive the great hive of its air and water supplies. The mineral oil came from a great black lake in the bowels of the place, a lake which had fed itself immemorially from some source far below ground. Along with the fresh-water lakes that teemed with blind cavernicolous fish and the well-stocked animal pens of the lower levels, the lake of oil assured the plateau its complete independence.

All in all, then, de Marigny's lot might be considered extremely comfortable, and it would not have been an at all unpleasant or even tedious existence on Borea . . . but for the fact that he could see, through binoculars loaned him by the Warlord, the time-clock where it nestled in a glittering of white rime at the foot of Ithaqua's pyramid altar.

The time-clock—his gateway to the stars, his magic carpet between worlds—so close and yet so far away.

He had his flying cloak, of course, and had demonstrated its gravity-defying skills before a thrilled audience of chieftains and Elders—its remarkable maneuverability in the cold air high above the plateau—but whenever he strayed out marginally over the white waste, he would feel the tentative tug of sinister winds. Then Ithaqua would stir atop his icy pyramid and stretch himself with the indolent but watchful attitude of a deceptively lazy cat.

Armandra had warned de Marigny about that, and when on the last occasion she herself had to send friendly winds to release him from the blustery clutches of one of her father's lesser elementals of the air, then she reluctantly but firmly denied him any further use of the cloak. And so he removed that garment of so many adventures, folded it, and laid it safely away in his rooms.

From that time forward, seeing the way de Marigny gradually retired within himself, the plateau's Warlord despaired for his newfound friend and cursed his own inability to assist him; and while previously he had only tentatively broached to Armandra the subject of the possibility of the eventual rescue or recovery of the time-clock, now Silberhutte gave her little respite but determinedly brought the matter up at every opportunity until she was heartily sick of it. Such was his apparent obsession that while Armandra now trusted de Marigny completely, she found herself doubting the Warlord's own motives.

Could it be that her man's ever-increasing concern for de Marigny and his Elysian quest was nothing more than a front hiding a desire to desert her and leave Borea forever? There seemed to be only one sure way to discover the truth of the matter: to assist in the clock's recovery and see what next happened. And if the Warlord did indeed desert her? Well then, if that were what he wanted, he would be free to go, but Armandra was unwilling to dwell too long upon the possibility of that ever happening.

Was he not the father of her child—and did she not know his very mind, his every thought? Ruefully she had to admit that recently she did not know his mind, for more than ever before he kept his thoughts closed to her. This could well be for her own good; he might not want her sharing his worries; but on the other hand was it not at least feasible that he secretly harbored a desire to be rid of her and Borea forever?

And always the problem returned to the same stumbling block—the question of the Warlord's loyalty, his love for her—so that in the end Armandra resigned herself to the one possible course of action. If the time should ever arrive when she could assist de Marigny in the recovery of his time-clock, then she would do so, and in so doing, she would give the man she called husband, Hank Silberhutte, every opportunity to leave her.

Having made her decision and considered its possible conclusions, she then turned her thoughts to certain inner nightmares—to dwell upon the vast spaces between the stars and the even greater voids between dimensions—and having done so, she shuddered. Long and long had her father tried to tempt her away to walk with him on the winds that continually blow between the worlds . . . and wasn't she his daughter? If Hank Silberhutte had not come to Borea when he did, then by now she might—

But thoughts of Silberhutte, her man from the Motherworld, and of their man-child, stilled her fears at once. No, it could never happen, she was sure of the Warlord's love; so sure that at the first opportunity she would put him to the ultimate test. Then she would see what she would see, for only then could her faith in him—her great love for him—earn its reward. . . .

Chapter Eight

Rough Justice

DE MARIGNY was asleep and dreaming wonderful dreams of Elysia, of Earth's dreamworld, and of all the strange and marvelous planets out on the very rim of existence, so that he all but cried out in anger when Hank Silberhutte shook him unceremoniously awake.

"Henri, wake up, there's something you should see. This may be our chance to get the clock back!"

Hearing the Warlord's words, the dull edge of sleep was driven instantly from de Marigny's mind. He got up and quickly followed Silberhutte to one of the square windows overlooking the white waste. Even without binoculars he could see a lot of unaccustomed activity about the Snow-Thing's distant altar. Ithaqua's peoples were there in their thousands, forming a dark oval blot on the white of the frozen earth.

Taking up his glasses and focusing them on the distant scene, de Marigny asked: "Why has he mustered them? Is there to be an attack on the plateau?"

The Warlord shook his head. "No, not that. He lost three-quarters of his army the last time he tried it—yes, and he learned a terrible lesson in the bargain. They've gathered to witness his departure, to be instructed in the arts of their master—and to be reminded of the penalties for any sort of treason or action in defiance of his laws. When last the Wind-Walker was away raping and murdering some poor girl of the tribes, three of his wolf-warriors—probably relatives of the girl—tried to defect to the plateau. It's not the first time; we've gained several useful citizens that way even in the time I've been here. On this occasion, however, they . . ." He paused and shrugged. "This time they were caught and taken back alive. Before he goes, Ithaqua will deal with them."

"He'll kill them?" de Marigny asked.

The Warlord nodded. "It won't be pleasant to watch, and that's not why I awakened you. My reason for doing so is simple: once Ithaqua leaves Borea, we may be able to recover the time-clock. And the sooner we get moving the better. Armandra says she'll help us—in fact she seems to have turned completely about-face on the thing. She wouldn't even talk of it at one time—now she says she'll do all she can to help you get the clock back."

"But that's marv—" de Marigny began, but the Warlord cut him off with:

"Look there. What's happening now?"

Again training his binoculars on the totem temple, de Marigny answered, "The ice-priests are bringing forward three captives through the ranks outside the circle of totems. The three are struggling like madmen, but their hands are bound. The rest of the crowd seems cowed, unmoving, heads bowed. Those inside the circle are prostrated. None but the priests move, and they leap and twirl like dervishes. The first of the three captives is pushed forward right to the foot of the ice pyramid."

"Henri, you don't have to watch," Silberhutte warned.

"I know quite a lot about Ithaqua already, Hank. If I'm to know him fully, then I may as well see him at his worst. Whatever is to happen will happen regardless of my witnessing it."

Watching the distant scene, de Marigny grew still as Ithaqua reached down to lift up the first of his victims. The man, an Indian by his looks and dress, had stopped struggling and now held himself stiffly erect as Ithaqua's massive fist drew him effortlessly into the air. Without preamble the Wind-Walker held the man up above his monstrous head, turning his glowing eyes upward to stare at him for a moment. Then those eyes blazed wide open and their fires flickered with an almost visible heat. The taloned hand opened suddenly and the Indian fell, a doll spinning briefly in the air before plummeting with a splash of carmine sparks *into* one of Ithaqua's eyes!

Slowly the grotesque figure atop the ice throne resumed his original position, then reached down again to take up the second wolf-warrior. Not so brave this man. He kicked with his legs and struggled violently. Ithaqua held him on high, made as if to drop him—then caught him—casually used thumb and forefinger of his free hand to pluck off one of the man's kicking, offending legs!

Sickened, de Marigny looked away, then held to his resolve and found the scene once more. Ithaqua was now in the act of tossing a limbless, headless torso into the crowd within the circle of totems. And it was now the turn of the third and final offender.

Grabbed up in massive fist, the man seemed to have fainted; his body hung slack from the Wind-Walker's fingers. Almost disinterestedly, Ithaqua threw him aloft in a high arc. De Marigny expected to see the body plummet to earth—but no, not yet. Ithaqua's fiendish elementals of the air had him, boosting him higher still, spinning him like a top until his limbs formed a cross, then buffeting him at dizzy speeds, north, south, east, and west above the white waste. Finally he zoomed skyward, a marionette jerked up on invisible wires, to be *thrown* down at high velocity into the scattering crowd.

And indeed the crowd was scattering, for who could trust in the Wind-Walker's mood at a time like this? He had been amusing himself but now . . . now the game was over.

Or was it?

He cast about, turning his huge head from side to side, and at last his eyes came to rest on the time-clock where it lay at the foot of the pyramid. De Marigny gasped as the clock was snatched up—gasped again as Ithaqua threw back his black blot of a head and rocked with the convulsions of crazed laughter. Dumb, no audible sound escaped the monster, but in the next moment he turned his face to look square upon the plateau—square, de Marigny thought, at the window where he and Silberhutte stood— and hell itself flared in the carmine fires of his eyes.

Then, time-clock firmly clenched in hand, he leaped aloft to stride up terraces of air, grew large as, still rising, he raced for the plateau, his shadow an acre of darkness on the white waste. Almost directly overhead he came to an impossible halt, stared down for a moment, and held up the clock like a toy—no, like a *trophy!*—in his great hand, his whole body shaking with massive glee. Then he was gone, out of sight over the roof of the plateau and up into higher reaches of the chill atmosphere. . . .

. . . Gone from sight, yes, and gone with him the time-clock, de Marigny's one hope of ever escaping from Borea and passing on into Elysia. For the first time the man from the Motherworld was truly stranded, and there seemed to be absolutely nothing he could do about it.

Less than four hours later Hank Silberhutte found de Marigny on the plateau's roof. Approaching him, the War-lord felt satisfaction at his friend's robust if somewhat dejected appearance. Silently he appraised and approved limbs and muscles that had benefited greatly from long hours spent in the gymnasiums and arenas. Nor was de Marigny too heavily wrapped as he leaned across the battlements and stared morosely out over the white waste. He had started to grow accustomed to the bitter temperatures discovered whenever he left his apartment on the plateau's warm perimeter.

"Henri, you look miserable."

Turning, de Marigny nodded a welcome and his agreement. "Yes, and I feel it." His tone was wry. "Should I be happy?"

"I think you'll be happy enough shortly."

There was a look about the Warlord that the other could not quite fathom, as if he harbored some pleasurable secret. Suddenly hope stirred in de Marigny and he asked: "Hank, what is it? What's happened?"

The other shrugged. "Oh, nothing much—except we still have a chance. . . ."

"A chance—for what? How do you mean, 'a chance'?"

"Ithaqua's gone, that much you know—but he didn't take the clock with him after all!"

De Marigny grasped the Warlord's arms. "You mean it's still here, on Borea?"

Silberhutte shook his head. "Not on Borea, no, but on one of Borea's moons. He visited both moons before he

66

went off on his wanderings—and when he left them, the clock stayed behind. Look—"

He pointed to the distant horizon, where two vast moons showed their dimly glowing rims, permanently suspended beyond the hills as if painted there by some cosmic artist. "That's where your time-clock is, Henri, in the moons of Borea. Which one—Numinos or Dromos—I don't know. One or the other, only time will tell."

De Marigny shook his head, frowning, failing to understand. "But if the clock is on one of Borea's moons, we're separated from it by at least twenty thousand miles of interplanetary space! A chance, you said, but what sort of chance is that? And how can you be sure that the clock is there in the first place?"

The Warlord held up a hand and said: "Calm down, my friend, and I'll explain.

"First off, Armandra kept track of her father telepathically when he left. She knows that when he finished his business on the moons, he no longer had the clock with him. Indeed she believes that he deliberately let her see that he'd left the clock behind. Possibly he thinks he might trap her into leaving Borea—but I won't let that happen."

"Do you mean to say that Armandra could walk between the worlds like Ithaqua?"

"If she wanted to, yes. That's always been her father's chief desire: to have her walking with him on the winds that blow between the worlds. If ever he managed to trap her out there"—with a toss of his head he indicated the alien star-spaces above and beyond—"he'd never let her go again, would kill her first."

"Then how," de Marigny patiently pressed, "are we ever to get the clock back? I don't see what—"

"Henri," the other cut him off, "what would you say if I offered you the chance to take part in the greatest adventure of a lifetime? Yes, and a chance to get your clock back in the bargain? Dangers there'll be, certainly, and your life itself may well be at risk throughout. But what an adventure—to fly out to the moons of Borea!"

"Fly to the moons of—" de Marigny's jaw dropped. "Hank, are you feeling well? How in the name of all that's weird could I possibly fly out to the moons of Borea? Through space? An airless void? I don't see—"

"This is Borea, Henri," Silberhutte reminded, again cutting him off. "It's not the Motherworld, not Earth. Things are often as different here as they are in Earth's dreamworld—or so I gather from what you've told me. We're in an alien dimension, man, and things are possible which would be totally unthinkable on Earth. You want to know how you get to the moons of Borea? As I said, you fly there—in your cloak!"

"My flying cloak? But—"

"No buts, Henri. This is how it will happen:

"Armandra will call up the biggest tornado you could possibly imagine—a fantastic twister, a great funnel of whirling wind twenty thousand miles long—and we'll fly down its eye like a bullet down the barrel of a rifle!"

"A tornado?" de Marigny's imagination spun as dizzily as the wonder Silberhutte described. "Fly down the eye of a vast tornado? And did you say 'we'?"

"We—yes—of course! Did you really think I'd let you go adventuring in the moons of Borea on your own?" And the Warlord laughed and slapped his thigh. "Now come on, we've one or two things to attend to."

PART TWO: *NUMINOS*

Chapter One

In the Eye of the Twister

APART FROM the two heavily wrapped figures standing dead center of the flat, frozen roof of the plateau, that elevated expanse was empty. No watchmen stood behind the low parapet walls; no sightseers gazed out over the white waste; nothing stirred but flurries of snow and rime blown about by stray gusts of wind. All well-wishers had departed minutes earlier—Tracy Silberhutte and Jimmy Franklin, Charlie Tacomah the Elder, Oontawa the handmaiden, and her man Kota'na, Keeper of the Bears, these and many others—all retired now and gone down into the safety of the plateau where the Great Wind would not touch them.

The fires that warmed the perimeter walls had been extinguished hours ago; all openings in the plateau's face were now glazed over with thick sheets of ice formed by pouring water over them, necessary in view of the tremendous suction Armandra's tornado would create; all inhabitants and denizens were safely within their caves, quarters, and stables, and the snow-ships were anchored and tied down deep in the recesses of their keeps. The two men on the roof, attached each to the other by a new double harness hurriedly manufactured by the plateau's saddlers, waited for Armandra.

She, too, had said her farewells, coming to the roof to hug de Marigny fiercely and kiss her Warlord tenderly, then departing to meditate for a few minutes alone in her apartments. Now they both waited for her and watched the rim of the plateau to the south. She would appear

71

there, floating free on the wind as she drifted up into sight. Then she would stand off from the face of the plateau, rising high into the sky before calling up the mighty whirlwind which would thrust the two adventurers across the vast gulf of space to the moons of Borea.

And now she came—Armandra, the Woman of the Winds—dressed all in white but aglow with a carmine flush that radiated outward from her perfect form as a visible aura. Her hair swayed lazily above her head, floating to and fro in eerie undulations as she rose up in awesome grandeur. Her arms were held loosely at her sides and her loose fur robes floated about her almost as if she were suspended in some slow liquid. Then, still facing them, she receded, moved out over the white waste, lifted up her arms shoulder high, and commenced a series of summoning motions with her long white hands. At this distance her body formed a small cross of carmine fire in the suddenly darkening sky—a cross that commanded incredible powers.

Mastery of all the elementals of the air—of the winds themselves—and in her father's absence, not even the most wayward wind might defy her!

Starting far out beyond Ithaqua's totem temple and hidden from the view of the adventurers on the roof by the horizon of the plateau's rim, the surface snow and rime began to stir in agitated flurries. Rapidly, forming a circle fifteen miles across that encompassed the plateau centrally, small white spirals marched on the plateau, closing their ranks and towering higher as the circle narrowed. The line, high now as Ithaqua's ice pyramid, swept across the area of the totem temple. Several totems were uprooted like matchsticks and tossed aside, and the snow wall marched on unhindered.

Finally the sky itself began to revolve, a sea of darkly churning thunderheads all moving together, turning like a great wheel on spokes of boiling cloud. As the speed of this fantastic aerial phenomenon picked up, the two adventurers gazed dizzily skyward, reeling together while the plateau's roof seemed physically to turn beneath their fur-booted feet. Now, too, they could hear the *rush* of air, the howling of the white wall as it thundered toward them; and at last its crest could be seen towering higher than the rim of the plateau.

Until now the wall had been formed of many individual snow devils, tornadoes in the making, but now these small twisters had begun to move to match the motion of the sky, had lost their individuality as they formed a single massive funnel that reached higher by the second, twisting into a whirling, swaying corkscrew shape that began to shut out the light as surely as any wall of bricks and mortar.

There came a roaring as of a tidal wave breaking on a headland . . . and instantly the massive funnel reared taller, reaching up to shut out all but a dim gray light. The tornado had climbed the walls of the plateau, was now narrowing down its diameter on the roof itself with the plateau as a base. To the many watchers who braved the winds that still roared about Ithaqua's totem temple, it seemed almost that the giant twister was an extension of the plateau, the stem of some incredible white-boled tree that swayed and writhed and went up forever; for indeed its top could no longer be seen but transcended the limits of human vision as it snaked out into the void, bending toward Borea's moons.

And within a great circle that had the plateau for its center, covering an area of almost a thousand square miles, the winds still fought and tore, shrieking as they rushed in to support the incredible column, to push it higher still, driving its corkscrew tip across the otherwise empty void. Now the adventurers felt the first tug of trembling air in the all but still center of the uproar—now their persons were explored by gently curious tendrils of air, caressed by scarcely definable fingers—now the flying cloak belled out about de Marigny's shoulders and he felt an upward tugging that bade fair to lift him with or without the cloak's assistance.

"Armandra's personal familiars," Silberhutte shouted above the howl of frenzied air. "Fair winds to protect us across the void, Henri. Now we can go. Give us maximum lift, or whatever it is you do, and let's get on our way."

"When I tell Titus Crow about this," de Marigny began as he urged the cloak gently skyward until the Warlord swung beneath him in the dual harness, "if ever I get to tell him, that is, he'll never . . . *My God!*" De Marigny's exclamation burst from him when, as if suddenly released like a stone from a catapult—or, as Silberhutte had put it, "a bullet down the barrel of a rifle"—the cloak and its passengers were shot aloft.

Up they went, ever faster, while the inner surface of the whirling white wall closed on them until it was only fifty feet or so away on all sides. And yet they felt no pressure, no friction or whipping of outraged air, for Armandra's familiar winds held them fast in a protective bubble that traveled with them. They *saw* flashing past them the dizzy wall like the flue of some cosmic chimney, and they *heard* the deafening bellow of banshee winds, but all they felt was the awesome, crushing acceleration as they plummeted ever faster up the eye of the tornado.

"He'll . . . never . . . believe me!" de Marigny finally finished with a whisper that went unheard in the mad tumult. Teeth gritted, flesh straining as the acceleration built up, the two clung desperately to their harnesses while the tube of insanely spiraling air became merely a blur, no longer white but a dark shade of gray rapidly turning black.

For Borea was far behind now and even the softly luminous auroral shades of this alien dimension's interplanetary void were shut out, excluded by the nearly solid, twisting, thrusting funnel of frozen air. Then the acceleration was over, and they fell free, weightless, while around them, silent now but working as furiously as ever, Armandra's tornado—that great-grandfather of all tornadoes—blew them toward unknown, unguessed adventures.

After a little while de Marigny's natural apprehension began to abate. The limited atmosphere was bitterly cold but bearable, by no means the icy, killing, frigid hell he would normally have expected of interplanetary space; and while doubtless the surrounding wall of the twister whirled and writhed as before, it could neither be seen nor heard from within, so that all seemed tranquil with no sensation of speed apparent. Nevertheless the travelers knew that they were speeding across space, protected only by Armandra's familiars whose substance formed about them a soft, hurtling bubble of air.

It never occurred to them that they might converse until de Marigny sneezed, but as the staccato echoes of that involuntary ejaculation died away, they recognized at once that conversation was indeed possible, moreover that it would help in further dissipating their tension and not unnatural nervousness.

"Would you like to know about Numinos, Henri?" Silberhutte's voice echoed and reverberated loudly within their protective bubble of air. "It suddenly occurs to me that you know nothing at all about where we're going."

"Any and everything you can tell me," de Marigny answered. "Forewarned, as they say back home, is forearmed."

"Yes," the Warlord agreed, "and armor is something we're pretty short of. An ax apiece, a flying cloak, and—" He paused.

"And?"

"These winds of Armandra's. Her personal familiars that have looked after her since the day she was born a daughter of that alien, black-hearted monster and a human mother. It worries me now that she's without them. Yet if they were to leave us . . . we'd be dead sooner than it takes to tell! They're ours to command now, until we find the clock, or—"

De Marigny sensed the Warlord's shrug of resignation in the dark, picturing the other floating weightlessly close by in his harness. Then the strangeness of his situation hit him, and he wondered to himself:

"What on Earth—or off it—am I doing here? Sustained by a bubble of sentient air; speeding along on a mad voyage between alien worlds; questing after a stolen space-time machine so that I can go off adventuring again in search of Elysia? Is there any such place as Elysia, I wonder, or am I simply another patient in a madhouse somewhere? A hopeless case that the doctors despair of, keeping him quietly sedated in his own lunatic world of opium dreams. . . ."

"Numinos," Silberhutte finally continued, "though the closest of the moons of Borea, is also a world in its own right—a world like many others, with an atmosphere, oceans, and people. On one of the largest islands dwells the principal race, sailors with a warrior instinct, worshipers of Ithaqua. From what Armandra has told me of them, it's perfectly natural that they should worship the Wind-Walker; their ancestors most certainly deified Odin and

75

Thor in the Motherworld. Yes, they are Norsemen or as nearly Vikings as makes no difference. They control and inhabit all of the Numinosian islands except one: the Isle of Mountains.

"In the Isle of Mountains dwells a peace-loving race, not Ithaqua's people, protected in some way from the periodic attacks of the seafaring barbarians. There aren't many of these peaceful folk—a few families, a handful—but Ithaqua's interest in them has always been intense, and never more than right now. I don't know why. . . ."

As the Warlord paused, de Marigny inquired: "But how does Armandra know all of these things? Has she herself visited the moons of Borea?"

In the absolute darkness Silberhutte answered, "No, but when she was a child—through all the years when the Elders were grooming her for her role as the plateau's first citizen—often Ithaqua would try to tempt her away from her tutors. He'd send her telepathic pictures of the secret places he knew, the distant, strange worlds where he is worshiped, feared, hated. Then, as now, he desired a companion to walk with him on the winds that blow between the worlds. Remember, Henri, that his is a loneliness lasting for aeons.

"At any rate sometimes these mental invasions of Ithaqua's upon his daughter's privacy were vivid and detailed. Particularly on those occasions when he told her of the relatively close dominions of Numinos and Dromos, worlds he was wont to visit whenever he returned to Borea from his immemorial wanderings.

"But however persuasive the monster's promises, however seductive his telepathic enticements, the Elders had brought the child up to loathe him, showing her his cruelties at every opportunity. And gradually, as she grew through her teens into womanhood, her father's tempting slackened off. After all, it must have been a great strain on him—even on the Wind-Walker—to carry on this prolonged attempt at Armandra's mental seduction, the ultimate goal of which was to be her defection from the plateau and its peoples. For you see, the plateau with its subterranean store of star-stones has always been anathema to him, and to force his mind in upon hers through barriers such as those laid down by the Elder Gods must have been psychic agony. And all to no avail, for she spurned him totally.

"His final disappointment must have been when she and I joined forces, when we took each other as man and wife; for it was then that she fought him with his own powers, inherited from him, and would have destroyed him with them if she could. Oh, yes, he must have realized then that she was a lost cause, that he could never hope to win her to him. I think that if ever he is given the chance, he will kill her. Certainly he would kill me—and, judging from what you've told me, he'd kill you, too, without hesitation."

As Silberhutte talked, his companion noticed what appeared to be a gradual lightening effect; the utter blackness became shot with dark gray streaks, and the whole began to take on an opaquely milky appearance.

"Hank," de Marigny called out. "I think something is happening—or do I only imagine it?"

After a slight pause the Warlord answered: "No, it's real enough, Henri. It could mean that we've reached the end of our—" Abruptly, breathlessly, he again paused, then cried, *"Look!"*

At Silberhutte's excited exclamation the surrounding milkiness rapidly took on rushing motion. One second all seemed calm and silent, the next brought a resumption of the tornado's chaotic whirling; and as a dim light illuminated the two voyagers, they saw that the wall of the twister had finally extended itself to its limit, that it now whirled about them within arms' reach!

In another moment gravity returned, and with it the knowledge that they were now falling headlong *down* the narrow tube that was the whirlwind's center. Sound, too, rushed in upon them from outside: a furious high-pitched whining that had them clapping hands to ears and gritting their teeth as the pitch rose higher with each passing second.

Then—

—The whirling wall was gone, disintegrating as at the touch of some magical wand, flying apart when Armandra, a world away on Borea, released her control over it. The mighty whirlwind was finished, done, its debris filling the higher atmosphere of Numinos as fine snow. And down through that rapidly dispersing cloud of ice particles, their ears still ringing with the sounds of the great twister's death cries, down from a height of something less than two miles plummeted the men who had ridden a tornado from one world to another.

Head over heels in a knot of leather, fur, and chill flesh they fell, the cloak wrapped about them like some tangled parachute. And yet even as their fall began, it was partially arrested; they found themselves buoyed up and stabilized by Armandra's familiar winds, those same semisentient elementals of the air whose life-support bubble had protected them across twenty thousand miles of interplanetary space.

Now, falling feetfirst and at a vastly reduced velocity, the two men quickly disentangled themselves, and de Marigny cautiously took control of the flying cloak. As that garment of the Elder Gods took their weight, they felt a momentary tightening of their harnesses, followed by the sensation of sustained, controlled flight.

The cloak belled out above and behind them like the membrane wings of some great bat, and down they swept toward the surface of Numinos far below. . . .

Chapter Two

The Vikings

THE DESCENT of the cloak and its passengers to the surface of Numinos was in itself a voyage of discovery. De Marigny soon noted that the cloak was flying with an efficiency never before experienced under the burden of a dual load. He attributed this fact to the low Numinosian gravity, which was about three-quarters that of Borea. He was also struck by the beauty of this strange moon whose far face, like that of Luna, had never been seen from the parent world and should therefore be cold, dark, and foreboding. Indeed away on the horizon great blue cliffs of ice reared like a mountain chain that stretched as far as the eye could see, and in the ocean vast icebergs drifted down from the frozen regions.

As for the Warlord: he was delighted to observe that Borea and her moons did after all have a sun of sorts, one perhaps not too greatly at odds with Earth's own. Away beyond the World of the Winds, which hung huge, gray-green, and ominously clouded in the sky, the pink and yellow orb of the luminary Silberhutte had always suspected showed more than half its disk, shooting out bursts of golden auroral streamers that flowed into the void, slowed, and were rapidly drawn back into the furnace heart.

"A sun!" Silberhutte cried once more. "Which means that Borea's far side is probably a paradise. Armandra never knew of the sun's existence, has never physically seen it, and her father seems to have taken good care never to let her see it through his mind. I'm willing to bet that Ithaqua is confined to Borea's frozen regions just as surely as he is to the Arctic Circle and its boundaries on Earth. If I'm right . . . do you know what it means? One day the monster may return from his wanderings to find the plateau deserted and its tribes flown the coop to tropical lands beyond his reach."

"Look down there," de Marigny called out by way of an answer. "Many of those islands appear to be volcanic. Is that or is it not a huge hot-water geyser?"

They were passing directly over a cluster of small islands as they headed for a greater land mass some miles distant. Close to one island a great spout of water belched up intermittently, emitting clouds of steam and boiling yellow gasses. High as they were above this phenomenon, nevertheless they smelled sulphur in the otherwise pure Numinosian air.

"Volcanic, yes," Silberhutte agreed. "I've seen and smelled much the same in the Motherworld—that is to say, on Earth. Look over there, on the horizon to our right. If that isn't a full-blown volcano, I've never seen one. . . ."

But now something else spouted in the calm, gold-glittering sea half a mile below—many somethings—and in unison the two men cried: "Whales!"

"Will you look at them, Hank!" de Marigny yelled. "They're Great Blues, surely?"

"I'm no expert, Henri, but whatever species they are, I count a school of about fifty. The sea must be rich in food to support them."

"But how did they get here, on Numinos, an alien moon in a strange parallel dimension?"

"The Wind-Walker could have brought the first pair of young ones—say, oh, maybe twenty thousand years ago."

"But why?" de Marigny asked incredulously. "Why should he do that, for goodness' sake?"

"Why not? If you're going to people planets, surely you have to provide food for your people, don't you? There has to be some sort of ecology. On the other hand, these whales might simply have evolved here—they might have been here since the dawn of time. Perhaps this is the source from which Earth's great schools sprang. As far as we know, the Eskimos were Ithaqua's first human worshipers—and

they've been killing whales for food since time immemorial."

"But the thought is fantastic!" de Marigny answered. "I
mean, Ithaqua is evil, as blackhearted and alien a member
of the CCD as ever was. And yet here we see him almost
as—"

"As a god, my friend? Well, he *is* a god, isn't he, com-
pared with the primitives who worship him? Certainly his
powers—regardless of how he chooses to use them—are
godlike. And for all we know, he could well be the Earthly
prototype of Odin or Thor."

"But to bring whales—"

"Why not?" the Warlord repeated, cutting in once more.
"Don't be fooled for one minute that he couldn't do it.
Down on the white waste, not far from the plateau, there's
an old icebreaker—a great ship of iron—and it could only
have arrived on Borea one way. For that matter, didn't
Ithaqua snatch my crew and me, not to mention our air-
plane, right off the face of the Earth and bring us here?
Don't underestimate the Wind-Walker, Henri."

"Little chance of that, Hank. I've had enough experience
of the CCD, Ithaqua included, to know well enough what
they're capable of. It's just that I'm beginning to see him in
a fresh light. So you reckon that he was the old Viking god
of the storm, eh?"

"Not for a certainty, but he could have been."

"And Valhalla?"

The Warlord looked up at his friend with a questioning
frown as they sped in vertical tandem across the Numinosian sea toward land. Finally he answered: "It's purely a
matter for conjecture, of course, but there are certain pho-
netic similarities. . . ."

"Yes, I can see that," de Marigny answered. "Using a bit
of imagination, one could make 'r'lyeh' sound much like
Valhalla."

"I was thinking more on the lines of Hali," the Warlord
contradicted. "After all, Ithaqua is an elemental of air and
space, not water. Perhaps the Vale of Hali? Val–Halla
. . . ? Of course if I had someone even moderately
versed in Old Norse matters here right now to talk to, he'd
probably shoot me down in flames on the instant. But even

an expert could only repeat what he has learned—what he himself believes—however erroneously. The real facts behind all myths and legends must forever lie in the unfathomable past. If your friend Titus Crow were—"

"Hank, look!" de Marigny's cry cut the Warlord off. "How's that for a Viking settlement?"

Half a mile away and looming larger by the second, perched in the flanking crags of an ocean inlet much like a fjord, a hamlet of cabins—many of them looking curiously like the dwellings of Scottish Highland crofters—stood as testimony to the habitation of the large landmass by human beings. Smoke, drifting up from a dozen or more family fires, made the air above the settlement blue with its lazily drifting haze.

Well-worn paths ran from the comparatively rude dwellings down to the sea, while on the beach three wooden slipways showed yellow against the darker shades of coarse sand and shingle. For a background to the whole, the cliffs and hills beyond were fringed with the tall pines of Norway.

To the rear of the beach, within the confines of a tall log fence, stood a large communal or festival hall. A pair of dragonships of classical shape and size lay beached, one to each side of the log enclosure. A third longship, its dragon's head lolling above the gentle swell, stood anchored just within the fjord's mouth. Several figures, antlike at that distance, moved on the beach and along the cliff paths.

Slowing the speed of the cloak as they approached the settlement, de Marigny asked the Warlord: "What now, Hank? Do we simply fly in and see what develops?"

"I think," the other answered, "that things are already developing. Listen . . ."

Drifting out to them over the sea came the deeply raucous bellow of a conch blown in warning, and immediately all of the now plainly visible human figures of the settlement turned to stare and point oceanward at the bat-shape that came down out of the sky toward the beach. Moments later, running down from their huts and houses—appearing from their places of work beneath the beached dragonships and out from behind the communal-hall's stockade, from wherever they happened to be at the time—the great majority of the settlement's people appeared, all hurrying to witness at firsthand the arrival of this strange, aerial visitor.

In between the rocky points of the fjord de Marigny flew the cloak, bringing it to a hovering halt over the sea some seventy-five yards from the beach. "I see a large number of weapons there, Hank," he cautioned. "Axes and swords."

"I see them, and a spear or two. Still, from what little I know of the Vikings, they wouldn't go to bed without taking their favorite blades along! And in any case there's no question of a fight. We're outnumbered at least twenty to one—and we're here for information, not blood. But look—what's happening now?"

On the beach the four or five dozen Vikings, including a scattered handful of women and children, were congregated about a massive slab-sided boulder that guarded the gate to the communal hall. Standing atop this great rock, a wild, long-haired, ragged female figure harangued the crowd. They cowered back, cringing in the face of her vehemence, then turned their backs on her to kneel grudgingly on the sand facing the sea and the men who rode the cloak.

"What the hell—?" the Warlord queried. "Vikings—on their knees before us?"

"The old woman's a 'witch-wife,' " de Marigny informed. "The Viking equivalent of both oracle and witchdoctor combined. A seer, a rune caster, supposedly endowed with all of the peculiar powers such terms dictate."

"Very well," said Silberhutte, "then since she seems to be for us, I say we give it a whirl and take a run ashore."

The beldam continued to rant at the assembled community as de Marigny flew the cloak in to the beach. There he hovered effortlessly while Silberhutte freed himself and fastened the loose ends of his harness straps at the back of his neck. Then, setting down beside the big Texan, the cloak's master allowed his marvelous garment to fall loosely about his fur-clad form. Now they stood shoulder to shoulder, the two of them, arms crossed on their chests.

Still the hag railed on, but her tone was lower now, full of awe. The eyes of the whole community fed unblinkingly, not a little suspiciously, on the men from the sky.

"That tongue she's using," Silberhutte casually drawled. "The more I hear, the better I understand it. There's some

83

Norse in it, a lot of Old English, too, but mainly it's . . ." He frowned in concentration, trying to fathom the strangely familiar dialect.

"Gaelic," de Marigny finally recognized the language. "And those swords on the sand there. Viking craftmanship, yes, but they're designed more like claymores than anything else!"

"Yes, I'd noticed that too," the Warlord answered. "But right now I'm more interested in the old woman. Listen to her—she's giving them hell!"

Even as he spoke, the crone uttered one final harsh word of command that rose in pitch to a breathless shriek. Then she threw her head back and her arms wide, beginning to stumble dangerously about the uneven upper surface of the rock. At that, almost without exception, the assembled Vikings cast their eyes down and bowed their heads. The two closest to the great boulder, however, leaped to their feet and rushed to help the witch-wife.

Her eyes had turned up, and she was falling forward, a bundle of rags that would have smashed down on the shingle if the two had not caught her and placed her on her feet. Now, recovering herself, she pushed them away and staggered through the prostrated ranks of Vikings to stand before the strangers. Her aides—blood relatives, sons by their looks—followed behind her at a respectful distance. Through black, bloodshot eyes she peered first at de Marigny, then at Silberhutte, all the while nodding her head of long, matted yellow hair. When finally she spoke, not all of her words were immediately intelligible to the pair, but their overall meaning was clear.

"So you have come, as I said you would: two strangers flying in from the sea on the wings of a bat. Two whose fates are totally entwined with those of the clan of Thonjolf the Red, for good or evil I know not. Two of you, blown on the winds, emissaries of Ithaqua!"

"Aye, we have come," the Warlord took the initiative, "and it is good that you greet us thus."

"You speak the tongue strangely," the crone answered, "but you do speak it. This, too, I foresaw."

"And who are you, witch-wife?" de Marigny inquired.

"I am Annahilde, mother of Erik and Rory." She placed

84

scrawny hands on the arms of the pair now come up close behind her. "Annahilde, widow of Hamish the Strong."

She turned to Silberhutte. "You are much like Hamish in his younger days. Six years gone, he too was . . . was called by Ithaqua." For a moment her visage grew yet more bleak and her eyes filled with horror. Then she shook back her wild yellow hair and peered about her, like someone waking from a nightmare.

The prostrated Vikings were beginning to stir, their patience with Annahilde's demands almost at an end. Not all of them held their eyes averted; two or three were openly, ominously grumbling together. The newcomers had noticed this, and Silberhutte, continuing his role as spokesman, decided to relieve the situation.

"If these are Thonjolf's people," he said, "where is the chief, Thonjolf himself? We would speak to him. Also, get these people up on their feet. Emissaries of Ithaqua we are, but before that we were ordinary, humble men."

"Ah, no!" she shook her head in denial and grinned, showing a mouthful of badly stained but surprisingly even teeth. "Ordinary men you never were, nor will you ever be humble. As for these—" She flapped a scarecrow arm to indicate the prostrated ones. "Up, dogs of the sea—on your feet. Ithaqua's emissaries grant you this boon, that you, too, might stand in their presence."

As the Vikings sullenly got to their feet, she continued: "You ask for Thonjolf? Thonjolf the Red, who is also called Thonjolf the Silent? Hs is at Norenstadt, summoned there by Leif Dougalson, king of all the Viking clans. Word is out that a raid is in the offing. Thonjolf attends a great meeting of the chiefs but should soon return. Only his oaf of a son Harold is here, and he lies drunken in the meetinghouse." She tossed her head to indicate the enclosure to her rear.

"You talk of a raid," de Marigny queried. "What sort of raid?"

She nodded, grinning. "Soon all Vikings will put on metal and sail their dragons against the people of the Isle of Mountains. Ithaqua has commanded it; he has set the hand of Leif Dougalson and the Vikings against the mountain isle."

85

Here she paused, then laughed loudly and grasped their elbows. "Aye, and your arms, too, will find work on that bat-haunted isle! Have I not foreseen it? Bat wings beating in the mist—blood and terror and great winds blowing—and all in the name of . . . of Lord Ithaqua!" And it seemed to the two men that she spat the Wind-Walker's name out on the sand.

By this time the Vikings were back on their feet, and the two newcomers were able to see their Numinosian hosts more clearly; from which moment onward they began to feel a certain gratitude for the doubtful affections of the witch-wife. For the clan of Thonjolf the Red, while only four or five dozen in number, was almost without exception a clan of giants among men. Even the stripling youths of fourteen or fifteen years were well over six feet tall, while some of the full-grown men were almost seven. Silberhutte, for all his massive stature by Earth standards, was dwarfed by them!

"Another effect of the low gravity, Henri?" the Warlord asked out of the corner of his mouth.

"I would say so. By the same token their strength has probably not increased in proportion. Might even have been reduced . . . I hope!"

Now the Vikings crowded forward, eager to get a closer look at their visitors, still open-minded about Annahilde's assertions regarding these men come down from the sky. So they flew, did they? Well, so did midges! What other powers did they have? Surely the Wind-Walker's chosen ones must be of greater stature than these men? What proof was there that they were what the witch-wife said they were? They moved closer still, then—

"Ho, there! Out of my way—move, man! Where are these strangers I heard the hag ranting about, these 'emissaries of Ithaqua?' " The voice was a deep, drunken bass rumble issuing from behind the massed Vikings.

As all eyes turned from the strangers and a way was cleared for the speaker, so Annahilde whispered: "Harold, the chief's son. He's a drunkard and a bully. Beware . . . !"

Chapter Three

Ithaqua's Emissaries

AS LARGE and foreboding as his voice—seven feet tall, with a middle like a barrel and a huge red face that well matched his tangled red hair and the blood in his pig eyes—Harold was a monster. He glanced once at the strangers, took a long draft from the jug he carried, then threw back his great head and burst into malicious laughter. His mirth was short-lived, however, and quickly gurgled into silence as he contemplated the two a second time. Now his peering inspection was much more thorough, more threatening; and while Harold was not as drunk as the Earthmen might have preferred, he certainly appeared to be all of the bully that Annahilde had named him.

Finally he turned scornfully on the assembled Vikings and roared: "A trick! You've been tricked, all of you. By these two, aye, and by the hag there. . . ." Harold waved a massive hand in Annahilde's direction. "Emissaries of Ithaqua, indeed! Why, only *look* at them! They're common men, can't you see that?"

"But we all saw them fly in from the sea," one of the younger men protested.

Harold stepped over to the youth and dealt him a backhanded blow that sent him reeling. "Fool! Oaf! It's Annahilde's work. She's blown her powder in your faces. You'd see anything she wanted you to see. Sent by Ithaqua, my backside! These two? They look more like men from the Isle of Mountains to me . . . and we all understand the witch-wife's interest in the Isle of Mountains. . . ."

Instantly Annahilde's sons, great hulking men in their late twenties, stepped forward and confronted Harold. At the same time a pair of surly looking brutes, Harold's cronies, took up positions flanking him. From one of these Harold snatched a spear whose shaft was thick as a man's wrist.

"Stand aside, bitch-sons, for I've no quarrel with you two—not yet! Aside, I say, and let's see what these strangers are made of."

In the chief's absence Harold had a certain authority with the clan. With his cronies beside him and following his cryptic accusations—against Annahilde as well as the two strangers—it would have been purest folly for the witchwife's sons to oppose him in earnest. Thus Erik and Rory reluctantly stood aside as de Marigny and Silberhutte separated and backed up against the hull of one of the beached longships.

Quickly then, allowing no time for thought, Harold drew back his arm and made as if to throw his spear. Instead of hurling the weapon, however, he retained it in the ready position. Silberhutte—a born fighter and greatly experienced—merely froze and narrowed his eyes, waiting for the cast, knowing he could step out of the spear's flight path. De Marigny, on the other hand, for all he had learned in the plateau's arenas, was short on practical experience. He feinted, almost tripped, and in the split second it took him to regain his balance, Harold laughed harshly and made his throw.

Without a doubt the hurled shaft should have pinned de Marigny to the planking of the dragonship, would have done so but for the intervention of Armandra's familiar winds. For when that deadly weapon was only three feet away from his middle, it met a violent, invisible force that wrenched it from its path and drove it point down into the coarse sand between the two outsiders. Silberhutte snatched the weapon up in a hail of pebbles and gravel, breaking it like a twig over his bent knee.

Harold shook his head in bewilderment, unable to accept the evidence of his own eyes. He knew his cast had been a good one. It had seemed as if some unseen hand had struck the shaft aside in midair. And now the larger of the strangers—whose strength, for all his comparatively diminutive size, must be prodigious—was striding over to him, looking up at him through eyes that were unafraid, eyes filled with anger.

De Marigny knew at once what had saved his life. Now, as Silberhutte approached the huge, red-haired Viking, he whispered his thanks into thin air, saying: "Just keep watch over us, friends. I've a feeling there'll be more work for you shortly."

Now the bullyboys flanking Harold puffed themselves up and gripped their weapons in massive hands. One carried an ax; the other, whose spear lay broken on the sand, had drawn a sword. Harold glanced at his brutal colleagues, turning his head from side to side and grinning. To the Warlord he said, "You wanted to speak to me, little man?"

"The two of us," the Texan grated out through clenched teeth. "You and I, dog, hand to hand. After that—then we'll decide which of us is the 'little' man!"

"You call me . . . dog!" Harold almost choked on the word, going bright as a beetroot in his rage. "And you, a midget, challenge me in hand-to-hand combat? Breath of Itha—" He drew back his arm to deliver a backhand blow like that dealt to the young Viking a moment or two earlier. Silberhutte ducked under the flying arc of muscle and bone, driving his rock-hard fist like a ramrod into Harold's solar plexus.

The bully immediately doubled forward, breath whistling from him. His descending chin met the clasped fists of the Warlord as they rose from knee level. It was a rapid combination of blows delivered by an expert; certainly it would have killed many a lesser man. As it was, Harold was lifted right off his feet, stretched out on the sand like a felled oak.

De Marigny had guessed the outcome of any contest between his companion and the bullying Viking, and he had foreseen the natural aftermath. Now, as Harold's henchmen made to strike—the one lifting his ax while the other drew back his sword—he cried out: "Hold . . . or be whirled aloft by angry winds and thrown down into the sea to drown!"

And with that he made a swift motion with his hand, as if casting sand in the faces of the two who threatened the Warlord. On the instant, as their eyes swiveled toward him and their blows were momentarily checked, twin spirals of sand and pebbles grew up from the beach, leaped upon the two and enveloped them, whirling them about and casting them down. For a few seconds, where a mere moment of time ago only a breeze had whispered off the sea, the wind whined its rage and drove sand up the beach in stinging flurries. Then there was quiet again.

The two Vikings, thoroughly cowed and shaken, carefully climbed to their feet and backed off, then turned and ran, fighting their way through the crush of silent, wide-eyed observers. And not once during the confrontation had the visitors from the skies reached for their own weapons . . .

The witch-wife, herself amazed at the way things had gone, but quick to take advantage of the situation, cried: "Now lift your blades high and give these men welcome for what they are: true emissaries of Ithaqua, Lord of the Winds!"

"Aye," cried Erik and Rory in unison, "here's a good strong arm for Lord Ithaqua's proven emissaries!" And the crowd on the beach joined in, lifting up their weapons and their voices in an accolade which was only cut short by Annahilde.

"And now," she shouted above the general babble, "to complete the day, comes Thonjolf himself." She pointed out to sea where, from behind the tall rocks at the mouth of the fjord, the dragon prow of a magnificently painted longship had appeared. There, in the prow at the neck of the nodding dragon, stood a man taller by inches than the tallest of his clan; a man whose stature, even as seen from the beach, was obviously that of a giant among giants, his red hair blowing behind him like a mane in the breeze from the open sea.

"Thonjolf the Red," Annahilde cried again. "And what news we have for him, eh, lads? For he's never had visitors such as these before. Men from the skies—sent by the Wind-Walker himself—emissaries of Ithaqua!"

Later, ostensibly as guests in Annahilde's house—a thatched, single-story affair of two small bedrooms, a kitchen half-open to the sky, and a living room of sorts where now they rested at their ease, or as best they could, on low wooden benches decked with smelly furs—Hank Silberhutte and Henri-Laurent de Marigny held a muted conversation. Outside the door to this crude but comparatively clean shelter, the two brothers Rory and Erik silently squatted like human watchdogs.

The visitors from Borea were unable to say whether they were under the quiet protection or merely the wary scrutiny of Annahilde's sons, but whichever way it was, at least they each had felt sufficiently secure to snatch a few hours sleep. While it had not been immediately apparent, their hurtling voyage through the void had been both physically and mentally strenuous; now, with a pint of sweet, sticky ale inside them along with a plate of smokey, half-cooked meat of undetermined origin, they felt up to facing their next problem as it presented itself.

Of the events immediately following on Thonjolf's return to his clan: that had been something of an anticlimax. And little wonder he was occasionally known as Thonjolf the Silent!

The chief had left his longship with his retinue of a dozen or so men, had briefly inspected the visitors, had grunted sourly at the sight of his son snoring on the beach, and had patiently given ear to Annahilde's shrill outline of events. Indeed her ragged figure and wild-eyed look had seemed to command their fair share of respect from the chief.

Then, following an aerial demonstration by de Marigny and the flying cloak, Thonjolf had gone off with the witch-wife and several members of the clan into the meeting-house. If the chief had been impressed by de Marigny's triumph over gravity, it had not showed, except perhaps in a slight arcing of his bushy red eyebrows.

And it was the general response to their coming—or rather the lack of response—that formed the topic of conversation between de Marigny and Silberhutte in Anna-hilde's house.

"I don't understand it," de Marigny said. "I always believed the Vikings to be a fiery, volatile people. The type of folk who would make a lot of an 'omen' such as we've provided. Yet here we are, a pair of near-dwarfs, flying in like something out of the *Arabian Nights,* 'emissaries of Ithaqua' and all that; not to mention your knocking the chief's son out cold. I mean, by my reckoning we should either be hanging up by our thumbs somewhere by now, or else occupying Thonjolf's throne—if he has one!"

Silberhutte nodded. "Yes, it puzzled me, too, at first. But the more I think of it—"

"Yes?"

"Well, to start with, visitors from the skies are by no means unheard of on Numinos, Henri. Ithaqua's comings and goings must be fairly frequent."

"Not too frequent, I hope," de Marigny answered with feeling.

"And then there's Annahilde and her hallucinatory powders," the Warlord continued. "You'll recall Harold mentioned them? If all of the clans come equipped with witchwives, and if all of them know where to lay their hands on the plants or whatever they use to concoct their powders . . . little wonder it requires a lot to make your average Numinosian Viking sit up and take notice! And just suppose Ithaqua had sent us here—how would you react if you were a Viking?"

"I'd be pretty wary, I suppose."

Silberhutte nodded. "Sure you would—and that was more or less the reaction we got. Except from Harold, who's a pretty stupid bully. And I fancy that even he was only trying to assert himself in his father's absence. As for the chief himself: Thonjolf strikes me as a man with a lot on his limited mind, namely this big meeting he's just back from and the upcoming raid on the Isle of Mountains. What with those things, and on top of them Ithaqua sending us as emissaries to *his* clan—which must strike him as a hell of a thing despite his nearly negative reaction—and at the same time having to bear the responsibility for the actions of his oaf of a son . . ."

"I suppose you're right," de Marigny conceded. "But it still doesn't get us any closer to finding the time-clock."

"No, but unless my ears deceive me, here's Annahilde now. On her own by the sound of it. This could be the ideal opportunity to fill in on background information—and at the same time try and find out about the clock. Let's see what she has to say."

The gabble of the witch-wife's voice grew louder as she approached the house, questioning her sons about the welfare of the strangers. They answered her respectfully if noncommittally, and she gave them permission to go down to the meetinghouse. Apparently the building within the stockade doubled not only as a throne room but also as a drinking place. A moment later she came through the door, closing it carefully behind her. Then she cocked her head to one side and listened, waiting for a few moments to ensure that her sons had indeed left their posts as instructed.

Satisfied, she turned at last and said: "Now then, the pair of you, let's have it."

"Let's have it?" de Marigny queried, doing his best to look blank.

"No games!" Annahilde cautioned. "You are not sent by Ithaqua, I know that. I knew it from the moment I touched you." She grasped their arms. "See! See! You"—she stared at Silberhutte—"ah, you have known Ithaqua's touch, his carmine gaze, his icy breath in your face, aye. But you are not his. He has chilled your blood, true, but you are your own man."

She turned to de Marigny. "And you—you, too, have met the Wind-Walker, but he has not touched you. Your blood is still warm. No, you are not Children of the Winds . . . so what are you? I do not even believe you to be of Numinos. But if not Numinos, where else?"

The two looked at each other, silent for a moment, then Silberhutte said: "Annahilde, it seems we're forced to trust you. No, we are not Ithaqua's emissaries, and we are not men of Numinos. I am Hank Silberhutte, Warlord of the Plateau on Borea. My people are sworn enemies of Ithaqua. This man"—he placed a hand on de Marigny's shoulder—"is Henri-Laurent de Marigny, and he is from the Motherworld. I, too, was born on Earth, but Borea is now my homeworld."

If Annahilde's eyes had gone wide when Silberhutte spoke of Borea, they became huge orbs at mention of the Motherworld. "Men of Earth, here on Numinos?" she gasped. "And not by Ithaqua's hand! But how? Why?"

"The how of it will have to wait," de Marigny told her. "As for why we are here: we seek a . . . a box."

"A box?"

"One big enough to contain a man. A box shaped like this—" and he drew a coffin-shape with his foot on the dirt floor. "It's mine, taken from me by Ithaqua. I want it back."

She nodded earnestly. "Yes, I know something of your box—but only tell me what you want with it, what you would do with it? Of what use is a box?"

"It is a device for traveling between worlds, for jumping backward and forward through time itself," Silberhutte told her. "My friend was questing after Elysia and had barely arrived on Borea when Ithaqua stole his traveling box away."

"Elysia!" she seemed astounded.

"Elysia is—" de Marigny began.

But Annahilde quickly cut him off. "The home of the Great Elder Gods—I know, I know!" Now she grabbed their wrists tight in claws like steel traps. "I thought when first I saw you flying in off the sea that someone had blown my own powders in my face. Now—" She shook her head in amazement. "Yours is the true magic!"

"Annahilde," de Marigny urgently took her hands in his. "Where is the time-clock—my box, I mean? I must find it."

Her eyes narrowed and she peered at her visitors cannily before answering. "Have no fear, you shall know the whereabouts of your box . . . in good time. Before that there is something you must do for me."

Chapter Four

The Witch-Wife's Tale

"THE Vikings have been here for thousands of years," Annahilde began. "I know, for I am one who can read the old writings. It is all in the Two Books: in the Book of Earth the Motherworld and in the Book of Numinos. The histories were handed down from father to son until later, when Ithaqua brought others who had writing, and then they were written in words in the Two Books." Here she closed her eyes and lay back her head, so that it was as if she quoted from a book in her mind:

"And it was Ithaqua brought the first men into Borea, and into Numinos, and many among the latter were Norsemen. This was before the time of the iron swords, but later they too came with men of the Motherworld brought into Numinos by Ithaqua. And the Wind-Walker said unto the tribes that he was their God and they would worship him, and in Norenstadt his pyramid altar was builded where it stands to this day.

"And the Vikings multiplied in Numinos and the tribes were many; for the Great God Ithaqua" (she spat these last words out, as she did whenever she spoke of the Wind-Walker) "had filled the ocean with fishes great and small and had carpeted the islands with grasses and peopled them with animals, all for the needs of the Vikings. But Ithaqua was a hard God and cold, and at times he would take the loveliest daughters of the tribes for his own to fly off with them into the lands beyond the Great Ice Wall. Aye, but he

95

rarely brought them back, and those he brought back were mazed and cold and rarely lived long.

"Among those that lived, several were with child, but such instances were always many years apart. Whole generations of Vikings would go by, and then, again, the Wind-Walker would get a woman with child. When born, all such spawn of Ithaqua were freaks or monsters, and all died with only one recorded exception. This child was so evil of aspect and inclination—a black vampire from birth that pulled blood and not milk from its mother's breast— that the chief of her tribe tore it from her and put it down with fire.

"And Ithaqua—when he came again to Numinos and when his priests told him what had transpired—then it was that he destroyed the entire tribe which lived in that place; and his wrath and the storms he brought, which lashed all of Numinos, were awful in their might!

"And yet the tribes knew that the Storm-God himself would have put down his child if he had seen it, for he was desirous of a beautiful child and of human form . . . why else would he choose the loveliest girls with which to mate? Then, because of Ithaqua's unending cruelties—which were such that his comings were dreaded and his goings much applauded in secret and out of earshot of his priests—it came about that the tribes turned against their God and defied him.

"Parents were wont to hide away their girl-children, especially those of lovely aspect, when they knew that Ithaqua was due to walk the winds of Numinos once more; and the God's chill-hearted priests, even those priests given over utterly to his worship, they became prone to peculiar accidents and fatal misadventures in their master's absence. But in the end the Storm-God knew how his people worked against him, and he waxed wroth indeed!

"He set the tribes one against the next until all Numinos burned from end to end, and the fires of blazing settlements were hotter than the lava that bubbles on the Islands of Fire. And at the last, when the tribes of Numinos were decimated, the Wind-Walker stood in the sky and laughed. He laughed—then rained down lightnings and sent storms racing across the ravished land and caused the very seas to wash the islands.

"And so all Numinos bowed down before him, and those who lived swore fealty to him, lest he destroy the Viking tribes forever. . . ." Here Annahilde paused and got her breath before going on.

"These things," she finally continued, "are written. It is also written that at last Ithaqua looked on Numinos and saw the tribes were penitent. Then he brought others here who were not Vikings though much like them; sturdy men and women of the Motherworld, they were, whose weapons and culture and tongue were different; and it was seen that the Wind-Walker would change the blood of the tribes, would produce women of great beauty and strength to satisfy his lusts and bear him the offspring he desired. . . ."

They waited for her to go on, but she seemed to have talked herself out. Finally Silberhutte asked: "And did he ever achieve his ambition? I think not, knowing how Armandra has never totally bowed to her father's will."

"No, he did not," she quickly answered, shaking her head in glad denial, "though he surely tried. He made it law that the most handsome and strongest youths of the tribes—which were now called clans—could take only the loveliest girls for brides, so that their children in turn would be beautiful and strong and the maidens pleasing in Ithaqua's eyes. So it came to pass that after eleven generations an entire tribe or clan of chosen people had grown up and dwelled upon one especially green and beautiful island. And Ithaqua looked upon the maidens of this wondrous clan and was sorely tempted, yet he held off and bided his time while eleven more generations passed. And now at last there were two couples on the island whose perfection of form and feature was a wonder to behold even in a clan whose least handsome member was beautiful, and both women of these couples were with child. The greatest seers of the time examined them, declaring that the children would be female.

"Then Ithaqua came again to Numinos and went into the beautiful isle. There he set aside certain elders to serve the mothers of his hoped-for future brides, and having done so, he put down the rest of the clan—all of them, man, woman, and child—out of hand!

"He did this—for what good reason?—and all for naught. There had been much inbreeding in the isle's two

97

and twenty generations, which previously had only shown itself in the infrequent birth of a beautiful idiot. Out of fear, these children the clan secretly put down. But now—

"—Not only were the children of those last two unfortunate women imbeciles, they were also hideous; aye, and both of them girls, as had been foreseen! In a single blow—a blow delivered perhaps by the clean old gods of Earth—all of Ithaqua's plans were destroyed. And he saw what was become of his dream and went away from Numinos for long and long. Then, when they thought he was gone forever and those who knew the old legends had turned again to serving the olden gods of the Motherworld, the Wind-Walker returned and brought his fearful oppressions back with him.

"He put down the worship of the Earth gods and their priests and once again was wont to fly away with and ravish the loveliest maidens, and ever and ever he sought to produce a child in his own and in Man's image. So things stood for an hundred years—until some sixty-three years gone." Again she paused.

"Sixty-three years ago?" de Marigny prompted her. "Something happened then?"

"Aye, for that was when he brought a ship of the Motherworld to Numinos; and in that small ship were a man and wife, two strong sons and a daughter of some twelve years. And they were the first people of Earth that Numinos had seen in over five hundred years. The wife was a lovely woman even in her middle years, the husband handsome, and the sons firm limbed and clever. And the girl-child was lovely.

"They were brought here, where Thonjolf's grandfather was the then chief, and some few years later the girl married a fine young man of the clan. Twin daughters came of that marriage, aye, and I was one of them. . . ."

"You?" Silberhutte stared at her, intrigued by her story.

"Ah!—I see what you are thinking," the witch-wife cried. "You wonder how I could possibly come of such a mating. Let me tell you that in girlhood I was not uncomely, that even now beneath the grime and the lines of age and pain I have beauty. But I am called 'hag' and that is the way the clan knows me; it is the way I live, have lived since—" Abruptly she stopped.

"Go on, Annahilde," de Marigny again prompted.

"I . . . I stumble blindly on, going ahead of myself," she finally said. "Let me continue in my own time. . . .

"I grew to a woman and was taken to bride by Hamish the Strong. Two fine sons he gave me and loyal, who have cared for and protected me these six years since Hamish was taken. As for my sister, Moira: she was almost perfect in her beauty and goodness. No one was ever so kind, no soul ever so lovely, and if Ithaqua had seen her as she grew to womanhood, surely would he have taken her. But his comings were rare in those days and confined mainly to Norenstadt where he sat his pyramid throne, and he saw Moira not.

"And so she too was wed, to a good and noble man of the clan, a learned man whose instructors were my grandparents brought to Numinos in their little ship; but she did not become pregnant by him until she was in her fortieth year. Then it was that Moreen was born, small and sweet and shiny like a little pearl—Moreen, whose tiny limbs were those of Earth and not the stretchy stilts of Numinos—Moreen of the Smile. And in her fifth year . . . then Ithaqua saw her.

"A child of five tender years, and already lovely as a flower. Fresh as the green fields and full of her mother's ways, she was the darling of her parents, the joy of the clan, the rose in the garden of Thonjolf the Elder's heart. Aye, for the present chief's father was so taken with the child that he had a house built for her family close to his own house, so that he could watch her at her play and laugh with her when she laughed, which was often.

"And when he came, Ithaqua saw her at play and lifted her up. He lifted her into the clouds in his great hand and gazed upon her curiously with his carmine eyes; and where other children would surely cry and beat their tiny fists and feet, that child of joy only laughed and pointed at the huge black blot of his head and tickled his bloated, taloned fingers! And the Wind-Walker—monstrous beast of hell that he is—seemed held in Moreen's tiny fist more tightly ever than he held her.

"Then at last he set her down close by her house and stood off in the sky above the settlement. For a long time he stood there astride the wind, gazing down upon Moreen

99

where she played below and waved up at him, and a strange fascination glowed deep in his fiery eyes.

"Soon, unable to bear this thing any longer, her parents ran out, snatched her up, and carried her into the house; whereupon Ithaqua stirred himself up as if from a dream and walked off across the sky toward Norenstadt. And as he went, often he looked back. . . .

"Some time later, two yak-riding priests came plodding from Norenstadt, and with them a retinue of Viking warriors led by Leif Dougalson himself. At first, when they went to my sister Moira's house and asked to see the girl-child, it was thought that they intended to steal little Moreen away. But no, instructed by Ithaqua, they had merely come to see the child. Then they spoke to my sister and her man; aye, and to old Thonjolf, too, come up with a body of men to protect the little one and her family if such were necessary.

"And the priests said to Thonjolf that his clan was honored among all the Viking clans, for the Great God Ithaqua had found Thonjolf's people fair and pleasing—particularly the tiny girl-child Moreen, who one day would walk with him as his bride upon the winds that blow between the worlds!

"Then, when they heard this, though glances full of meaning passed between Moreen's elders and old Thonjolf, nothing against the plan was said; for after all nothing could be said, not at that time; and that night there was a feast and drinking and much praying for the peaceful propitiation of Ithaqua. The next day Thonjolf received Leif Dougalson's instructions to care well for little Moreen: it would go badly for all concerned were Ithaqua in any way thwarted in this matter, for it was known that the Wind-Walker would return again and again to Thonjolf's clan to watch the small one grow into womanhood.

"And the priests also spoke to my sister and her man, saying how well it were that the little one should grow up carefully protected and in innocence; and they issued a warning to all the clan that its sons be not tempted as Moreen grew to maturity. Then, before these most important visitors took themselves off to their rightful places in Norenstadt, the priests said how if they had their way, the child would go with them, but that Ithaqua himself had commanded that she be allowed to grow up within her family and clan according to her nature.

"Following their departure, how my sister cried! She wept and her man was distraught with horror, anger, and helplessness, and even the old chief shed a tear at the thought of the now inevitable fate of little Moreen. The entire clan, with the exception of a handful of callow or jealous wives, grew sad and morose, remaining thus for many a day. It was as though a great king had passed away, or as if each family had lost a favorite son or daughter all in the same disaster. And the only one to remain unchanged through all of this was the angel Moreen herself, for she was less than six years old and understood nothing at all of the matter—not yet.

"As for me: such were my own emotions over the thing that I think at times I went a little mad. And when these bouts of madness were upon me, I would see strange visions and utter weird warnings and omens. As time passed, I sensed a monstrous disaster looming—though its essence utterly eluded me—and I deliberately began to pose as a seer before the clan, so that not even my poor husband or sons saw through the trick. Yet it was not merely a mad game I played, no; for the approach of the unknown horror was very real to me, and I sought to escape it. And that escape lay in the fostering of my own image as a soothsayer and wonder-worker, a power among the people.

"Thus I set about to learn all manner of spells and conjurations, brewed vision-engendering potions, gathered the delirious pollens of rare and poisonous blooms; and because my grandparents from the Motherworld had been my tutors, passing on great wisdom and even greater curiosity to me, I also journeyed to Norenstadt and learned how to read the olden books, thus discovering for myself the legends of the Vikings and their coming into Numinos. And in this manner and by these means did Annahilde become a witch-wife.

"During these preparations of mine for that terror which I knew was coming, and which by now I knew must concern Ithaqua and his desire to pluck Moreen from the clan when she was ripe, seven years went all too quickly by. Ithaqua had been back only once in those seven years, when Moreen was not yet nine years old. And if anything

101

the extra years had merely added to the goodness of her nature, so that she was loved by all the clan; aye, and even the wild animals of the fields and the birds of the air loved her; and never hurting anything or anyone, she herself was never hurt, nor even understood the meaning of fear . . . which was as well.

"For picture the sight of that horror winging down the whistling winds of ether to Numinos: the monster Ithaqua, his mind filled with many alien thoughts, and also one thought which is all too easily recognized by men. Aye, and if man knows the meaning of lust, how then Ithaqua? For he has known the lusts of all the ages, knows them yet, and while his burning eyes were veiled, certainly lust seethed in his black heart. But little Moreen saw it not, saw only the vast being of whom her parents and the clan spoke in shuddering whispers, the massive manlike shape in the sky whose hand came down, gentle as a falling leaf, to lift her to the high places from which, in her innocence, she could gaze down upon Numinos like some queen of the clouds—which one day, if he had his way, she would surely become. And who to say him nay?

"And on this occasion he seemed even more taken with Moreen than before and flew with her round the span of Numinos, showing her all of the places, even the icelands beyond the dark horizons. Aye, but he returned her warm and unharmed, and he smiled—if ever beast such as he could be said to smile at all!—on the clan of old Thonjolf, and the islands knew fair weather, bountiful crops, and good hunting for long and long after his going.

"But of course, three years later he came again . . .

"Now there was a lad in the clan, a mere lad, one Garven the Fair. And he admired Moreen and fancied her as is right for young men to fancy pretty girls. That was all there was to it, for Garven was good and honored the warnings and words of his parents, and the rose Moreen herself was not yet budded. Yet they were childhood sweethearts when times allowed and would meet in the fields some miles inland at a secret place. In this one thing Garven disobeyed his elders, and Moreen hers, and in other circumstances surely the time would arrive when they would cleave each to the other as man and wife. Alas, that time could never be.

"When next Ithaqua came, Moreen was not in the village. The Wind-Walker's coming was unexpected as the rough winds he brought with him and the dark clouds of storm and thunder. He came in suspicion and found things sorely wanting. The clan's cowards rushed here and there, searching for the maid that Ithaqua might be appeased, but she was not to be found. Nor indeed was the lad Garven to be found.

"Then, as Ithaqua's rage mounted to a fury, the innocents came hand in hand, over the cliff paths from their fond wandering in the fields. And Ithaqua saw them. . . .

"For all that they were children and pure as driven snow, Ithaqua's reaction was that of a cuckolded berserker! Jealousy crackled in the lightnings that played about his head, and the wonder is that his great pits of eyes did not glow brilliant green rather than their customary smoldering carmine. He snatched the two up and glared at them, and for a moment the very clouds stood still and no breath of air was felt. Then—

"—Before Moreen's very eyes, slowly and deliberately, he crushed young Garven to a tattered red pulp—squeezed the living guts from him—then tossed the red wet thing that had been a fair young lad down from on high to splatter on the beach below the settlement! While Moreen screamed and screamed, he next ripped off her clothes and examined her child's body minutely, finding no blemish, no evidence that she was ought but a child, no sign that his own evil ambitions were preempted. In the sky he nodded his great black blot of a head. So, and now he must ensure that the clan of Thonjolf understood his commands, that they obeyed them more fully in future. And who better to start with than Thonjolf himself, with whom all responsibility must ultimately lie?

"But there, what use to spell out the Wind-Walker's iniquities? The list is long as his life, which began back in the dim mists of time and seems interminable. Let it suffice to say that he murdered the elder Thonjolf's family (with the exception of the third chief of the line, the present Thonjolf the Red, who with his eldest son Harold was away hunting at the time) and also little Moreen's father, oh, and everyone and anyone he could get his great black hands on. Aye, and my man, too, Hamish, great fool that he was.

"But such a *brave* fool! Why, when he saw the carnage, Hamish ran at Ithaqua, waving his sword at him and challenging him where he stood red-handed and furious in the sky! I think my husband's mind had snapped—or perhaps he was drunk, I'm not sure. Whichever, he was very brave, and of course Ithaqua struck him down."

Briefly Annahilde paused, before quickly continuing: "Then, gathering great balls of snow from the dark clouds and freezing them hard in his hands, the monster rained them down upon the settlement until a third of the people were dead and their houses in ruins; and all of this the child Moreen saw. And though her screaming had stopped, her eyes, which once were so innocent, now opened wide in horror and loathing as she gazed down from her precarious perch in the crook of Ithaqua's shoulder.

"Finally he set the child down—not gently this time, tossing her naked into the shingle of the beach—before storming off into the lowering sky toward Norenstadt. Then . . . but how may I describe the agony and despair that Ithaqua left in his wicked wake? And before too long, in the midst of all that grief and mourning, back came those same priests from Norenstadt last seen seven years earlier.

"On this occasion Leif Dougalson did not accompany them, no, for he lay grievously ill upon his sickbed. The wonder is that he survives to this day; for Ithaqua had chastised him, had pulled out his left arm by its roots in payment for his disappointment! And so the priests came quickly and in anger this time, spurring their yaks cruelly on, with no false words of praise for the clan of Thonjolf and its new chief.

"Ah, but I had not been idle in the period following Ithaqua's departure. The home of Moreen and her mother had been destroyed during the Wind-Walker's fury—along with my sister's mind—so I had taken the pair in to care for them. I had lost my own man, true, but had known for long enough that some such was in the offing and recovered quickly from the ordeal. And I had known too that the Wind-Walker's priests must soon come to remove the child into their own care. Well, that black God of Horror had already taken more than eough from the clan, and now I, Annahilde, determined he should take no more. And I had instructed the child thus and so, until she knew what she must say and how she must behave.

"So when they came and laid hands on her, she at once broke free of them, pointing at the one and crying: 'When my Lord returns, I shall tell him that you tried to have me for yourself, against my will, and I shall ask him for your head to play with! And you'—she turned on the other—'I shall say to him that you plot against him, seeking a way to blind him and send him lost and stumbling between the stars!'

"'No, mistress, we beg of you!' they cried out to her, flinging themselves at her feet, her mercy. 'These things are not true, as well you know.'

"'Yet I will surely tell him that they are true,' she answered, 'if you dare to take me from the clan of Thonjolf.' And she stamped her foot as I had shown her, saying: 'Now—go!'

"Now these priests had not come out of Norenstadt at Ithaqua's command but of their own accord; for rather than face his wrath again following some further contravention of his wishes, they had decided the girl were best under lock and key and in their control. Well, that plan was now plainly out of the question, and without further ado and in great haste they left. Nor has the clan been bothered with them since . . .

"Perhaps this victory of mine over Ithaqua's so-called priests went to my head, perhaps not; but whichever, once they had gone, I set about to plan for Moreen's future, for her safety. Blood of my blood would not bear Ithaqua children to walk with him on the winds of ether, spreading his seed through all the universe—no, not if I had any say in the matter.

"And so I determined to smuggle Moreen away into the Isle of Mountains: the only place in all Numinos where her safety would be guaranteed, where Ithaqua could not touch her. That is where she is now, and that is where the pair of you enter into my plan."

"Oh? And why should Moreen's whereabouts affect us?" Silberhutte asked.

"Your quest will never be completed without her," she answered. "You will find her in the Isle of Mountains, and you"—she took de Marigny's arm—"you will surely fall in love with her; it can hardly be otherwise. I had thought that perhaps you would stay there and protect her, since Ithaqua will never give up trying to regain her for his own, but now that I know of this box of yours which flies between the worlds . . ."

"Well?" de Marigny prompted.

The witch-wife nodded, apparently reaching some unspoken decision or other. "Yes, it shall be this way: I will give you a letter to take with you. You will not be able to read what is written—but Moreen will. The letter will tell—"

"—Where we may find the time-clock?" de Marigny finished it for her.

"Of course!" she answered. And she laughed a laugh as normal and hearty as any they ever heard, with no slightest trace of her assumed eccentricity, so that finally they saw in her much more than a mere soothsayer or seer. She was a woman of the human race, and as such was shrewd as any of her shrewdest sisters—for which they could but admire her.

Chapter Five

Departure at Darkhour

"YOU'VE interested us greatly in all you've told us, Annahilde," Silberhutte said, "but there are a number of things we don't quite understand, things which could be important."

"Ask away," she replied.

"First: you mentioned Moreen's 'warmness' following Ithaqua's handling of her. What did you mean?"

"I meant what I said. The child was warm, *is* warm to this day, as if the Wind-Walker never laid hand on her. Surely you understand me? Look, you—" She took the Warlord's hand. "You have surely known Ithaqua's touch, for you are cold. This one, however"—and now she touched de Marigny—"he is warm, which shows that his contact with the Wind-Walker has been only tenuous, or that he has been protected."

"All true," de Marigny agreed. "It's generally accepted that physical contact with Ithaqua or lengthy close proximity will result in a permanent lowering of the body's temperature and an inexplicable immunity to subzero conditions. And yet you say that Moreen—"

"—Is warm, yes. Ithaqua did not chill her blood but left well alone. Perhaps it was all in keeping with his plan to let her grow into womanhood according to her nature, I do not know."

"I don't understand," de Marigny shook his head. "Surely all of the people on Numinos have altered metabolisms, just as they do on Borea?"

107

"Not all of them, Henri," the Warlord contradicted. "Occasionally the Wind-Walker's influence breeds itself out. There are several such 'warm ones' in the plateau on Borea."

"Aye, and here on Numinos," Annahilde agreed. "Most of them in the Isle of Mountains."

"That brings us to the second question," Silberhutte told her. "Just where is this 'Isle of Mountains,' and how is it that Ithaqua has no control over it?"

"Ah!" Annahilde answered, her voice dropping to the merest whisper. "The answer lies in the shape of the island. You see, there is a symbol which is utterly abhorrent to the Wind-Walker, a symbol he has forbidden in all of Numinos. The name of this symbol has never been allowed to be spoken, and so it no longer has a name. Of course I know this symbol—aye, and its ancient forbidden name for that matter—though I've only ever spoken it to myself, but . . ."

She paused and gasped, her eyes widening, then drew quickly back as de Marigny traced out a sign with his foot in the dirt of the floor. The shape he had drawn was that of a five-pointed star!

"Are you telling us that the Isle of Mountains is in the form of a star?" he asked.

"He makes the sign," Annahilde whispered, pointing at the star-shape, "and speaks its name!"

Silberhutte too had drawn back from the abhorred symbol, but now, with an expression of disgust flitting briefly across his face, he quickly advanced and scuffed out the sign with the toe of a fur-booted foot. "Is my friend right, Annahilde?"

She nodded. "Indeed he is. Of all the hundreds of islands in the seas of Numinos, the Isle of Mountains alone is protected from Ithaqua's wrath—by its very shape! That shape is hurtful to him."

"That is something we readily understand," Silberhutte answered. "But tell me, since the majority of living beings who have known the curse of Ithaqua are similarly affected by the symbol, how is it that the Isle of Mountains is not lethal to them also? How may one seek shelter in a poisoned place?"

"It is the degree of kinship that accounts for it," the

witch-wife explained. "The Wind-Walker's priests could not even set foot upon the isle, let alone live there. But warm ones such as Henri and Moreen, and others long fled there, are unaffected."

The Warlord frowned but remained silent.

"My friend wonders how the Isle of Mountains will affect him," de Marigny explained. "He has had much to do with Ithaqua, in one way or another."

She shrugged, glancing thoughtfully at Silberhutte. "I cannot say. I do not know. We can only wait and see. . . ."

Finally the Warlord looked up, and the frown slipped from his face. He grinned, however ruefully. "Well, I've had my share of this sort of problem before and come through it. There was a time when we turned the entire roof of the plateau on Borea into a huge star. There's nothing to be gained in worrying about it now. As Annahilde says, we can only wait and see." He turned to her: "But how do we go about looking for the Isle of Mountains? Will you give us directions, Annahilde?"

"No," she shook her head. "You will not go on your own. You will be carried there in Thonjolf's longships."

"In the longships?" de Marigny frowned. "Are you saying that the whole clan is defecting?"

"No, no," she repeated. "Oh, there was some such plan once mooted—but soon forsaken."

"But why?"

"Because three years ago when Ithaqua came to Numinos and discovered Moreen fled, he told his priests in Norenstadt that it was his intention in the near future to send all the Vikings against the Isle of Mountains—to kill all therein except the girl—which means that to flee there now is to commit suicide. And the meeting of chiefs from which Thonjolf has just returned confirms the Wind-Walker's intentions. However . . . ," she paused.

"Go on, Annahilde," Silberhutte urged.

"You two will be there *before* the Viking hordes. I have convinced Thonjolf that you are come here to lead his clan in the first assault upon the island—that you wish neither to wait for nor to join the main attack under Leif Dougalson—and that in this way, and by fetching Moreen out of the Isle of Mountains, the clan may regain Ithaqua's favor. I said these things to explain why you are here; also to ensure you reach the island before the bulk of the Vikings."

Now it was once more the big Texan's turn to frown. "Surely we could get there much faster on our own?" he said.

"Perhaps you could—if you knew the way," she answered. "But that is the one thing I cannot tell you. Only the sea captains know the location of the Isle of Mountains, and of course they have always shunned it—except for a trickle of refugees from Ithaqua's tyranny."

"And when do the longships leave?" de Marigny asked.

"The men prepare them even now," she replied, "and they set sail at the next Darkhour."

"Darkhour?" Silberhutte queried.

"That is the time when the sun is more than half-eclipsed by Borea. Always the sun hangs close behind Borea, but when the two seem to merge in the sky until the sun is two-thirds obscured, that is Darkhour. On the other hand, 'Lighthour' is when the rims of the sun and Borea separate, however fractionally. From one Lighthour to the next is a 'day' on Numinos. According to the old books about one hundred such days are equal to one 'year' in the Mother-world."

Here de Marigny spoke up. "I know a little astronomy—a little science, physics," he said, "and by all Earthly laws this planetary system can't work." Then, seeing that Silberhutte was about to voice his usual protest, he added: "Oh, I know, I know: this isn't Earth, not even the same universe we were born in—but it's baffling nevertheless."

"That's as it may be," Silberhutte mused, "but what Annahilde says explains a thing or two. Borea and its moons—if they really are moons and not a couple of minor planets—occupy fixed positions on a slightly crooked line, at the inner end of which stands the sun. That's why, seen from Borea, the moons are always partially eclipsed. The plateau must stand just sufficiently far around the curve of Borea to permanently hide the sun from view, which is why the plateau exists in a permanent half-light. When the moons are in Borea's shadow, there's always a false-dawn effect caused by the sun getting as close as it ever comes to rising. And when the sun shines full on the moons, they reflect its light upon Borea, maintaining a sort of balance. If my own knowledge of astronomy had been a little better,

110

I might long ago have realized that there must be a sun. The regular shadow that half-obscures the moons should have told me as much on its own!"

"But you've always more than half-suspected it," said de Marigny.

"Yes, I have. And just think: if on my expeditions I had ever managed to push on a few more miles away from Borea's twilight zone—why—I might well have seen my first Borean sunrise!" He paused for a moment and his expression grew more serious. "Right now, however, we're more interested in the next Darkhour than in any future sunrise."

"That's right," de Marigny agreed, turning back to Annahilde. "So we set sail for the Isle of Mountains at Darkhour. And when we get there and find Moreen? And after she translates your letter and tells us where we may find the time-clock? What then?"

She shrugged. "That is out of my hands. But Moreen must not be harmed, and she must not be brought back here where Ithaqua can find her. She is a woman now. He would not hesitate . . ."

"About Moreen," de Marigny said. "There's one more thing I don't understand. One thing about her, and one about Ithaqua."

"Say on," she nodded, "but be quick. I must report to Thonjolf. Later there will be feasting and drinking, then all will sleep—including you two, for you'll need your strength—and when you next awaken, it will be Darkhour."

"Two questions, that's all. How is it that the clan, which you say loved Moreen, now turns so readily against her? And why did Ithaqua not take some terrible revenge on discovering that the girl had fled from him? I would have thought he would utterly destroy the clan of Thonjolf."

"Ah, but that was some three or four years ago," she answered, "and when Ithaqua visited Numinos at that time he had other things to worry about. I was studying the books in Norenstadt when he came, and I saw him. I believe he was wounded!"

"Wounded?"

"Aye, for he sat on his pyramid throne and rocked to and fro, and he held up a great hand to his eye, from which trickles of carmine fire dripped like vile blood!"

111

The Warlord nodded. "That was my doing," he said, showing neither pride nor modesty. "When Ithaqua attacked the roof of the plateau with his kite-warriors, I struck him through the eye with a star-stone–tipped spear."

"Your doing?" Annahilde was astounded. "You struck him? A mere man against the Wind-Walker?" For a moment she was dumbstruck, then she laughed delightedly. "And did I not say you reminded me of Hamish?"

Again the Texan nodded. "You did, but my weapon was far more potent than any sword, Annahilde. Your Hamish was a hero, while I was merely desperate! But in any case you were going to tell us about the clan's change of heart toward Moreen. How did it come about?"

She shrugged fatalistically. "There were always the jealous ones. Then, after the near-slaughter of the clan and the destruction of the settlement when Ithaqua found Moreen and Garven together—aye, and once she was fled, the sure knowledge that Ithaqua must sooner or later exact an even more terrible vengeance—" Again she shrugged.

"Moreen was a loved one, yes, but the families of the clan have their own loved ones to worry over. It has been four years since I sent the lass away; sufficient time for the clan to transfer all the blame upon her innocent head. They forget that the only one to blame is the one who walks on the wind. But who am I to judge them? Now, with your coming, they grasp at their one chance to redeem themselves in Ithaqua's eyes. No, I do not blame them—I pity them."

After pausing reflectively, the witch-wife continued in a lighter tone. "Now then, before I report to Thonjolf—and just in case no further chance presents itself between now and Darkhour—I have something to give you."

From pockets hidden in her ragged clothing she drew out two small skin pouches. "This one," she said, passing it to de Marigny, "is for you. It contains herbs and salts crushed to a powder. Individually the ingredients are of no consequence; as I have prepared them, they form a powerful potion. The powder is to be taken carefully and sparingly."

"But what does it do?" de Marigny asked, weighing the pouch in his hand. "And why do you give it to me and not the Warlord?"

112

"He has no need of it," she answered, "for he feels only the utmost extremes of cold. You, on the other hand, are a warm one. The powder will keep you warm when the cold would otherwise kill you!"

Silberhutte eyed the other pouch. "And that one?" he asked.

She smiled cannily. "Ah, this one is a small magic in support of those you already possess. No mage in all Numinos prepares a more effective dreaming powder than Annahilde the witch-wife. Nor is it necessary for a man to sleep in order to dream. Simply blow the powder in the faces of any you would confuse or dismay. Look—"

She opened the neck of the pouch and took the merest pinch of a blue powder from it, blowing it from her palm into their faces before they could turn away. The powder settled on their lips, in their eyes. It entered their nostrils.

Then—

Silberhutte reeled as if struck with a sledgehammer. He threw himself against a wall, weaving, dodging, feinting, his arms and hands a blur as he batted away the myriad axes that flew at him from all directions, hurled by invisible hands. At the same time de Marigny leaped back from a black chasm that gaped open at his feet, where far below he glimpsed needle peaks that seemed to pull at him with a weird magnetism, demanding that he hurl himself to his death! Instead of "escaping" from the chasm's edge . . . he fell backward over a bench to sit jarringly on the dirt floor.

For both men the uncanny experience of being removed instantly from Annahilde's house into unknown realms of terror was totally real; so that when, scant seconds later, the powder-inspired visions faded and were replaced by the room they recognized and their laughing hostess, then their astonishment was complete.

She gave them no opportunity for comments or further questions, however, but clasped their strong arms to assure them that reality had indeed returned, then briefly studied their startled faces with bright eyes. Satisfied with what she saw, she nodded. "Most effective, yes?"

Without waiting for an answer, she continued: "The freedom of the settlement is yours. Only ask no more questions—certainly not of the common folk—for of course you

113

are near-omniscient and therefore need no questions answered." With that she opened the door and slipped out of the house.

"A pity," de Marigny at last managed to say as the door closed behind her.

"What is?" the Warlord turned to him, fully recovered now from his brief ordeal.

"I meant to ask her about the bats. Don't you remember? She mentioned them in connection with the Isle of Mountains when first she met us on the beach. 'That bat-haunted isle,' she called it. 'Bat wings beating in the mist—blood and terror and great winds blowing!'"

"Yes, I remember," the Warlord nodded thoughtfully. "Perhaps we'll get a chance to talk with her later. Then we can thank her for these 'small magics' she's given us. . . ."

Darkhour . . .

Darkhour, and chill gray mists had come up off the sea, changing the shapes of the grim-faced men who boarded the longships into those of weirdly horned monsters. Leather and metal helmets glistened with moisture, and furs clung damply to brawny backs and arms. The mist seemed to form a film of slime over everything; the timbers of the ships were slick with it.

The temperature had fallen until it stood not far above freezing; even the ocean, normally slightly warm from the high incidence of submarine volcanic activity, was more chill than its medium. Outlines were soft and blurred, and sounds were muffled.

The Warlord, where he sat beside de Marigny toward the stern of Harold's ship, had been quiet for some time, had uttered no word since boarding. Now he shuddered involuntarily. He felt no natural chill but an ominous foreboding, engendered perhaps of the quiet, sullenly lapping waters and the leaden mist.

De Marigny was more cheerful. He was filled with warmth and feelings of well-being, the result of putting his tongue gingerly to the merest pinch of Annahilde's warming powder. The blood flowed in his veins like red wine and his features, pale and waxy since first he set foot on Borea, were now ruddy and seemed almost to glow. He turned to his silent companion.

"Hank, Annahilde's warming powder is certainly the Great Equalizer where I'm concerned. I never felt so warm and well. I feel almost reborn, well up to anything Borea and its moons may throw my way. Even in the plateau the cold was a damnable handicap—but no longer."

As if waking from a daydream, the big Texan had started nervously when de Marigny began to speak. Now he shook himself and nodded his approval. "Good," he grunted. "I only wish I felt as comfortable and as confident."

De Marigny searched the other's mist-damp face. "Is something wrong?"

"Several things. For one, I don't like being on Harold's longship. He hates us and it shows. You saw the way he watched us all through that shindig they threw for us? If he can, he'll do away with us at his first opportunity. No, I don't like him; and I don't care much for this mist, either. It hides too much. Also I've a strong premonition of trouble looming. And finally—"

"Yes?"

"Armandra has me worried."

"She's been in contact with you?"

The Warlord nodded. "We agreed only to 'talk' to each other if there was real danger or something important to say. Well, she too has been bothered by dark premonitions. She thinks Ithaqua is close at hand, standing off in the void and riding the ether wind like a great hawk. She thinks he's watching us, that we are his quarry, his prey."

"Are we that vulnerable?"

"We're completely vulnerable. Oh, with luck Armandra might be able to snatch us back to Borea faster than her father could come for us. But on the other hand . . ." He shrugged.

"You mean we might be out of luck?"

Again Silberhutte nodded. "Could be. And you'll note that Annahilde's boys aren't coming on the raid? She made damn sure they were to remain with the rear party, didn't she? What does she know that we don't, eh?"

De Marigny refused to be subdued. "I'm sure I don't know," he said. "But about Ithaqua: personally, I think he's gone off on his wanderings again. I mean, if he were really interested in taking us and knew of our whereabouts, surely he'd have done it by now. What do you think?"

The Warlord shrugged. "I wish I dared seek him out with my mind, telepathically," he said. "But if he's close, he might recognize me and track us down by my thoughts. As a matter of fact I think Armandra's right and he is somewhere out there, not too far away. I also think he knows much of what's going on. He won't make his move yet, though, for he holds all the trump cards and he's very greedy."

"Greedy?"

"Sure. Why should he step in now and spoil it all? Why take us now when he might yet get his hands on Moreen— and the two of us in the bargain? And what a coup it would be if he could lure Armandra herself away from the plateau and Borea."

"You think that's his plan?"

"It makes sense."

Suddenly deflated, de Marigny said: "If it wasn't for my stupidity you wouldn't be in this spot."

The Warlord looked at him and grinned wryly. "Don't flatter yourself, Henri. I'll go out of my way to help a friend, yes, but don't forget that you're the one man who can help me . . . you and your time-clock. That machine of yours isn't just a gateway out of Borea and this alien dimension we're trapped in—where at the moment I'm as surely a castaway as you are—it's also a powerful weapon. The ultimate weapon against the Wind-Walker."

"True enough," de Marigny answered. "If any weapon can destroy Ithaqua, the time-clock can. Is that what you want, to kill him? Or is it that you want to escape from Borea and get back to old Earth?"

The other shrugged again. "I'll tell you better when we've recovered the time-clock—if we ever do recover it. As for now, it looks like we're on our way."

With a shout that roared out from sixteen throats as if from one—a shout whose echoes vibrated eerily through the mist—the oarsmen lifted up their oars vertically, poising them momentarily like twin rows of masts above the deck. Then the oars were lowered into oarlocks and dipped deep into darkly swirling ocean; and flanked by its dragon sisters, as a pacemaker in the mist-wreathed prow took up the beat with his hardwood pounding blocks, the longship pulled sluggishly away from the beach.

In the wake of the ships the settlement with its backdrop of cliffs quickly merged with the mist, and soon the three vessels passed out through the mouth of the fjord into the open sea. There, for all that the mist lay thick and menacing, the sails were unfurled and soon filled out as the dank, moisture-laden air swirled into them.

Finally, as they emerged seaward of the gray bank of fog, Harold roared a command from where he stood swaying in the prow. Echoing cries came back from the other ships; the pacemaker stopped his pounding; the sail belled out with the freshening breeze; and as the longships surged forward into the gloom of Darkhour, so the oars were lifted up once more and stowed away.

The longships were now fully under sail, creaking through slapping wavelets toward unseen horizons. Overhead, a dull-glowing crescent of sun showed golden-red from behind Borea's shadowy bulk.

Chapter Six

Wings in the Mist

THEY SAILED out of one Darkhour toward the next, always holding the same course, three ships abreast under strange auroral skies. To the port side sailed the chief's ship with Thonjolf himself in command; to starboard his cousin Hanarl's dragon clove the wave crests. Pride of place, though, went to Harold's ship, for it was the craft that carried Ithaqua's emissaries and rode to sea flanked by the other two.

Only once, when the wind failed, did the Vikings unship their oars, and then briefly. For growing impatient, the Borean Warlord (a genuine high priest of the Wind-Walker in the eyes of most of the Vikings, though Harold and his closer colleagues obviously maintained certain reservations) saw fit to call up Armandra's familiar winds to fill the slack sails and drive the ships on. To witness again at firsthand the strange powers of these men from the skies, and this time to be completely sober, was galling for Harold and his cronies and astonishing to the crewmen; nevertheless, as time passed, proximity bred something of contempt among the crew of the longship.

True, the small-statured strangers seemed to command the very spirits of the air, and it certainly appeared that they carried the word of the Storm-God, but in the end they were only men. And so the bearded giants of the ship soon grew tired of peering wonderingly at the pair where they sat in the stern, and on occasion one or other of the Vikings would even venture so far as to ask of them a gruff

118

question. For their part they always answered carefully and with a paucity of words so as not to demean their assumed standing.

Harold himself, exercising his trunklike legs by walking the wide central way that separated the oar banks, often strode close to the strangers. Whenever this happened, he would pause, legs braced and arms akimbo, scowling down at them. Invariably, though they returned his gaze blandly enough, de Marigny could sense the Warlord's desire to hurl himself at Harold's throat. Silberhutte's experiences on Borea had taught him well enough the best way to deal with treacherous enemies. To challenge Harold here, however, would be to challenge the entire crew—not to mention the crews of the other ships—and it would not bring their quest any closer to its conclusion. Thus Silberhutte bided his time, though now and then his companion could almost swear he heard the grinding of the Warlord's teeth.

For all their intense distrust and dislike of Harold, in one respect the pair followed his example: they, too, in a limited way, managed to spend some little time in exercising. De Marigny's method was to stroll out onto the walkway and limber up in the manner taught him in the plateau's gymnasiums: "physical jerks" which were initially greeted with loud hoots of derision. The Vikings soon grew bored with such "caperings," however, and left him to get on with it.

Silberhutte's exercises were rather more spectacular. Using his fantastic skill, he juggled with his own and de Marigny's murderous picklike weapons; or at other times he would hurl himself furiously from one end of the walkway to the other in whirlwind feats of gymnastic agility. For all that displays such as these were performed solely as a means of loosening up otherwise inactive muscles, still the warrior crew would look on in open awe and admiration, much to their captain's envious chagrin.

During those infrequent periods when the Warlord sat nodding with his broad back to the curving side of the ship, then his companion would ensure that he stayed awake and mentally alert, and vice versa. Both men were certain that their position was very tenuous—the look in Harold's pig eyes said as much—which was sufficient in itself to keep them on their toes.

119

So Lighthour came and went, and gradually the sun crept once more into Borea's shade, and slow but sure the mists rolled up off the sea to deaden the slap of wavelets and shroud the ships in undulating milky billows. Darkhour was coming on again, and according to things the Earthmen had overheard, that was the time estimated for their arrival in the forbidden region, that area of ocean where loomed the rocky star-shaped bastions of the Isle of Mountains. They had heard other whispers, too, concerning devilish creatures that came down out of the sky to murder unfortunate sailors and drive venturesome ships away, but of these they could discover no further details. . . .

Almost completely immunized against the cold by Annahilde's powder, de Marigny enjoyed as best he could his newfound comfort; nevertheless, and not wanting to become too dependent upon the drug, he used it sparingly as directed. In that period before and after Lighthour corresponding roughly to one Earth day, he had not taken a single sniff of the stuff, but as Darkhour drew closer, so he resumed his wary consumption of the warming powder, keeping at bay the freezing chill that came with the billowing mists.

Once, before the mist came down in earnest, they had thought to see in the distance a jagged wedge of land against the horizon, and at sight of those distant spires rising, the Vikings had grown silent. Too, there had been a cloud of tiny dots in the lowering sky above the far-off landmass, dots that seemed to circle sentiently but with motions unlike those of birds. Then the damp miasma of ocean had washed over the ships, covering them with a grayly swirling blanket.

And it was then also, with the Isle of Mountains comparatively close at hand and visibility down to only a few feet, that Harold decided to have done with these so-called emissaries of Ithaqua. It would have to be now, under cover of the mist, so that Thonjolf would never know the truth of it; he was a strange old dog with an odd sense of honor. Harold could always fabricate some tale or other with which to satisfy the old chief, and he knew well enough how to cow his men into complete silence. He had long ago decided that if anyone were to receive Ithaqua's blessings for fetching the girl Moreen out of the Isle of Mountains, that one would be Harold. The reward must certainly not go to a pair of strangers of doubtful origins. . . .

De Marigny was on watch while Silberhutte lay wrapped in sleep in the very stern of the ship. For some little time the Warlord's sleep had been restless, and he had tossed and moaned, so that de Marigny had thought to waken him. He had resisted the impulse, reckoning it was best for Silberhutte that he slept his fill in spite of whatever bad dreams disturbed him.

Moments after making this decision, however, he reconsidered. Suddenly there was a tension in the air not at all to his liking, an ominous, almost physical weight that seemed to press down upon him. The figures of the Vikings closest to him, where they sat in their places behind the round shields that lined the sides of the ship, were almost obscured by writhing tendrils of mist; they seemed like grim-horned phantoms sitting there, and their sullen silence only served to accentuate de Marigny's growing premonition of creeping doom.

Then, before he could stretch out a hand to shake Silberhutte's shoulder, there came to his ears a clear and distinct sound. An unmistakable sound which issued neither from the too-calm sea nor the ships that lolled upon it but from above, from the banks of mist that rolled over them. The sound of great wings in the mist, beating steadily, eerily over the longships.

De Marigny started, his heart leaping, as Silberhutte's hand grasped his wrist. "Henri! I . . . I was dreaming. Or was I?"

"More like a nightmare," the other retorted in a strained whisper. "But this—whatever it is—seems real enough. Listen!"

The Warlord needed no urging; his face was already tilted upward. "Bat wings beating, the old girl said," he recollected. "But I don't believe she told the half of it, and we forgot to ask!"

Harold, too, heard the wings in the mist. Halfway down the walkway toward the strangers, sword to hand and flanked by two of his flunkies while a third followed up

121

behind, he paused; his darkly suffused face blanched and his pig eyes grew wide.

"They've come," he whispered, his voice a half-croak. "Well then, so be it. But before the winged ones tackle us, we take the imposters. . . . *Now!*" And with that cry on his lips, crouching as he rushed forward through the shrouding curtain of mist, Harold led his men in a treacherous attack.

Surging out from the swirling gray wall that obscured the deck, startling the crew almost as much as the outsiders they attacked, Harold and his homicidal colleagues were a fearsome sight. He himself wore no helmet and his long damp hair was plastered back on his head. His mouth was open in a twisted, hideous snarl, and his tremendous stature and sheer bulk—plus the fact that the great, dully glinting sword he held on high was all of five feet long—put the finishing touches to the paralyzing shock of his appearance.

All in all the element of surprise itself ought to have been sufficient to see Harold's murderous intentions carried through, would have been sufficient but for unforeseen circumstances. One: the bully had made a mistake in allowing his cronies to flank him so closely. The walkway was not wide enough to accommodate three men abreast, certainly not men as huge as the Vikings. Even as they rushed into view of their intended prey, the man on Harold's right slipped on the damp planking, lost his balance, and fell, bringing down the one to the rear. By then de Marigny and Silberhutte were on their feet, reaching for their hand axes, automatically taking up defensive stances.

Then came the second unforeseen circumstance—the sudden intervention of an outside agency. For down out of the mist came Nightmare borne on leathery wings, Nightmare with the pointed ears and dripping fangs of the devil himself. The creature was a bat—fur bellied, yellow-eyed, with a wrinkled black-leather face—but it was almost as big as a man!

Flying between attackers and attacked, the giant bat used the talons of one of its hind limbs to rake Harold's face, opening his cheek in a red slash. He cursed and hacked at the thing with his great sword, but the creature was agile as its smaller cousins of the Motherworld and avoided the Viking's blade without difficulty.

Again and again Harold struck upward at the huge bat until suddenly, following fast upon his last thrust, its talons reached down and caught at the blade near his wrist, snatching it from him. He cursed as, with a shrill whistle of triumph, the creature tossed the weapon aside so that it fell into the sea.

By then the man on Harold's left, who had momentarily stepped back to give the chief's son elbow room, was once more coming in to the attack. He leaped high in the air, striking at the bat and missing, then followed up his action by turning his attention once more to the strangers. Landing in a crouch, he straightened up and whirled his sword at de Marigny. Instinctively, with skill born of his many lessons in the plateau's arenas, the Earthman ducked under the deadly arc to swing the needlepoint of his weapon into the giant's neck. In the next moment blood gushed in a crimson fountain, and the stricken man gave a single, gurgling scream before toppling overboard.

But now more bats had descended from the mist and were flitting hugely over the heads of the Vikings, striking at them with wickedly sharp talons as they rose up from their seats to fight back with savage blows. All was confusion; the mist swirled everywhere; the air was filled with shrill whistlings, screams, and bull roars of rage and pain as the bats took advantage of the momentary havoc to tear and rip.

Harold, defenseless now, still faced the first of these horrors from the sky, and as the great bat struck at him yet again, de Marigny stepped forward and made to intervene. The Earthman was in no way interested in saving Harold's skin, but it fully appeared to him that unless the bats were driven off, all aboard the dragonship were surely doomed.

Before he could strike, however, the Warlord—until now curiously inactive—caught at his arm and stayed the blow. "No, Henri," he shouted, "leave it. If we don't bother them, they won't bother us. It's the Vikings they're after!"

But freely given or not at all, Harold needed no assistance. He was far from crippled by the loss of his sword, and as the bat tore at his chest with its talons, he struck it a massive double-fisted blow in the face. Half-stunned, the creature thudded to the deck, and taking advantage of this brief respite, the chief's son roared: "Do you see what these

123

so-called 'emissaries of Ithaqua' are up to, lads? Why, it's *them* called these monsters down on us! See here, they've sided with the bats! Now fight, you dogs, and when we've driven off the fliers, then we'll deal with the traitors. . . ."

As he finished yelling, the dazed bat on the deck seemed to recover its senses. Wings outstretched, it flopped toward him and attempted to knock him from his feet. With a blustering battle roar, seeing that the thing was half done for, Harold stepped inside the span of its wings and caught at its soft throat. Forcing its dripping fangs to one side and well away from his face, he locked his mighty arms about its neck.

His remaining pair of cronies, having been amply engaged in their own right prior to this moment, now rushed to assist him. They stabbed at the bat together, their swords passing through its membranous wings and into its soft body. Blood gushed from its wounds and from its gaping mouth, drenching Harold from head to foot; but a moment later he heaved its corpse over the side of the ship to stand there red with gore and furious in the berserk rage that now gripped him.

The mist was lifting a little, and the bats were retreating with it, but in their wake they left a dozen dead or dying Vikings. Nor had the crew of the longship failed to take its toll. The deck was littered with the broken bodies of great bats, and those that yet lived were even now being put to the sword.

"Time we abandoned ship, Henri," Silberhutte said as Harold's pig eyes lighted upon them where they stood in the stern. "The big fellow's tasted meat, and we're next on the menu. Can you fly us out of this? The bats are waiting for us."

"Waiting for us?" the other repeated. "Then maybe we'd do as well to take our chances here."

"No, you don't understand. They're waiting to lead us to the Isle of Mountains—to the great cave where the people of the island live—to Moreen . . ."

"But how do you—?"

"No time now, Henri. Later. And here comes Harold— *look out!*"

Harold had taken two paces toward them, his massive hands reaching. Then, finding himself weaponless, he snatched a sword from one of his men. As he did so, de Marigny shrugged out of his fur jacket and let down his cloak from where he had gathered it at his waist.

As the Earthman's fingers brushed the studs that controlled the cloak in flight, so the Warlord yelled: "Get aloft, Henri. Quick—I'll grab your legs!"

"They're trying to get away!" Harold roared, and he rushed forward, swinging his sword around his head. De Marigny was already airborne over the deck and bringing the cloak under his expert control when Silberhutte and the chief's son came together in a clash of steel and flying sparks. He looked down and was barely in time to see the fight finish as quickly as it began. For such had been the violence of the shock when the two crashed together that their weapons had shivered into fragments; the metal of their blades—ax and sword alike—had actually shattered!

Harold had then stepped back to hurl the heavy, jagged hilt of his sword at Silberhutte's face. But the Warlord, avoiding the deadly missile, had stepped in close to use the splintered haft of his ax as a club. Swinging it against Harold's neck, he had battered the giant to his knees. Then, as the Texan leaped to grab at de Marigny's legs, so he simultaneously contrived to smash his knee into the Viking's forehead. Once again this combination of blows must surely have killed any normal man, but even as Silberhutte secured his hold on de Marigny's calves and the two drifted aloft, so they could make out the shape of the fallen man moving on the deck below, trying to climb to his feet.

"He must be made of iron!" Silberhutte muttered, shaking his head in disbelief as the cloak now bore them more surely upward into the dispersing mist.

And now, too, the remainder of the crew awoke from the stupefaction of seeing Harold so swiftly dealt with for the second time by the "little" stranger. But their awakening was too late, and their cries of rage were of no avail as the cloak-fliers quickly soared out of range. Only one of the many spears thrown after them passed close; the remainder fell well behind, splashing into the sea. Then the ship was momentarily lost to their view as they rose swiftly upward into the chill but rapidly thinning mist.

Seconds later they climbed into open air. Circling high overhead, the bats were beginning to disperse, heading for that island briefly glimpsed before the mist had come down. At this distance and from this elevation, the island's shape could not be discerned, but the cloak-fliers had little doubt that it was the Isle of Mountains.

"Will you be all right, Hank, hanging onto me like that?" de Marigny called down to his passenger.

"I'll be okay," the Warlord answered. "Don't worry about me. Just follow the bats."

"Just as you say—but what makes you so sure they won't turn on us?"

"Because they told me so," the Warlord returned, laughter in his voice.

"They *what?*" de Marigny shouted. "How in the name of—"

"They're telepathic, Henri. Most animals are, to one degree or another. Dogs and dolphins are, for sure. You must have noticed how a dog reacts when it senses you're afraid of it? Well, the bats are telepathic, too, only more so. They're highly intelligent, cleverer than dolphins, I'd say. They're probing my mind right now, as they were when I was sleeping. That's why you thought I was having a nightmare. And watch what you're thinking, for they're probably probing you, too!"

"And do they know why we're here, that we're looking for Moreen?"

"Yes, and they know we mean her no harm. If we did . . . well, that would be just too bad."

For a moment they were quiet and only the whine of the wind in the cloak disturbed the silence. Then, noting that the mist had finally dispersed, leaving the surface of the sea a dull and wave-flecked bronze color, de Marigny called: "Hey! Look down there. The bats didn't just pick on Harold's ship."

Far below the three longships showed against the sea, though height and distance now made it impossible to pick out individuals among the antlike figures that scurried about the decks. One of the ships—drifting quite aimlessly, crippled, with its sail torn and askew—seemed to be completely void of human activity. The other vessels moved in, throwing lines aboard and closing with her.

"Hanarl's ship," the Warlord grunted. "She must have been taken completely by surprise. Well, there's nothing we can do—and you must know how we'll be dealt with if ever the Vikings get their hands on us after this. Let's hope they don't catch up with us."

"You think they'll try?" de Marigny asked, urging more speed from the cloak as the great bats began to draw away.

"Sure of it," Silberhutte declared. "It's Thonjolf's one remaining chance to save face—Harold's, too. And don't forget, Henri, somewhere out there, possibly at this very moment, a thousand longships are making sail in this direction. Oh, yes—we'll do well to find Moreen and be far gone from here when those ships arrive. . . ."

Chapter Seven

The People of the Cave

WHEN THEY were well underway and de Marigny could give his attention to things other than the firm control of his flying cloak, he managed to reach down and receive from Silberhutte the fastenings of the other's harness. Not without some difficulty he then clipped his passenger's straps safely into position. Now at last, while the big Texan hung in comparative comfort below, de Marigny was able to work his own dangling legs and stretch them, bringing life back to them after their crushing by Silberhutte's mighty arms.

The three dragonships were mere matchsticks floating far below and behind them by then, while ahead the rocky, natural bastions of the island loomed ever closer. Gradually climbing higher into the sky of Numinos, they had at last seen that indeed the island was in the shape of a regular, five-pointed star. It appeared that in some bygone age there had been five mountains, all of a height and probably volcanic. As time passed, the elements had whittled the formation into a single star-shape on the outside while forming an irregular lake within. Steam and a little smoke, puffing up still from the center of the vast, still lake, showed that volcanic activity was not yet extinct in the area; but soon, as the bats began a breathtaking descent and de Marigny followed suit, the central lake was lost to sight behind the topmost spires of the exterior mountains.

Down the great bats fell in a spiraling stream, and rushing up to greet them came the jagged fangs of secondary peaks, crested now with tufts of white cloud that formed ever faster as Borea slipped in front of the sun to shut out its light and warming rays. Darkhour was almost here, and so chill the wind howling over the mountains that de Marigny felt obliged to take yet another pinch of Annahilde's warming powder.

Then the winds were suddenly shut off, and the view beyond the mountains disappeared in an instant as the fliers fell below the level of the range to continue their descent oceanward. They were coming down in a bay formed of two of the island's starfish arms, and they could now see and hear the wash of ocean on the rocks far below and marvel at the gaunt appearance of the inhospitable coastline. Here the ocean-facing cliffs rose black and threatening, almost perpendicular from the sea, so that it seemed almost impossible for anyone approaching by ship to gain any sort of foothold upon them.

Stark and bare, the place looked uninhabitable, and yet the fliers were certain that there were people here: the people of the cavern that Silberhutte had seen in telepathic pictures snatched from the minds of the great bats; those same creatures that now skimmed unhesitatingly toward a shadowed entrance whose mouth loomed darkly ominous in the rocky wall some forty feet above the level of the choppy sea.

A few seconds later, hot on the trail of the hindmost bat, the fliers entered a deep high-ceilinged cave. From the entrance to a depth of some fifty feet, the ceiling had been propped up with stout beams fashioned from whole pines—wood which was now black with age, decayed, and sagging—and brackish water dripped from above, splashing on the slimed stone floor. Overhead, showing through a crisscross of heavy beams, the pair saw how badly rotted was the rock of the ceiling, how saturated with the salts of ocean and the nitrous drip of acidic moistures.

Beyond this point de Marigny was forced to cut back their velocity to little more than walking speed. The bat they followed made no attempt to wait for them but disappeared with an amplified burst of fluttering into the darkness of the cave's winding tunnel. In its wake a single high-pitched whistle echoed eerily back to them. Finally, finding themselves flying blind as the light quickly diminished, they were obliged to settle to the moist shingle floor where they waited until their eyes grew more accustomed to the gloom.

"People live in here?" de Marigny inquired as his eyes began to pick out details of the fissurelike tunnel. "They actually *live* here?"

"No, this is only the entrance," the Warlord stated matter-of-factly. "We've some way to go yet before we reach the cavern where the people live. The tunnel goes right back to their cave and even continues beyond it, in the form of old volcanic vents which come out on the inner slopes above the central lake. That lake feeds a lesser pool in the great cave, where the cavern people do their fishing."

De Marigny looked at his friend in astonishment. "You got all that telepathically, from the bats?"

The other nodded. "Yes, and I'm getting other stuff right now." He peered into the gloomy reaches of the tunnel. "Actually I should feel quite at home here; there's much about this place that has the atmosphere of the plateau on Borea. And yet . . ."

"Yes?"

"Well, Annahilde was right. It's an effort to stop myself running right out of here. The island's star-shape, you know. . . ."

De Marigny nodded. "I forgot about that. Of course I personally feel nothing."

"No, you shouldn't. It's just something I'll have to live with for now; but after all, I've had it worse than this before. I was once inside the plateau's forbidden tunnel, which leads down to a cave full of star-stones—the genuine articles—beneath the very heart of the place. By comparison this is only a very small fear."

De Marigny looked at his companion's dusky outline and found it hard to imagine that the Warlord could fear anything. Presently he said, "I believe I can see a little better now. Should we press on?"

"Do us good to stretch our legs," the big Texan nodded. Then: "Henri, do you mind if I take your ax? You've learned to handle it pretty well, but I've had a lot more firsthand experience. We don't really know for sure what's up ahead, and—"

"Take it by all means," de Marigny cut in, handing his

weapon over. "In my hands it's only a pick—or an ax, or whatever you want to call it—but with you behind it, the thing's almost an arsenal!"

Moments later, having wrapped the cloak about his waist, de Marigny was ready. Silberhutte, clipping the straps of his harness securely behind his neck, hefted the ax once in his hand and said, "Well, ready or not, here we come. While we walk, I'll probe ahead and see if I can pick up the bats."

The Warlord managed a grin that de Marigny sensed rather than saw. "It was quite a shock for them when they found I could read their minds almost as well as they read mine. They never met a human telepath before. Come to think of it, apart from Armandra's and the mind of one other girl I knew—and not forgetting the alien cesspits of the CCD minds—these are the first genuine telepaths I've been able to contact. One thing I'm sure of is that they're good guys. They don't dislike people."

"Oh? What of their attack on the longships?" de Marigny asked.

"Their allegiance lies with the people of the cavern," the Warlord answered, "especially with Moreen. They knew why the Vikings were coming, and their attack was to show how strongly they disapproved. I don't know what that girl has, but I reckon the bats love her dearly." After a moment he added: "Hey, Henri, you'd better worry about that, eh?"

"About what? How do you mean, Hank?"

"Well, didn't old Annahilde say you'd fall for Moreen? It certainly seems like the girl's got something worth falling for!"

"Is that so?" de Marigny soberly answered. "Well, whatever she's got, surely the last thing we want is any sort of complication. Just look at the circumstances. Can you really see an affair brewing between me and some unknown girl—here on Numinos, in an environment alien as this—as if the trouble we have already isn't enough?"

"Just kidding, Henri," the Warlord nodded, stepping out a little faster along the tunnel. "But you have to admit Annahilde's prophesies have been right on target so far, eh?"

When no answer came, he added: "Forget it." But de Marigny was pleased to hear the Texan's low chuckle sounding in the darkness. Already his massive companion was forgetting his deep, subconsciously rooted fear of the place, and that could only be a point to the good.

So they set out to walk down the dusty, guano-smelling passage through the mountains, moving in comparative silence, with only the dull echoes of their footsteps to accompany them.

After traversing the first two bends, all remaining exterior light was shut out, but they were thankful to note that the gloom was relieved, however faintly, by a fungus phosphorescence that glowed from the flaky walls. If anything, they were able to go ahead a little faster, though there were stretches here and there where the absence of the patchy fungus threw them into pitch-darkness. Gradually they became used to feeling ahead with their feet and hands; and so they progressed.

Midway through one of these regions of Stygian darkness, where they were to each other's eyes vague outlines seen against a very faintly glowing background, Silberhutte fetched an abrupt halt and grasped his companion's arm. "Henri, I just got something from the bats. There's danger up ahead. . . . Wait a minute. . . ."

"Yes?"

The Warlord grunted. "Some sort of trap. No, it's not meant for us after all. We just have to step warily, that's all."

Moving even slower now, after some time they reached a spot where a steady breeze blew in their faces. Soon after, from high above, the dim light of Darkhour filtered down through a fissure that reached clear up to the open air. By that feeble light they saw that the tunnel had widened out considerably, that to their right a subterranean ravine now opened, at the foot of which unseen waters gurgled and rushed, hurrying blindly to some unfathomed destination.

Once the fissure was behind them, the breeze all but disappeared, and with its passing, the gloom descended once more; the wide ledge they trod seemed to vanish in the darkness ahead, as did the chasm to their right; the silence was relieved only by the sound of their hushed breathing and the far-off *drip, drip, drip* of falling water. Then, in the distance—a mere flicker at first but quickly brightening—

they spied an orange-burning flame whose light beckoned them more rapidly on.

The flambeau—of seaweed drenched in some slow-burning, glutinous resin—was set in a blackened hardwood bracket fastened to the wall of the tunnel. Its sputtering flame illuminated the ledge, the rough lip of the ravine . . . and something else. A trip wire had been stretched inches above the floor across the entire width of the ledge. Climbing the craggy wall to their left to a height of some thirty feet, the trip was fastened to a wooden beam that protruded from a V-shaped crevice.

Piled above this beam, precariously balanced, great boulders filled the crevice in such a way that even a gentle tug on the trip wire would bring them tumbling down in an avalanche that would sweep anyone on the ledge over the lip of the ravine into oblivion.

"Hardly what you might call a friendly welcome," the Warlord dryly commented, "but at least we were warned about it."

De Marigny nodded. "It would have been a sight less friendly if they'd left the torch unlit for us! Careful how you go, Hank."

Gingerly they stepped over the trip wire, uncomfortably aware of the great weight of boulders above, and quickly continued on down the tunnel for a further hundred yards or so. There, rounding a gentle bend and plunging once more into darkness, they spotted in the near-distance the flickering glow of a second torch. Now their progress became much more rapid as they moved between a succession of sputtering torches, evading the booby traps their light invariably disclosed, until at last the tunnel narrowed down to a mere shaft, and the ravine disappeared altogether. Then it was that they emerged into a cave of truly fantastic proportions, where a party of the cavern dwellers awaited them.

At first they did not see the men who waited, so stunned were they at the sight that greeted them as they came out of the tunnel into the vast cavern. Flambeaux seemed to burn everywhere—forming a rough circle around the floor of the cave some fifteen feet or so below them, a circle at least fifty yards across which marked the perimeter of the cave's walls; blazing brightly higher up in the walls of the place, from where the mouths of lesser caves looked down; burning in braziers borne on the decks of rafts that floated on the rippled surface of a pool which occupied at least one-third of the cavern's floor space; and, across the cave proper, illuminating the mouths of a hundred smaller caves which were plainly the dwelling places of family units—so that the whole scene was as of some Troglodyte grotto, or perhaps a diamond mine of the fabled King Solomon. The smoke from all of these sources seemed drawn on a draft of air to a central vent high in the ceiling, so that the atmosphere was surprisingly clean and free of debris.

But even as they gazed at the scene in silence—watching fire-bright fishermen casting their nets from the decks of the rafts and listening to the low chanting of figures where they squatted in some sort of ceremony around a blazing fire—so they became aware of their reception committee. Out from the shadows they stepped, forming a ring about the pair, and a moment later sparks were struck from flints to ignite yet more torches.

Not quite so tall as the average Viking and carrying far less weight, the men of the cave were pallid, their eyes showing a distinct lack of color. They were clothed in garments made from animal skins or furs, many of which appeared to have been woven from the soft fur of the great bats. None of them were youngsters, the majority appearing to be in their thirties or older; and all of them seemed to have stooped shoulders, a stigma which was very prominent among the more obviously aged.

"We come in peace," de Marigny offered when a few moments had passed in uneasy silence.

"Aye, we know that," said one graybeard stepping forward and holding his torch high. "If you did not, then the bats would have struck you down."

The same man turned to Silberhutte, eyeing first the hand ax and then the face of the man who held it. "Since you come in peace, you will surely not need that."

"Ah?" the Warlord started, then saw the old man's meaning. He quickly put the weapon away in his belt. "Your pardon," he said. "We did not know what to expect."

Now a somewhat younger man stepped forward, his face firm but friendly in the light of the torches. "Before we welcome you more properly," he said, "there are certain formalities of ritual. We will tell you what we have to offer you, and you will say how you will make payment for our hospitality."

As the other two stepped back, so a third man came to the fore. He said: "We offer you the shelter of the cave and its warmth, the fellowship of the bats, the flesh of the beasts of the inner slopes and their furs, the mushrooms of the caves, the water of the pool that you may drink and its fishes that you may eat. All of these things we offer. How are you to make payment?"

The two looked at each other. Finally de Marigny spoke. "How shall I answer?" he asked.

The graybeard who had first spoken came forward again and grasped his arm. "Answer in your own way," he advised.

"Very well. . . ." De Marigny considered for a moment, then said: "We thank you for all you offer. For however short a span we remain with you, we gratefully accept these things. We will pay for them with our friendship, with our respect for your laws, and with—with—"

"With information," the Warlord cut in, seeing de Marigny's difficulty. "Information which could well mean life or death for all of you!"

"Information? Life or death? Speak on," commanded the elder.

"The Vikings are coming—all of them," Silberhutte continued. "A thousand longships sent by order of Ithaqua against the Isle of Mountains. They'll find your cave—from the sea or by climbing the mountains to the inner slopes, it makes little difference—and they are sworn to kill all they find. All except the woman Moreen, which Ithaqua the Wind-Walker claims as his own. That is the information we bring."

The elder slowly nodded. "Aye, we thought that might happen sooner or later." Then, more urgently he asked, "How much time do we have?"

Silberhutte shrugged. "Not long. We believe that the Vikings may be converging on your island even now. Certainly three ships from the clan of Thonjolf are already in these waters."

"Then there remains only one more question, or perhaps

two," the elder muttered. Suddenly he seemed lost for words, strangely embarrassed, but at last he found his tongue:

"We keep watches on the sea approaches; the higher peaks are constantly manned, as is the passageway from the sea. Just before you came, we were forewarned by the young man on watch at the mouth of the tunnel. He is a very young man and easily excited, but he says that when you came, you followed the bats, and that like the bats you—"

"Like them we flew, yes," de Marigny spoke up, anticipating the question. "This cloak I wear has the power of flight. It carries us through the air at great speed. I brought it with me from the Motherworld. The Warlord, too, is a stranger in your world, for he hails from Borea, the World of the Winds. Our purpose in coming here is to find the woman Moreen, for we think she may be able to help us in our quest. . . ." Here de Marigny broke off, for as he had spoken, his voice had been progressively drowned out by a rapidly rising babble from the surrounding circle of cave dwellers.

His and Silberhutte's revelations, coming thick and fast, had finally broken through the reserve—real or assumed—that the men of the caves had initially displayed. Now the air was full of such muttered words and phrases as: "The Motherworld! Borea! A *thousand* longships! The woman Moreen! A flying cloak!"

At last the hunched-up old graybeard—who appeared to be the main spokesman for the group, possibly the leader of the entire subterranean clan—held up his hands and cried: "Hold! There is much to be said and little enough time for saying it. There must be an orderly council meeting as soon as one can be arranged, but before that—" He turned back to the strangers.

"You," he spoke to Silberhutte. "You have the appearance and the build of a great warrior, even though you are not a very tall man, and your friend calls you 'Warlord.' And you," he looked at de Marigny. "You wear a flying cloak that carries you through the skies like a bird. That is a wonder I must see. And in addition, though you would not seem to be wizards, you say you come from distant worlds! Very well," he nodded, "we accept that you control

136

great powers; it remains to be seen how well you use them. And so, before I call a grand meeting of the council, there is one more thing I must know. When the Vikings come, will you—"

"Yes, we will," Silberhutte interrupted. "If we are still here when the Vikings come, we'll help you defend yourselves as best we can." He turned to his companion. "Right, Henri?"

"Right!" said the other. And from somewhere high in one of the many deep dark recesses of the ceiling, a series of shrill, eerie whistlings greeted their decision with approval. . . .

Chapter Eight

Moreen

FROM that time onward—following the meeting of the council and during the feast prepared in their honor that followed it; and then through the drinking, talking, and great round of introductions—time and again the newcomers would ask to see Moreen, only to be told that for the moment this was out of the question. Darkhour was not long passed, and no one would venture to guide them to Moreen until the way was fully lighted by the strange auroral rays of the sun.

For she did not dwell in the cavern itself—was unable to bear the weight of the mountain above—but preferred the air of the inner slopes, of the forest and the five mountains, particularly that peak whose inner face housed her in a cave of her own. There she dwelled, far across and high above the deep central lake, and there they would doubtless find her with her retinue of great bats—but not until after Darkhour. Now they must rest themselves and benefit from the good food and drink they had consumed. They could sleep easy in the knowledge that they were with friends, and when they awakened, that would be time enough for them to go out and seek Moreen.

For all that, the proposed itinerary of the cavern folk seemed to make good sense. The thought of finding the mysterious Moreen remained uppermost in de Marigny's mind; of finding her, yes, and of having her decipher those cryptic symbols scrawled upon a scrap of soft hide by Annahilde. Surely, he told himself, he must be closer now to recovering the time-clock than at any time since leaving Borea; and such was the mental fever this thought wrought in his mind that sleep seemed almost impossible.

Nevertheless he did sleep, finally succumbing to the combination of weariness and strain that hung over from the nerve-racking journey through the midnight tunnel; and to the sporific effect of an amount of ale consumed during the feast; but it was in no way a peaceful sleep.

Twice he started awake from unremembered nightmares upon his bed of furs, bathed in the glow of the fire that burned brightly before the hollow in the cave's wall that housed his own and Silberhutte's recumbent forms. On both occasions he cast about nervously with his eyes in the gloom beyond the flickering flames, observing on ledges across the great cave the moving fires that told of patrolling watches. But it was not until he awoke for the third time that he noticed the huge bat where it hung upside down, clinging to an overhang of rock like some weird watchdog not far above where he lay.

The eyes of the creature, inverted, burned upon his briefly, then turned to Silberhutte's still form. The Warlord stirred for a moment and his body tensed . . . but then he settled back on his furs, sighed deeply, and relaxed. After awhile the great creature turned its eyes once more upon de Marigny, and he fancied it sensed his restlessness.

At once, as if from nowhere, driving out all agitation and frustration, comforting sensations began to fill his mind. Without feeling any resentment, he knew that indeed this monstrous creature, whose smaller cousins of Earth were snyonymous with Night and all the terrors of midnight abysses—was lulling him to sleep, soothing his fears, and calming his troubled mind; and so persuasive was its hypnotic power that he gave himelf up entirely into its care and quickly fell into a deep, satisfying, and dreamless sleep.

. . . And it was the leathery beating of that same creature's wings that awakened him hours later; that and Silberhutte's terse command, breaking into his subconscious, that he should get up. Raising himself onto one elbow, de Marigny saw the Warlord crouching upon his own bed and staring into the eyes of the huge bat where it hovered, buffeting the air with mighty sweeps of its wings. The creature's movements were full of a visible urgency, de Marigny could see that, but the nature of what it imparted to the Texan was far beyond his grasp. Though Titus Crow had once hinted that he was slightly telepathic, de Marigny had little practical knowledge of the art.

He could guess, however, and guessing, his heart sank. For the Warlord had made a promise, and de Marigny knew that it could not be broken. "The Vikings?" he queried.

Silberhutte, without taking his eyes from those of the furred monster whose motions scattered the ashes of the fire and caused its embers to glow bright red, merely nodded for an answer.

"They're here?" de Marigny pressed. "Already?"

"Only hours away, Henri, and there's much to do."

"I know," a trace of bitterness crept into de Marigny's voice. "We promised we'd help . . ."

"No," the Warlord quickly answered, turning toward him, "I promised."

The great bat, satisfied at last that its message was understood, flew off into the cavern's gloom as Silberhutte grasped de Marigny's shoulder. "I promised, Henri," he repeated, "and it's up to me to make that promise good."

"But I—"

"No buts, friend. I fixed it with old Skaldsson the chief, right after the feast. You are to go hunt out Moreen, while I take a closer look at the tunnel's defenses. The peaks should be easily enough defended—a dozen men could start avalanches down the outer slopes that would keep out the entire army of Vikings for a long time—but the tunnel is different again. Those booby traps they've rigged up will create all hell when they hit, but only for a moment. When the boulders stop rolling the Vikings will come on again, more angry than before, and they'll take it out on the cavern folk."

"You think they'll get this far?" the other asked.

Silberhutte nodded. "I don't doubt it. There are too many of them: thousands of them in a great fleet of long-ships with Harold bringing them in. I was shown them through the mind of the great bat. Some of its brothers are keeping an eye on the fleet even now, picking off Vikings

140

whenever they get the chance—and paying dearly for their audacity!"

"But I can't just go off chasing this girl while you—"

Again the Warlord cut him off: "You have to, Henri. We have to get that cryptogram deciphered before we can find the time-clock. For all we know the clock is within easy reach, and with it—"

"We could turn back the entire Viking force!"

"Right!" The Warlord clapped him on the shoulder. "While you're away, I'll get in touch with Armandra. With or without the clock we may have to be out of here quickly. Also I have my work cut out in the tunnel. There must be dozens of places where additional booby traps can be rigged up. If I take a gang of the cavern folk and start near the entrance, we can play a delaying game all along the tunnel's length. By then, using the flying cloak, you should be safely back from your meeting with Moreen."

"But surely I should be back long before then," de Marigny protested, frowning. "I mean, the Vikings are still hours away."

"That's right, and you still have to get out of here. The exits from here to the inner valley are long, dark, winding, and treacherous. But . . ." The Warlord paused. "Wait, I have an idea."

"An idea? About what?"

"We've been thinking in terms of a human guide to get you to Moreen. However . . ." Again he paused, then frowned and half-closed his eyes. He held up his hand to silence de Marigny as the other started to question his meaning.

Moments later there came the throb of leathery wings and one of the great bats hovered close by. The Warlord opened his eyes wide and stared at the bat, and once more de Marigny watched their silent "conversation." Finally the bat flew off and Silberhutte turned to his friend with a grin.

Before the Warlord could speak, de Marigny guessed: "A bat? My guide is to be a bat?"

"Right. There's one on its way from Moreen right now. Flying your cloak, you'll follow it out along one of the exit tunnels to the inner slopes. Once out in the open, it will take you straight across the lake to Moreen."

"I'm to fly blind through the tunnel?"

"Carry a torch," the other answered. "Is that feasible?"

"I wouldn't really care to try it," de Marigny replied. "What if the cloak catches fire? I don't know how—"

"Then try to attach yourself to your guide in some way or other," Silberhutte cut in. "Give it some thought. Getting to Moreen has to be your problem, Henri. As for me: I'm off to get things moving. The cavern folk are not telepathic; so far they don't know that the Vikings are almost here. Well, they should have recovered from their feast by now. I certainly hope so. They're going to need all of their strength and wits before very much longer!

Flying in darkness behind the great creature to which he was loosely tethered—not having to worry about obstacles but merely ensuring that his forward speed and direction were compatible with those of the bat; being towed, if anything, like some blind, sentient balloon behind his constantly, weirdly whistling "guide"—de Marigny thought back on that period of activity immediately preceding his departure from the great cavern. He had gone with Silberhutte to warn the cavern folk of their imminent danger, and while the Warlord had assumed command of the fighting forces, he had spoken long and earnestly with the chief, old Arnrik Skaldsson. Their topic had been Moreen.

The chief had been able to tell him much. Since her coming to the Isle of Mountains, Moreen might easily have had her pick of the younger unattached men of the cavern, of which there were several, but had preferred a lone existence accompanied only by her bats on the slopes of the inner valley. It seemed that before she came here, a witchwife had promised her that the time would come when a man would find her—a man as good and free in spirit as she herself was good and free—one she could love. And of course she had shunned the great cavern from the first, had hated the idea of being shut in; for she was a "warm one" and her love of open skies and freshening breezes could not be fulfilled below ground.

The cavern folk, on the other hand, for the most part could not bear to be too long out in the open. They feared Ithaqua mightily, most of them having fled his wrath to come to the island in the first place, and they associated the Wind-Walker with vast, wide-open skies. Their agoraphobia could not, however, preclude their essential watch duties on the peaks, nor did it stop certain persistent types from visiting Moreen when circumstances permitted and attempting to woo her over.

She would have none of it; for to give herself to a man of the cavern would mean following him into the constant gloom of the cavern world, and hers was an exceptionally free spirit. Why should she take a husband when already her bats provided so adequately for her? Five in number, those creatures which had bound themselves to her brought her wildfowl from the wooded inner slopes, fishes from the deep lake; even her clothing was woven of their soft fur. They were her constant companions.

Aye, and they were her protection, too, or so old Skaldsson had told de Marigny. Twice when men had thought to bring her forcibly to the cavern (they were, after all, Vikings or the sons of Vikings, and as such willful and less than diplomatic in dealing with women), they had returned scratched, bruised, and bloodied from their encounters with Moreen's providers and protectors.

She could have had those men killed, little doubt of that, but such was not her nature. She was kind and gentle and free, and she intended to stay that way. She desired neither the cavern's safety nor its restrictions, nor indeed the caresses of any dweller therein. But if de Marigny had questions to ask of her, surely she would answer all of them willingly and truthfully if she could, and certainly she would enjoy his company for a little while, she who lived apart from the cavern clan and dwelled halfway up a mountain.

These things that the chief had told him, together with many other scraps of knowledge, passed in kaleidoscope review through de Marigny's mind as he automatically answered the gentle tug of his guideline in the dark. Quite apart from Moreen he thought of Silberhutte and his plan to fight a delaying action along the length of the tunnel from the sea. He could not help feeling a little guilty that he was to have no part in that fight. Perhaps if he could get this meeting with Moreen quickly and satisfactorily over and done with . . .

The Warlord had said he would contact Armandra, ask her to conjure up another tornado—one with its roots right here on Numinos—to carry them to their final destination, wherever that might be. Just how the Woman of the Winds would contrive to do that, de Marigny could hardly guess, but Silberhutte seemed sure enough of the thing's mechanics. According to him the idea's feasibility was not the crucial factor; the crux of the matter lay in their ability to rendezvous with the tornado when it came.

All of these things had passed through de Marigny's thoughts several times before he spied ahead, partly obscured by the nightmare shape of his guide as it maneuvered the jaggedly tortuous sinuses of this long-dead volcanic vent, a distant fragment of dull daylight that hung in darkness like a damply luminous rag. Soon, as the light improved, he was able to pick out the features of the treacherous walls as they moved slowly by, following which the passage rapidly widened and the bat picked up speed.

De Marigny could almost sense the relief of his huge "blind dog" as it now sped ahead, no longer constrained by concern for its merely human charge. The muscles powering its wings must have been close to exhaustion. No bird, except perhaps the hawk with its ability to hover, could have managed the job; even a hawk must surely have crashed and come to grief in the absolute darkness.

Now there was no holding the bat, and such was the turmoil of air left in its wake that de Marigny's control of the cloak was in constant jeopardy. He quickly cut himself loose from his guide, then accelerated to maximum velocity as the bat, free at last of its aerial anchor, shot ahead on throbbing wings.

Out they sped across the inner lake, the five peaks towering overhead. Straight as the path of an arrow flew the great bat with de Marigny not too far behind. Somewhere over there, at the other side of the lake, the woman Moreen had her cave. It would not be long now before de Marigny knew the answer to his one, all-important question.

Moreen . . . The "woman" Moreen, in actuality little more than a girl. Almost twenty years of age and all of them spent on Numinos, an alien moon in an alien universe.

Moreen of the golden hair, shoulder length and shining with its own lustrous light; Moreen of the wide, bright blue eyes. Her natural, intrinsic warmth covered her like a blanket only ever torn aside by Ithaqua, black walker on the winds that blow forever between the worlds.

Tiny Moreen, at least by Numinosian standards. Sixty-four inches of unaffected grace, loveliness, youthful litheness, and not-quite innocence; for she had seen the Wind-Walker at his worst, and no one could remain wholly innocent after that. To be audience to it, even captive audience, was to be defiled.

Moreen: mortal and fragile as are all human beings, nevertheless carrying a strength within her which, mercifully, made it possible for her to put aside the past—blot it from her mind to a wide extent—until those long-lost loved ones, her father and poor, maddened mother, aye, and Garven too, all of them were only bright memories that terminated where the Wind-Walker had intruded to score them from her mind.

Moreen of the mountain—laughing Moreen—who had a love of all living things with but one exception: the monster Ithaqua, for whom her heart held only hatred.

Moreen . . .

At Darkhour, as was her wont, she had lain in the mouth of her cave on a comfortable bed of bracken covered with soft skins, her body bathed in the glow of a fire that burned ruddily in a hearth of piled stones. She had absently listened to the rustle of great wings from the rear of her cave where her bats hung together from the stalactite ceiling like a cluster of strange fruit; and she had watched the reflective surface of the still lake far below for the ripple and wash of auroral heavens and the images of pale stars which only ever showed at Darkhour.

She had observed, too, the campfires of the watchers on the peaks across the lake. Such fires told of the presence of men from the great cavern; and she had shuddered at the thought of that vast and (to her) tomblike subterranean grotto.

Oh, periodically they would come to her, those younger men of the cavern, boasting and strutting and attempting her seduction, to no avail. Though loneliness hurt her more and more, she would not go with them; not to their cavern world, to the smoky, airless pits of darkness where they hid like pallid cockroaches from a giant's tread—from the wrath of Ithaqua.

Yet their campfires at Darkhour comforted her, making her feel less lonely. And on those rare occasions when she recalled how some of her suitors had been fairly handsome men, for all their pallor, then she would remember Annahilde's promise: that one day a real man would come to her—a *man*, not some stooped, burrowing mole in man's guise.

Well, her witch-wife aunt's prophesy had best reveal itself soon, for the warming powders were four-fifths used up. Without the powder, given her by Annahilde, Moreen were long since dead; or at least gone from here to seek warmth at the fires of the cavern, which to her seemed worse than death. She knew this all too well and constantly wore the precious packet about her neck, fingering it now and then for reassurance. She wore very little else, for their seemed nothing of value in false modesty (who was there to see her near-nakedness here?), and the warming powder turned even the chillest wind to a balmy breeze. But when the last of the powder was gone, which it would be before she was very much older, what then?

Perhaps her man would find her before then. Annahilde had said it would be so.

With these thoughts in her mind and lulled by the soft glow of the distant fires and the whirl of pastel reflections in the lake, Moreen had slept, only waking when it was lighter and the weirdly streaming orb of the sun was visible as a glowing bulge on Borea's gray flank.

She had noticed at once that the bats were active again with an unaccustomed agitation and wondered why. They had been acting this way on and off for some time now, and their excitement puzzled her. If only she could read their minds, as she knew they read hers. Then, for no apparent reason, one of the bats had left in great haste, flitting hugely across the lake toward the opposite shore. Something was in the wind, that was plain, and Moreen guessed that it must somehow concern her.

Normally she might have gone down to the lake to bathe, picking her way down the steep path she knew so well, but on this occasion she had not done so, being satisfied merely to splash her face and breasts with the chill waters of a streamlet cascading from on high. Up here she could keep watch over the entire lake and its surrounding inner slopes, though she knew not what she expected to see.

Then, after a long time, she had grown bored and thought to make her way down to the trees that grew tall and dense where the slope was less steep not too far below and to one side of her lofty aerie. There she could play with the smaller animals that lived in the trees, and with the tiny colored birds, all of which came to her as household dogs answered the calls of their masters in the Viking village she had known as a girl.

It was as she was putting on knee-length trousers made from the pelt of a white fox, with a halter to match, that she noted increasing activity in the four bats within the cave. Suddenly they fell in rapid succession from the shadowy ceiling and glided out of the cave on still wings, barely disturbing the air. Outside in the wan Numinosian light, they circled overhead before heading out over the lake. Gazing after them, Moreen frowned—until she picked out the oncoming form of the fifth creature.

So, they had gone to welcome their brother on his return: four forms converging on a fifth high over the gray lake. Five of them now, her five familiars, who had followed after her like faithful watchdogs when she left the great cavern to come and live here. Five monstrous bats that loved her as—

Five?

No, six!

Six of them? Moreen's eyes narrowed and her frown deepened. The single bone button of her halter slipped unfastened, forgotten, from her fingers as the flying figures drew closer. They wheeled high overhead, almost level with the rocky saddle between the two nearest peaks, then began to descend.

At last Moreen could see all six figures quite clearly. Now her mouth fell open and she froze where she stood, trembling in every limb, close to the mouth of her cave. The blood had seemed to drain from her in a moment.

The sixth flier was . . . a man?

Moreen's hand flew to her mouth. A man—or a monster! Her experience of man-shapes that walked on the wind

147

in no way concerned human beings. Only Ithaqua to her knowledge could do that. But this could hardly be the Wind-Walker, neither him nor any manifestation of him. No, for a bat—one of *her* bats—had brought him here; and while all of the huge creatures were excited, none of them seemed afraid or concerned for her safety.

It must then be a man, a man in a cloak with wings almost as big as those of the bats themselves. A handsome man, more young than old, who smiled at her now as he made an expert landing a half-dozen paces away.

The bats, hovering nervously, thrust the air this way and that with their throbbing wings. Facing the stranger, still frozen in amazement, Moreen saw his lips form her name, heard him say it as a question:

"Moreen?"

She shook off her paralysis. "Yes, I am Moreen."

A gust of disturbed air tugged aside her halter, which she automatically trapped with her elbow before it could blow away altogether. For a moment, caught unawares, de Marigny stared at her. Then, coloring, he averted his gaze.

Moreen, seeing his confusion and knowing its cause, laughed and finally managed to button her halter. She said: "You know me—and yet you are a stranger."

"Yes," he nodded, stepping closer. "I'm a stranger—but I'm a friend, too."

"You're no Viking," she stated with certainty. "Nor are you of the cavern folk. Your back is too straight, and your skin's not pale like theirs. Do you have a name? Who are you?"

"I'm called Henri," he answered. "And no, I'm not a man of Numinos. It's a long story, one we've really no time for now, but I hail from the Motherworld. Annahilde sent me to—"

"Annahilde?" In a moment the look on her face went from puzzlement through astonishment to sheer joy. "Annahilde sent you?" She breathed the words.

A moment more and she had flown into his arms, almost throwing him from his feet. "Then you must be the one!"

"I must?" de Marigny repeated, not quite knowing what to do with his hands. Then, from nowhere, certain words of the witch-wife, forgotten until now, came back to him:

"You will surely fall in love with her; it can hardly be otherwise!"

"You are the one, aren't you?" the girl asked, her wide eyes anxiously searching his face.

"Why, I—" He paused, lost for words, brain whirling, before finally wrapping his arms firmly about her suddenly snuggling form.

"Yes?" she pressed him, sweet breath fanning his neck, the smell of everything good filling his nostrils, his heart.

And de Marigny knew then what Annahilde had meant, and that seer or none she had been absolutely right.

"Oh, I'm the one, all right," he answered at last. "It could hardly be otherwise. . . ."

Chapter Nine

Under Attack!

LONG BEFORE Hank Silberhutte and his ten men of the cavern had reached the seaward entrance to the fissure, the Warlord knew the worst: that the Vikings were closer than he had believed and that there would be no time to build further defenses against them.

This bad news came to him first from the lips of the lone watchkeeper from the mouth of the tunnel, racing back to the cavern with the grim news; secondly, it was relayed to him via the minds of a pair of wounded bats limping home from a fight aboard one of the longships. The bats were the sole survivors of a party of six of the great, intelligent creatures, and they were able to tell Silberhutte much.

The enemy fleet was closing rapidly with the island (the bats informed), ringing it about and sailing in from all sides. Furthermore, while there were those aboard the ships who knew of the tunnel entrance to the cavern and while doubtless many of the Vikings would land there, the tunnel could only accommodate so many. The invaders appreciated this fact too; thousands of them, believing that the ridges between the peaks would be mainly unguarded, intended to scale them and thus make their way to the inner slopes. By now there would be many defenders in the mountainous heights, and many more climbing the inner slopes from the volcanic vents, but there could never be enough.

Quite simply, the men of the cavern were outnumbered by at least thirty to one! Therefore, while the main shaft from the sea could probably be held for a very long time, plainly the crucial battles must in the end be fought on the heights and in the volcanic vents. To place too much emphasis in the main tunnel would therefore be a waste of time and manpower. Instead it would be better if that tunnel were blocked completely, and the way to do this was readily at hand.

Years ago the cavern folk had prepared for just such an emergency, propping up the unstable and rotting ceiling of the fissure at its entrance. The Warlord recalled having seen the evidence of this operation when first arriving on the island with de Marigny—the massive beams and props that held up the slimy, nitrous ceiling. Now those supports must be removed, allowing gravity, nature, and thousands of tons of rock and ocean-rotted debris to seal the fissure forever. Once that was done, then the party could return to the cavern, and pass through the volcanic vents climbing the inner slopes to reinforce the defenders of the saddles between the five peaks.

Less than one hundred yards from the tunnel's mouth, however, with the sound of the ocean loud in their ears, they knew that before they could destroy the entrance, they must first clear it of invaders. For a handful of Vikings were already in the tunnel and more were climbing the sea cliff from their longships. Waiting in the gloom, invisible to the silhouetted, helmeted Vikings, the Warlord and his party listened for a moment to the loud, boastful conversation of the invaders—and to the frightened voices of more than a few whose dread of the Isle of Mountains was obviously a terror within them—before making a hurried, whispered plan of campaign.

Silberhutte measured and cut a length of heavy rope, knotted one end, and stood with it close to a wall of the tunnel. The heaviest of his colleagues did the same with the other end of the rope, taking up a like position by the opposite wall. Then, with the rope held taut between them and the remainder of the party following up behind, uttering bloodthirsty shrieks and war cries which the tunnel magnified tenfold, they rushed forward upon the startled, unsuspecting Vikings.

Half a dozen of the invaders were speared where they stood; the rest became caught up in the rope and were hurled by it and the crush of men behind it from the mouth of the tunnel to fall into the sea. At once axes and spears were flying between the tunnel's mouth and the decks of the dragonships bobbing below, and the air became thick with curses, screams and shouts.

Moments later, avoiding the flying weapons that clattered all around them, the Warlord's party tossed the corpses of the slain Vikings down into the sea. Then Silberhutte was able to take stock. Two of his men had lost their lives, and one other had a bad wound. The Warlord quickly ordered that the injured man be helped back to the cavern, which left only himself and five others to attend to the sealing of the entrance.

While Silberhutte and two others collected shields and spears of fallen Vikings with which to guard the narrow ledge in front of the entrance, the remaining men formed a demolition team and began tying ropes to the bases of the lesser beams that supported the rotting ceiling. Throughout, heavy grappling irons continued to land on the ledge and in the entrance, several of which found purchase. The Warlord and his colleagues were responsible for disengaging these grapples, thus ensuring that no more of the raiders gained a foothold. This was in no way a simple task; every grapple that flashed into the wide entrance was accompanied by half a dozen spears and the occasional ax.

Just as the demolition party was completing its preparations, a hurled grapple struck the man on Silberhutte's left, one of its barbed tines hooking into his thigh. Before anything could be done, he had been yanked screaming into empty air, his shield and spear flying free. He landed half-in, half-out of a longship forty feet below, breaking his back and dying instantly.

Now the Vikings redoubled their efforts, and two of them actually struggled their way to the rim of the ledge before Silberhutte cut them down. The Warlord was completely dispassionate and efficient in his killing, ruthless as his early days on Borea had taught him to be; but he was just as ready to disengage when the toiling team behind him called for his assistance.

Drawing back into the entrance, he cursed as a spear flashed into view and skewered his right-hand man through the breast, killing him outright. Then, wasting no more time, he joined the remaining trio of cave dwellers where they strained at the heavy ropes. By the time Silberhutte was able to wrap a rope round his waist and add his weight to the effort, more of the invaders were clambering up onto the ledge. Their energies had been spent in vain, however, for no sooner were five or six established and moving cautiously, blindly into the dark interior of the tunnel than—with a snapping of timbers and a rumbling of fractured rock—the first section of the ceiling crashed down upon them, burying them beneath untold tons of boulders and rubble.

Deep within the tunnel, momentarily suffocated by complete darkness and billowing clouds of dust, the jubilant four moved quickly back as debris continued to rain down from the sagging ceiling. Finally a torch was struck and, as a second section of the tunnel collapsed behind them, Silberhutte and his small force hurried back the way they had come.

It was time now for the Warlord to seek out de Marigny. Pressure was building up far too rapidly in the cauldron that was Numinos, particularly on the Isle of the Five Mountains. The sooner the secret of Annahilde's runes was revealed—and the time-clock discovered and reclaimed—the better. . . .

Silberhutte got back to the cavern minutes after de Marigny's own arrival. The latter, having flown up above the peaks on leaving Moreen (who still would not go down into the island's interior), had seen the longships in their hundreds where they were anchored about the island, their crews grimly preparing for their assault upon the arduous slopes. He had warned the cavern folk of the enormity of the peril and had then sent out the cavern's rear guard, a pitiful band of one hundred and fifty men, to strengthen the thin ranks of the three hundred already gone to defend the ring of mountain peaks.

While Moreen's own mountain—farthest from the cavern and unguarded when last de Marigny had seen it, though a stream of men from the cavern had been heading toward it along the high saddles—was also the tallest of the five peaks and the most sheer oceanward, nevertheless the Earthman was frantic with worry over the girl. He had promised to return for her, would not have left her in the first place but for the need to carry her translation of Annahilde's message to Silberhutte.

She had however assured him that she would be safe—that if the Vikings came in his absence, her bats would protect her—before wishing him well as he went reluctantly off again, once more in tandem behind the strongest of her retainers. The trip back through the volcanic blowhole had been quicker this time, the way lighted by flaring flambeaux by whose light parties of the cavern's women worked to fortify the vents against attack; and de Marigny had reckoned not unreasonably that indeed this was where the final battles would be fought.

All of these things de Marigny told to Silberhutte in return for the Warlord's own news, but when he paused, there were several very important things left unsaid. Now Silberhutte pressed the other for additional information:

"And the time-clock? Did you find out where it is?"

"Dromos," answered the other, seemingly surprised. "Didn't I mention it?" He was visibly on edge and kept eyeing the shadowed mouths of the vents close to where they stood. "The Ice-Priests of Dromos have it. But—"

"But what, my friend? I half-suspected that Ithaqua hadn't left the clock here on Numinos. What I didn't suspect was that Annahilde's prophesy would work out so well—that she'd get all her own way."

"Her own way?" de Marigny repeated as the Warlord donned his part of the cloak's harness.

"She was hoping and praying that you'd fall for the girl," Silberhutte explained his meaning. "Well, it seems to me that you have. And you're the one who wanted 'no complications!'"

"Listen," de Marigny ignored his friend's knowing grin. "I have it all worked out. We two weigh something less than normal here on Numinos, right?"

"Three-quarters normal, yes."

"Well then, that means—"

"—That the cloak can probably manage all three of us? Yes, it probably can, at least here on Numinos. I'm way ahead of you, Henri, and it looks like I'll have to go along with you. I only hope that this girl of yours doesn't slow us down, that's all. Dromos is different again from Numinos—

154

but I'll tell you what I know about that when we're on our way. Right now we have to get out into the open air before I can start things moving."

"How do you mean?" asked de Marigny, lifting the cloak up above the floor of the cavern and taking the other's weight, then flying slowly into the main vent. "What's your plan?"

"My plan? Any plan I might have had would be changed beyond recognition by now. The idea was that if we found the clock here on Numinos, we'd pick it up and that would be that. But, having an idea that Ithaqua might have taken it to Dromos, I put it to Armandra, and she told me how we could go about getting there if we had to. Well, now we have to—but it's going to be a hell of a job, that's a promise. And it won't be any easier now we've the girl to allow for."

"About Moreen—" de Marigny began.

"Don't tell me," the Warlord cut him off. "It's written all over your face. Anyway, if she's half what Annahilde described, a man would be a fool to leave her behind."

"When you see her, you can judge for yourself," de Marigny answered. "As for now, I'll have to concentrate on what I'm doing, get us through this damned snake of a hole as fast as I can."

"Yes. Well, I won't bother you," the other grunted. "I'll spend the time 'chatting' with my better half, let her know what's going on."

Now in silence the cloak flew rapidly between a string of flaring, shadow-casting torches, passing the occasional group of frantically toiling women along the way. Without exception the women wished them all speed, urging them onward with approving cries and gestures; and so they swept eerily on through the winding volcanic flue.

De Marigny's urgency was clearly visible in the way he took chances in the darker stretches of the vent, but his handling of the cloak was now inspired. Despite the fact that his hideous guide had long since deserted him to return to Moreen, he flew faster than he had on either of his previous trips. Even so, it seemed to take hours before they finally flew out into daylight.

And it was at once apparent that fighting was already in progress. Even in the dim light of Numinos the glint of metal could be seen in the saddles between the three lesser peaks, and the faint shouts and screams of furious contests echoed down to the fliers through the ominously still air.

Gaining height the better to see the action in the saddles, the pair were relieved to note that the cavern folk were getting the better of their adversaries. At present only small groups of Vikings were reaching the ridges, and that only after fighting their way through continual avalanches of boulders released by the defenders. Tired from the climb and bruised by flying rocks, they were easily picked off as soon as they attained the saddles; but greater numbers were not too far behind. It would not be long before they were too many for the defenders to handle.

Racing high over the lake, the adventurers felt a warm updraft from its still volcanic center; then, ahead, Moreen's peak rose up before them; and—

—And on its uppermost slope there was a clouding of dust, the glitter of whirling weapons, and a vast and frenzied throbbing of bat wings!

Ten, a dozen Vikings engaged Moreen's monstrous protectors at not too great a height above her refuge; and two more, armed to the teeth, slid recklessly down a shale slope immediately above the low overhang that sheltered her cave. Then de Marigny saw the girl herself, hair streaming behind her as she plunged in a near-panic flight down the steep slope toward a green stand of tall, thickly grown pines.

They were after her, those two heathens, and their prime reason for being here seemed completely forgotten in the excitement of the chase. There was no saying what they would do to the girl when they caught her. . . .

Chapter Ten

Warlords of the Winds

UNSEEN, swooping down upon Moreen's pursuers from above and behind, the fliers made to deliver a surprise attack. De Marigny felt the cloak yaw slightly and saw that the Warlord had freed himself from the harness, that he hung now by his arms alone. Then, close in behind the excited, scrabbling raiders, the cloak yawed again, more wildly this time, before shooting skyward as Silberhutte cast himself free.

Hurtling between the unsuspecting Vikings, whose eyes saw only the fleeing Moreen, Silberhutte caught them up in his powerful arms. This had the effect of braking his own speed while rapidly accelerating theirs, so that they shot headfirst out over the overhang to crash down in front of the girl's now empty cave. The Warlord landed light as a cat between them, noting that one lay still, his head at an odd angle. Better for the other if he, too, had shown no sign of life; instead he made to climb shakily to his feet, his helmeted skull offering itself as a target for the exiled Earthman's weapon.

Up above, once more in control of the cloak, de Marigny saw metal shatter, blood and brains flying, heard a single gurgling shriek, then glided on after the stumbling, fearful girl.

"Moreen, it's me—don't run!"

At the sound of his voice she fell back onto her fur-clad rump, skidded a few feet while clutching at tufts of tough herbage, then slowed to a halt, and looked back. De Marigny swept down upon her, landed close by in time to catch her up as she threw herself into his arms.

"Hang on," he told her. "Tight now!" And again he was airborne and winging back up the slope to where Silberhutte waited.

"She stays here for now," the Warlord yelled before de Marigny could once more set down. "Henri, we have to take that peak up there. It has to be our launch site. The bats are doing a good job—but not quite good enough. We'll need to give them a hand."

To Moreen de Marigny said: "Climb up after us—but be careful." And when she would have questioned him, he earnestly added: "Trust us, Moreen."

She stood then for a moment, looking lost and lonely as the pair flew off toward the peak. . . .

Bloody battle still raged at the mountain's crest, but the bats had done well. Only three of the dozen Vikings remained on their feet, and of those that had fallen, all but one were dead. The bats had paid dearly for their selfless service to the girl, however, for only two of them remained aloft. Pounding the air, they wheeled and hovered, buffeting and tearing at the bloodied Vikings who desperately hacked at them with whistling blades.

Alighting, the Warlord rushed in to support these weird defenders of the peak. De Marigny quickly shucked off his marvelous aerial garment, and snatching up a fallen foeman's sword, he, too, joined the fray.

First blood went to Silberhutte as he ran past a crippled but still active invader where he lay with the tendons of his legs slashed through. With a savage cry and a wild sweep of his sword, the man made to sever the Warlord's own legs. But leaping above the deadly arc of metal, the Earthman came down with both feet on the other's outstretched arm, breaking it close to the elbow. In the next moment the Viking's scream of agony bubbled into silence as Silberhutte sliced open his jugular.

Simultaneous with that bubbling shriek came another—but not from an enemy. This dying scream came from one of the two remaining bats, skewered through the eye by a Viking sword. Down the great creature fell with the sword stuck fast in its head, so that the owner of that weapon had to leap astride the body of the bat to drag his blade free. As finally the sword came loose and its wielder turned toward the onrushing de Marigny, so the last bat settled with a piercing whistle of rage on the Viking's shoulders, literally decapitating him as it hurled his body to the ground.

Both of the remaining Vikings fell on the creature from behind, dispatching it in a moment, then backed away from the oncoming Earthmen. Silberhutte and de Marigny, however, giving the invaders no time to recover from their terrific exertions, leaped in upon them with war cries and whirling weapons.

The Warlord battered aside his man's buckler and blade, splitting his skull in the time it takes to tell, and de Marigny took only slightly longer. At the end, gore spattered and wild, the victors stood breathlessly back to back and surveyed the now silent field of battle. Broken bodies and bloodied weapons lay scattered about; great bats lay like crumpled heaps of dark fur together in a tangle with white-limbed Vikings; but finally the peak, that topmost summit of Moreen's mountain, was free of all living invaders.

As for the girl herself: she came quickly, nimbly up the steep slope toward the gore-streaked pair, a little out of breath and disheveled but otherwise unharmed. Before she could reach them, Silberhutte moved apart from de Marigny to stand alone, his eyes closed and his mind far, far away on another world, in mental conversation with the mind of his woman.

For a moment he stood thus, then opened his eyes, turned to de Marigny and said: "Well, this is it, Henri. Let's hope there's time enough." He nodded, directing his gaze down the outer slope. There, rapidly toiling upward, came a large body of Vikings. Among them, one stood out like a tree among saplings.

"Harold," de Marigny grimly noted. "I was expecting him. Those two"—he indicated a pair of corpses with the fatal marks of the great bats fresh upon them—"were from his ship. Did you recognize them?"

The Warlord nodded an affirmative. "If Harold gets up here before we can lift off—well, it will be up to you. I'll be busy and of no use to you. You'd better get your cloak on and clip me in while I work." He paused, added: "And Henri—no distractions. This has to be all systems go first time . . . or not at all!"

There were questions de Marigny would dearly love to ask, but he put his faith in the Warlord and remained silent. As Moreen came closer, climbing the slope to a destiny she would never have believed, he ran to where he had thrown his cloak and donned it. Then he flew to the girl and returned with her to Silberhutte.

And approaching, seeing his friend standing there alone atop the peak, finally de Marigny understood. He had not wondered how Armandra might go about sending them a tornado, for he knew well enough that she was capable of that. What had puzzled and worried him was how such a whirlwind could possibly pick them up and then power them on their way to Dromos; and, with fighting still in progress and increasing in ferocity along the ridges, how such a rescue could be achieved in time. Now he saw that no such intervention from Borea was planned, that their passage to Dromos would have its origin right here on Numinos!

For Armandra controlled the winds with her mind, and now the giant Texan had given himself completely over to her—*so that his mind was merely an extension of hers!*

The Warlord stood—legs apart and arms reaching out to the sea and sky, eyes closed and face a death mask—flesh white as a candle's wax and chill as an icicle. He stood there under a sky that darkened visibly, rapidly, as Armandra worked her will on the elements through his mind.

Far out at sea, from a leaden sky shot with the golden traceries of electrical energy, searing lightning suddenly lashed down to lighten the surface of the darkly roiling sea. Then another bolt, and another, and in rapid succession a fourth, fifth, and sixth—becoming a torrent of bolts that turned Numinos bright with their fire as they strode about the Isle of Mountains on forked and fiery legs—until, in a final concerted blast that left the atmosphere reeking of ozone, the fires from the sky were done.

Armandra was satisfied for the moment. She had successfully tested her powers. . . .

Moreen pressed close to de Marigny and gazed awestruck at the Warlord. Unseen forces lifted his long hair and floated it up about his head as if it drifted in deep and languid waters. Then de Marigny felt the tug of familiar, invisible fingers at the fabric of his fabulous cloak: Armandra's little winds, eager now to add their own effort to the greater tumult to come.

"Go on then," de Marigny whispered to them, unheard by Moreen. "Do what you can." And a flurry of dust spiraled up at his feet to race away and dwindle into the gloom that now hung everywhere like a harbinger of Doomsday.

All lightnings had ceased now, as had the golden flickerings in the clouds that heralded them. Strangely, while the sky boiled darkly, about the peak the air was still. Steadily the mass of invaders, who as a man had paused to witness the aerial phenomenon, continued their climb toward the peaks and saddles, drawing closer with each passing moment. But now—

—Now it was time to go, and now too an utterly weird thing began to happen far out at sea. At first it appeared that a wall of mist had sprung up in a vast circle about the mountainous island, a wall that deepened and whirled and came closer by the second. But soon it could be seen that the entire ocean was in motion, turning like a tremendous disk about the hub of the island, and that rushing wall of mist formed the disk's outer perimeter.

In fact the mist was moisture ripped from the ocean's surface by the winds of Numinos under Armandra-Silberhutte's control, the same force that drove the sea in its rapidly accelerating whorl about the island. And that motion had reached the ocean cliffs of the island now, was already lifting the sea in a huge swell, tossing the Viking longships at anchor and threatening to smash them against the cliffs. A few moments more and they were being reduced to kindling as the waves reached higher yet up the rocks. Some of the ships parted with their anchors, went careening and dipping on the wild ocean until they, too, were battered against the cliffs and flew asunder.

For a moment the Vikings on the slopes were awestruck, paralyzed by the destruction of their ships; and in the saddles the island's defenders took advantage of the diversion to wipe out those invaders who had recently reached their positions. Then, realizing that some nameless doom was about to befall them, the men of the caves turned and fled back down the inner paths toward the vents. They would gather ranks there, make a stand against the Vikings at the mouths of the vents, then fall back and fight delaying actions along the lengths of the subterranean channels to the great cavern itself. That was probably how they planned it—but they were not to know that they would be spared any further fighting.

The rising, towering, whirling wall of vapor was half as high as the mountains now, closing with the island, sucking more water up from the frenzied ocean. It was a fearsome sight, completely unnerving, and the effect it had on the Vikings was electric. They were afraid, yes, even unto flight—but where should they flee? With the alien wall of vapor rising at their heels, threatening to suck them up and blow them away, and their ships gone in a maelstrom of wind and water, they could only come forward, up the last few feet of shale-covered slope to the saddles and peaks.

And come they did, howling their berserker rage to the more loudly howling sky, foaming through their beards in fear and bloodlust. And the mountain peaks deserted and empty now of life—all save one.

Carefully de Marigny fastened Silberhutte's harness about him, stood close to the Warlord, gathered Moreen to him and hugged her, telling her to cling to him tightly, more tightly than she ever clung to anything before.

And still the Warlord stood as petrified, and faster whirled the great spout and higher still. Now the wall had breasted the far range of peaks and saddles, dipping down into the valley and moving rapidly across the central lake, whipping that, too, to a white-foaming fury.

It was abundantly clear that the peak whereon the three stood was the center of the tremendous spout, but as such it was utterly, incredibly calm. Calm, despite the fact that the sky was quickly being shut out—calm, while rushing ever closer the inner wall of the funnel wore a glassy mirror sheen—calm, when above and all about the sky, ocean, and central lake were a howling, banshee tumult.

Then, as de Marigny felt invisible but familiar fingers returned to tug at the trappings of his cloak and freed one hand to find the controls of that fabulous garment, Moreen gasped in his ear and pointed to where a burly, red-haired Viking warrior now toiled toward them up the crest of the ridge less than one hundred yards away. Harold, alone of all his comrades, driven on by a berserker rage—an all-consuming hatred for the strangers who had upended his plans and his world—had finally arrived on the scene in time to be part of its conclusion.

He seemed oblivious to the rushing wall of water that climbed the slope behind him, tearing up trees and boulders alike and rushing them aloft; he saw only the Earthmen and the girl, and, possibly, in his mind's eye, the destruction of the longships and the fantastic doom which had already overtaken his comrades in their thousands.

"Emissaries of Ithaqua!" he roared, his voice somehow coming to them over the howling of tortured elements. "Aye, perhaps you are after all, for surely have the winds protected you. Well, if the Wind-Walker is in truth your Lord, then he is no longer mine! Damn Ithaqua, and damn his carmine eyes! His winds shall not protect you this time—*not this time!*" And he lumbered forward, red-eyed and foaming at the mouth.

When Harold was no more than fifty paces from the little knot of people on the peak, the whirling wall caught up with him. Perhaps at the last he sensed his doom, for in the moment before that almost solid sheet of revolving air and water struck him, he turned to face it, throwing wide his arms as if to enclose it and uttering a wild shriek. A shriek of horror, perhaps, or maybe rage—rage that indeed the elements had won the day and robbed him of his prey.

And a second later he was gone. Only a brawny arm showed itself to the horrified watchers, an arm that stuck out from the glassy surface briefly and was then sucked under. An arm, and the dull glint of Harold's great ax caught up in the rush and swirl. These things they saw, and heard the drowning echo of Harold's final shriek, soon lost in the cacophony of insane elements.

Then, with a rush and a pounding of pressure that threatened to burst eardrums and pop eyes from their sockets, the cloak belled out and rocketed aloft, and Moreen's legs wound about her Earthman's waist in a scissor grip as the trio fled down the eye of the waterspout and out beyond the rim of Numinos.

To an observor, had there been one far out in the Numinosian sea, it would have seemed that the great spout stretched itself impossibly thin as it speared the heavens—that high above the outermost layers of atmosphere it

163

twisted tortuously and bent its neck like a great serpent—
before striking across space at a huge and dully glowing
orb hanging low on the horizon.

Dromos . . .

PART THREE: *DROMOS*

Chapter One

Ice-Planet

WRAPPED SAFELY in a bubble of air formed of the substance of Armandra's familiar winds, the trio sped down the eye of the fantastic waterspout-cum-tornado. The journey would be shorter this time, for the distance between Numinos and Dromos was not so great. In the almost complete darkness the inner wall of the twister was a bluish sheen of incredible motion viewed beyond their protective bubble; and now, recovering from the heart-stopping, strangling effects of nightmarish acceleration, de Marigny comforted the girl in his arms and tried to explain, as best he could, what they were about.

They each took a pinch of Annahilde's warming powder, and as it gradually took effect and apprehension of the unknown waned a little in Moreen's heart, so she began to question de Marigny, to absorb and believe the many wonderful things he told her. Then, surprised at her rapid recovery and acceptance of her present position, he asked her if she were not afraid.

"Afraid?" her voice was tiny in the darkness. "There are so many things I don't understand, and Annahilde used to say that ignorance is fear. In that way I suppose I'm afraid. But afraid of flying to Dromos and of what we might find there? No, I think not. Should I be afraid when you are here with me, who came from the Motherworld to fetch me out of the Isle of Mountains?"

"Moreen," he began, "you should know that there may well be dangers ahead, and that—"

"Dangers we will face together," she put her fingers to his lips. "You and I and the Warlord, until we find this box you seek so urgently. And of what dangers do you speak? No creature of flesh and blood will harm me, nor you when you are with me—except perhaps evil men or Lord Ithaqua. . . ." She paused and de Marigny felt her shudder where she lay weightless in his arms.

"I have flown with him, too," she finally continued, "in the skies over Numinos. But he is not like you. No one—no *thing*—is like unto Ithaqua." She found de Marigny's mouth and kissed it.

Then for a while they were silent, Annahilde's powder producing warm sensations of well-being within them, and soon de Marigny became very conscious of the girl's lovely body pressed tight to his, of her form that clung to him and set his flesh tingling despite the thick fur garment he wore.

Moreen, too, for all her innocence, felt the fire that burned in her Earthman's blood. Now she knew him for a real man, and her pulse quickened to match his. Then—

Breaking the spell, coming to them from the darkness close at hand, faint stirrings and a sighing groan!

"Hank!" de Marigny whispered, horrified at the thought of what would happen if the Warlord should inadvertently waken from his telepathic trance and lose control over the vast funnel that bore them through the void. *"For God's sake!"*

"No panic, Henri," came the Warlord's waking rumble. "Armandra has it in hand. She only needed me to help out with the takeoff—to supply a one-hundred-percent location statement and to get things started. Now she's completely taken over. She'll get us to Dromos, all right, and help set us down safely, too—but from then on we're on our own. Dromos is too far out, at the very extremes of her reach. You may as well know it right now: if we fail to find the clock, we're stuck."

Sighing his relief that all was well, at least for the moment, de Marigny answered: "And meanwhile Ithaqua just sits somewhere out there and watches us wriggle, right?"

"That's the way I read it, yes. Right now, if he wanted to, he could take me, you, Moreen—all of us and the time-clock too."

"Then why doesn't he do just that?"

"There's something else he wants."

"Armandra?"

"Right—but that's not going to happen."

"Armandra?" came Moreen's voice in the darkness. "She is your woman, Warlord?"

"Call me Hank," he answered. "She's my woman, yes, and a daughter of Ithaqua, too. He wants her more desperately than all three of us together. But he'll never have her, not while I live."

Silberhutte paused, and when next he spoke his tone had lightened somewhat: "About our destination, Henri. Now is as good a time as any to tell you what I know of Dromos—possibly the only chance I'll get. Moreen, you'd best listen in, too, and learn what you can. . . .

"Armandra tells me that Dromos is an ice planet, and that the habitation of its dwellers lies far below the surface in huge caves of ice in the bowels of a vast, near-extinct volcano. That's one of the reasons she won't be able to help us leave when the time comes, for we'll probably be deep underground—or at least, under ice.

"As for the inhabitants of Dromos—they were men, once."

"Were men?" de Marigny questioned. "What are they now?"

"Surely men are men," Moreen added. "What else could they be?"

"I honestly don't know," the Warlord replied. "I know only as much as Armandra has told me. I'll try to explain.

"The ice-priests of Dromos were first taken there millions of years ago by Ithaqua in his youth. Like all men, they had their origin on Earth the Motherworld, but at a time predating the dinosaurs. If Atlantis was yesterday, their world was years ago! They were of a primal continent at the dawn of Earth's prehistory, lost in such unthinkable abysses of the past that you could never convince any modern scientists back home that they ever existed at all.

"All of these things Armandra plucked from her father's mind when she was a child and he used to tempt her with telepathic tales of his deeds and his wanderings between alien spheres. She even learned the name of that primal continent, and that of the city which the ice-priests ruled with cruelty, terror, and through their skill at casting monstrous visions, mass hallucinations with which to confuse the minds of the common people.

"The land was called Theem'hdra, and the city of the ice-priests was Khrissa, a place of massive basalt slabs in Theem'hdra's frozen northern regions. There the ice-priests conjured their evil illusions and worshiped dark gods, among which was this same Ithaqua we know now. And indeed all of this was so long ago that the Wind-Walker himself has all but forgotten the details. For while he is very nearly immortal, ageless, yet all of this was in his youth.

"Of the ice-priests themselves: they were a tall, thin, hairless race, white as death and cold and cruel as ice itself. They set themselves up as the saviors of Theem'hdra, saying that only their black prayers could keep the ice at bay, that great wall of ice that crept down from the north each winter and grudgingly retreated as the seasons waxed warmer. But those must have been monstrous prayers indeed, for in company with them the priests would kill off hundreds of women, human sacrifices to propitiate their hideous gods.

"And you ask, Moreen, how men can be other than men? I don't call such as these things I've described men."

Here de Marigny asked, "And Ithaqua brought these ice-priests to Dromos, you say? How many of them and why?"

They could almost sense the Warlord's shrug in the darkness. "I'm not sure, but you may be certain he had his reasons. Armandra tells of a great war that raged between certain of Theem'hdra's barbarian nations and the people of Khrissa, when the city lay under seige for many years while the barbarians bided their time outside the massive basalt walls. Perhaps that had something to do with it— perhaps Ithaqua took his priests out of the doomed city as repayment for their tainted worship. Who can say?

"At any rate, there's little more to tell. As I've said, Dromos is an ice planet, perpetually frozen, but it wasn't always so. Armandra tells that simultaneous with the coming of the ice-priests into Dromos, Ithaqua wrought a fantastic climatic change in the moon. Prior to that time there had been a great volcanic belt about Dromos, which was not to the Wind-Walker's liking; he finds all sources of warmth abhorrent.

"As time passed, however, the volcanoes became extinct

until only one remained: the hugest cone of all, still rumbling threateningly, with a throat that went down almost to the moon's core. When he brought the ice-priests from doomed Khrissa, Ithaqua made it a condition of his mercy that they become instrumental in damming up that last great vent, thus turning Dromos into the frozen world which it is now. How he or they achieved this, I'm at a loss to say; but as we all know well enough, Ithaqua defies all Earthly laws and sciences. . . ."

Following Silberhutte's narrative, for a few moments there was silence, then de Marigny said: "Well, if that's Dromos as you've described it, it sounds like a pretty inhospitable place to me. And I can't say I much fancy the idea of these ice-priests, either!"

"Neither them nor their priestesses," added Moreen.

"Priestesses!" de Marigny repeated her, surprise showing in his voice.

"The facts of life, Henri," came the Warlord's humorless chuckle. "Your girl has a head on her shoulders. Perhaps the ice-priests are less inhuman than we picture them."

"Yes," the other replied, equally dryly, "but then again, perhaps they're not. . . ."

Not long after, their journey came to an abrupt end. On this occasion, however, de Marigny was ready for it, was prepared at any moment to use his cloak in the manner accustomed, so that it came as no surprise when the vast and whirling tube fell apart around them.

Down they swept through the debris of the collapsed funnel—which drifted as shimmering ice-crystal curtains and flurries of fine snow—toward glacial Dromos. The air was thin and icy, though mercifully no winds blew, and so the surface of the world a mile below was crystal clear to their eyes in every minute detail. Had the scene been other than utterly barren and white, then it might have been beautiful. It *would* be beautiful, but not to any lover of life. For Dromos, at least on the surface, was quite dead.

What little light filtered its way out here from the sun, or down from the weirdly lucent heavens, was reflected in millions of tiny points of light from the frozen surface. Great drifts of snow—forming white and blue dunes whose

171

slopes scintillated dazzlingly, with crests miles apart—marched to the distant horizons and formed the only topographic features to be seen . . . almost.

For as they dropped down closer to the surface, they now saw against the horizon a series of distant mounds silhouetted against the subtly auroral backdrop of the sky. Since these huge domed hills were obviously not merely gigantic snowdrifts (which everywhere else seemed perfectly uniform in height and formation), they must be rounded mountains, perhaps the range of dead volcanoes for which the trio searched.

And so for more than an hour they followed in silence the cloak's strange shadow across the deep snows, buoyed up and assisted on their way by Armandra's small friendly winds; until at last they were in the frozen white foothills that led upward to vast, extinct volcanic cones. They flew high above a range of six such bowls, each one filled to its craterlike brim with drifted snow, before spying some miles ahead a dome almost twice the size of any of the others. This could only be—must surely be—that final prehistoric vent into whose throat, in countless ages past, Ithaqua had transported the Khrissan ice-priests. And according to Armandra this was where the ice-priests dwelled to this day.

And now, as they gained elevation to fly across that looming crater wall at a height of many thousands of feet, they saw . . . an impossible sight!

For here was no great bowl of drifted snow but a spiraling ice-cut stairway that coiled down and down into that terrific throat and finally disappeared far below in a dark blue gloom. Hardly daring to believe their eyes, the cloak-fliers descended into that mighty blowhole, and as they drifted slowly down past the first of those Titan-carved steps—each one of which had a rise as tall as a tall man—so their senses once more were astounded.

Not by sight this time but sound!

Or was it purely *physical* sound? No, not sound as ordinary men know it; though certainly Silberhutte recognized the phenomenon at once, and his companions took only a little longer. For it was a voice they heard—a deeply booming, clinically cold and correct voice—and while it seemed to have its source deep down in the volcano's

172

throat, the trio knew now that they heard it only inside their heads!

A voice, yes—a telepathic voice that said: *"Welcome, strangers—welcome to Dromos. The ice-priests await you, as they have waited since the dawn of time!"*

Chapter Two

Beneath the Volcano

BECKONED ON by the voice that called in their heads from unknown depths below, the trio drifted down past tiers of descending, colossal steps that swept around the perimeter of a vent all of a mile across. After "hearing" the voice that first time, they had heard no more, but still eerie mental echoes reverberated in their minds.

To say that the three were wary would be to severely understate the apprehension they felt, particularly Silberhutte. For the Warlord was experienced in telepathic communication, and he had detected behind the voice's welcome certain sinister undertones. "The ice-priests await you," the voice had said, which was to admit knowledge of their coming. Who, then, had foreseen and foretold their eventual arrival on Dromos, when they themselves had not known of it for a fact until so recently?

Who else but Ithaqua himself, when he deposited the lure here, the time-clock, knowing that they must follow on behind sooner or later! Little wonder that the Wind-Walker had been so crazed with lunatic glee when last they had seen him high over the plateau, his mighty fist clenched about the time-clock.

"The ice-priests await you, as they have waited since the dawn of time." Since the dawn of time? Merely for the arrival of three mortals come to Dromos on an impossible quest? But then again, perhaps that was it exactly; perhaps any mortals would suffice, would satisfy the needs of the ice-priests—whatever those needs were. Such were the thoughts that passed through the Warlord's head; and because of them he grasped his massive ax, rescued from the debris of battle atop Moreen's peak, more tightly as he hung in his harness below de Marigny and Moreen.

As for de Marigny: he now wore in his belt his original picklike weapon, reclaimed when the Warlord discarded it, and its presence there comforted him inordinately. While he had taken the voice's welcome at its face value, (for the moment at least,) and while he did not have Silberhutte's acumen in matters of mental communication, still he remembered well his friend's tale of the cruelty of the icepriests. And his arm tightened protectively about the girl whose slender legs encircled his waist and whose arm hugged his neck.

Moreen, too, was full of doubt, but she must now go where the men from the Motherworld went, placing herself entirely in their care. If that meant exploring the bowels of a huge volcanic vent, wherein as yet unknown intelligences—"men," perhaps—had their lair, then that must be the way of it. Still, she comforted herself, while Dromos was a strange, cold world and most mysterious, Numinos had never been a paradise. She had known hardships before and would probably know them again before finding that Elysia of which her Earthman had spoken and which he sought so avidly. And, she reminded herself, it was by no means certain that they ever would find Elysia; for de Marigny had told her that there would be dangers, and he had tried to hint that they could well be insurmountable. Well, she had been brave enough when she shrugged his warning off—but now?

Now Silberhutte interrupted the thoughts of his companions to say: "Henri, if we can be contacted that way by the ice-priests, then it should be just as easy for us—for me at least—to contact them. While it's obvious we can't stay up there on the surface, that we must get on as quickly as possible and find the clock, still I would like to know more about where we're going and what we're letting ourselves in for. So steady as you go and give me time to get a few answers, or at least time to pose a few questions." And with that he fell silent.

Knowing his friend to be probing telepathically ahead, searching for the minds of the as yet unknown ice-priests,

175

de Marigny slowed the rate of the cloak's descent to little more than a gentle drift and waited breathlessly for the Warlord's report. And almost immediately Silberhutte's sixth sense detected something in the dark blue gloom below. A mental *motion*, a purely psychic seething—a lurking presence . . . no, many presences—a conclave of shadowy minds, a cesspit of evil influence!

For a split second he had caught the ice-priests, who or whatever they were, unawares; but that was all the time it took for him to determine their purpose—which was, as the Warlord had feared, nothing less than to snare the three who now descended toward their subterranean lair! A split second only to divine not only this but also something of how it would be done.

These things Silberhutte learned from that single moment of telepathic contact, these and one other: that while the ice-priests may well have been men once long ago in fabulous Theem'hdra, they most certainly were not men now! No race of men could possibly have minds like these, which reeked of an evil as ancient as the CCD themselves.

This was as much as he was allowed to know, for no sooner was his presence felt by the ice-priests than they shut his mind out, blocking his telepathic power as surely as if it had never existed. Silently the Warlord cursed himself for letting the ice-priests discover him, then gripped his harness tightly and turned his face up to look at de Marigny and Moreen where they swung together beneath the canopy of the cloak above him.

"Get out of here, Henri!" the Warlord shouted. "Take us up, man—before it's too late!"

But a moment later, as de Marigny desperately tried to manipulate the studs that controlled his wonderful garment, he knew the worst: that they were already too late. For now, as if somewhere below the blades of a great fan had begun to turn, air was being sucked down the narrowing bore of the volcano in huge gulps, creating too much of a drag for the already overloaded cloak to defy.

For a few moments de Marigny fought the rapidly increasing suction but then, as the turbulence became such that he was obliged to seek the center of the bore where there was less danger of being tossed against the steep steps of ice, he gave up the unequal struggle and fought instead to keep the cloak stable as it was drawn down toward whatever fate awaited it.

Down they spiraled, helplessly, like ants trapped on a leaf and whirled in a gale, and even Armandra's little familiar winds could do nothing to help them. . . .

Minutes passed and still the power of the vortex increased, so that twice de Marigny felt Moreen's legs slip where they gripped him. On both occasions he released all control over the cloak to grab the girl to him, gritting his teeth in the face of the now howling current of air that rushed them ever faster into nightmare bowels of ice and stone.

In the same interval of time Silberhutte, too, was active, partly freeing himself from his harness and then fighting the suction that threatened to tear him bodily loose from his straps. He would part with the cloak soon enough—but when he chose to do so and not before. When he went to the ice-priests, he would go as his own man, not hooked and wriggling like some fish on a line.

But now, as the bore narrowed until its huge, blue-glowing ice steps were less than fifty feet away on all sides, the cloak and its passengers were caught up in a chaos of crazed air that immediately checked their sickening plunge, whirling them in a circle that took the trio ever closer to the smooth ice walls. Finally, when it seemed they must surely be dashed to pieces against the lowest tiers of steps at the very bottom of the pit, then the mad winds hurled them irresistibly along one of several horizontal shafts that lay at right angles to the main bore.

They were rushed into a region of eerie, blue-lit caves hung with ice stalactites that glowed phosphorescently, and as the frenzied current of seemingly sentient air slackened off a little to thread them safely through this maze of descending daggers, so Silberhutte decided that the time had come to part company with his friends—at least for the time being.

He finished unfastening himself and, ignoring his great speed, cast himself free. His arms, thrown wide, momentarily embraced a pair of icicles almost as thick as his thighs, which might have withstood his body's weight but never its hurtling velocity. They snapped from the ceiling and crashed down with him to the floor of the tunnel in a massive shivering of ice. In the next moment there came a veritable deluge of crystals shaken loose by the reverberating echoes of Silberhutte's collision and fall; following which, as the howling subterranean winds bore the cloak swiftly away into the distance, the tunnel became still once more and coldly silent.

As for the two who still clung together beneath the cloak's straining canopy, they did not even know that the Warlord had left them. They knew only the nausea of their buffeting rush through bowels of earth and ice—a kaleidoscope vista of weirdly carved ice caves, lit now by blue luminosity, now dark as Stygian tombs—the irresistible wind and, in deep mental recesses, the obscene tittering of telepathic voices which could only belong to the ice-priests of olden Khrissa. ·

When the Warlord's senses returned, (he knew not how long after his fall,) he found himself lying in a pile of ice fragments, large and small; but while his body was a mass of bruises and abrasions, nothing seemed to be broken, though a painful and lumpy forehead explained his splitting headache. He climbed carefully to his feet and examined his body minutely, easing the aches and pains out of stiffened joints and battered limbs.

Then, as he made to follow a trail of ice debris brought down from the ceiling of the tunnel by the demon wind and the cloak's passing, he cast his mind back over the most immediate past. Uppermost in his memory was the wind that had dragged the cloak down the bore of the dead volcano and into this icy underworld, a wind which had doubtless been called up by the ice-priests. Ithaqua had obviously conferred certain of his powers on the ice-priests, much as he had on Borea.

Ah, but these priests of Dromos were different again from those the Wind-Walker occasionally elevated from the ranks of his common worshipers on Borea; they had been real priests in their time and were still, however dark the powers they served. Moreover they were telepathic. For this latter reason Silberhutte kept his thoughts carefully guarded as he traversed the tunnel, which in reality was not so much a tunnel as a series of domed caverns or galleries, natural in appearance and of unknown extent.

So the ice-priests were telepathic; they served Ithaqua and commanded, to one degree or another, a certain control over the elements; and they were basically evil in nature, as Armandra had forewarned. In short, and in the light of what the Warlord had glimpsed in their minds, they were certainly inimical to de Marigny's quest and both he and the girl Moreen could well be in the most dire trouble at this very moment.

With the latter thought strong in his mind, Silberhutte found himself increasing his pace as he passed through successive caverns of blue-glowing ice, always following the trail of crystalline debris. The air was absolutely calm now and completely icy, with a temperature well below zero, so that for all the masses of ice that hung from the ceiling and festooned the walls and floors in fantastic formations, no water moved or dripped anywhere. Silberhutte, however, felt no discomfort; his metabolism had been permanently altered long ago, so that he was perfectly at home in this frigid place, but he worried about de Marigny and Moreen. He knew that they had Annahilde's warming powder but wondered if they had retained their freedom to use it. By now they might well be in the clutches of the ice-priests.

Feeling almost fully recovered and having worked all of his aches and pains out of his system, the Warlord now forged ahead at a rapid pace, surefooted despite the treacherous surface on which he trod. Once or twice as he went, he felt tentative, searching mental fingers groping at the edges of his mind, but he kept his thoughts completely shielded from whichever minds sought his in this alien underworld. The very fact that they sought him, however, told him that his fears for the safety of his companions were realized; that they must have fallen into the hands of the ice-priests and that his own absence had been noted. That simply meant that he must proceed with great caution. And yet how could he do that and maintain his speed? No, speed was of the essence and caution must for the moment take second place in matters of precedence.

At least he could not complain of misplacement; on the contrary, for he was used to a subterranean or semisubterranean existence. These were different caves from those he had known in the plateau on Borea, certainly, and different again from the volcanic system of caverns and vents in the

Isle of Mountains on Numinos, but they were caves none-theless. Thus he was not at all dismayed when he was obliged to traverse several darker caves where the illumination was little more than a dull blue glow around the perimeter of the walls (he had known darker places in the plateau), though of necessity he had to slow his pace in passing through such areas.

Before long, however, he came to a large gallery where he was brought up short in unaccustomed indecision. Here the ceiling receded into frosty heights from which massive ice pillars, many of a thickness three or four times as great as his waist, joined with columns that grew up from an oddly corrugated floor; but the size and configurations of the place were not that which stopped him. What caused his consternation was something entirely different.

For some time the ice-crystal spoor of the cloak's passing had been diminishing, but here in this huge cave it petered out altogether. That might well mean that Silberhutte's search was almost at an end, but at the same time it confused matters greatly. For the place was like some sort of underground junction from which several shafts led off in different directions. One of these tunnels had been the cloak's exit route from the gallery, and its discovery would certainly lead the Warlord to his vanished friends.

But which one?

Chapter Three

Lair of the Ice-Priests

FOLLOWING the perimeter of the vast ice hall, Silberhutte peered into each of the tunnel entrances in turn, examining their floors for sign of the cloak's passing. He discovered nothing to suggest the way his friends had gone, but he did detect at the last entrance a certain odor. For a single second in the frozen, sterile atmosphere of the place, the strange smell—of incense, perhaps, and yet sulphurous, too—assailed his nostrils, then was gone.

Wasting no time, he moved forward into the tunnel, going as silently as possible between bluely luminous walls of ice, and as he went so the peculiar smell came stronger to him from some as yet unknown source. A minute more, and as the Warlord carefully came around a bend, he froze, baring his teeth in a half-snarl, half-gasp of surprise.

Slowly, great ax upraised, he emerged into view of a fantastic scene. Then he allowed himself to relax, his body coming erect from its half-crouch as he again moved forward, disbelief growing on his face. For this was the tunnel's end, the very lair of the ice-priests. And indeed there were ice-priests here—but they were the last thing Silberhutte had expected.

Armandra had said they were tall, hairless, thin, and cold. Yes, and so they were, but her description simply did not do them justice! They stood all of eight feet tall, were thin to the point of emaciation—mere bones with an outer layer of naked, heavily wrinkled skin—and their *color* . . .

They were white, but not the white of clean snow or of

181

good milk or of any normal thing. They were *corpse*-white, the sickly white of the destroying angel, Amanita Phalloides, the mushroom of death! And not only in their unwholesome color did they match that terrible fungus, for their heads, too, were of a loathsome mushroom shape; with foreheads that overhung their faces, and skulls that were much too squat and flat.

Like grotesque, alien mummies they were, and preserved just as surely—though not wound in bindings or lain in carven sarcophagi. No, they were preserved in pillars of ice! And like mummies they too were ancient; but somehow Silberhutte knew that they predated any Earthly mummy, that indeed they were the original ice-priests of Theem'hdra, and that time itself had wrought in them their hideous dessication.

Nine in number—standing upright, monstrous heads drooping upon bony, shriveled chests, spindly legs together and stick-arms hanging by their sides . . . and all encased in ice, except for the domes of their projecting heads and their turned-down faces. At first the Warlord thought that they were dead. Stepping closer, however, he saw that they were merely in a state of suspension, a cryogenic limbo; for even as he stared at the awful skull of one of them, he saw the distended blood vessels darkening as the ice-priest's circulatory system worked. They were alive, yes, but their metabolisms had been so slowed as to be almost at a standstill.

They stood (were encased) each to his own icicle in a ring about a central pit, facing outward. The pit was the source of that peculiar odor—much stronger here—that had attracted the Warlord's attention to the lair in the first instance. He now found himself thinking of the place more positively as a "lair," as if the ice-priests were more animal than human; nor did studying them briefly at close quarters change his opinion of them in this respect.

Basically human they might well be, but their branch had grown apart from the great tree of humanity in an age predating the coelacanth, and from that day to this they had remained unaltered and irretrievably, yes, alien! They *were* human—as was Neanderthal, as is the pygmy and the aborigine—but their evolution had taken them much farther from the main stem than any of these.

Carefully, still more than a little wary, the Warlord stepped between two of the refrigerated figures to stare down into the central pit. Here the fumes from below were understandably stronger, cloying almost, so that he held his breath as he looked down upon the slow, glutinous bubbling of some thickly viscous lavalike substance fifty feet below. Then, seeing that the walls of the pit at its bottom were glowing a dull red, he decided that it must indeed be an as yet active volcanic source, the valve of some larger vent, and further that the fumes it gave off must somehow be essential to the process of suspended animation.

Finally he straightened up to walk silently around the circle, only halting when he came to a wide gap in the ring of ice-blurred figures. Here, where instinct told the Warlord that there should be more pillars of ice reaching from floor to ceiling, he saw only the stumps of three great icicles which formed uneven mounds upon the floor. And deeply indented in them were the marks of wide, wedge-shaped feet . . . such marks as the feet of the ice-priests would make. Now the Warlord knew that there must be twelve ice-priests in all—an even dozen—of which three were even now awake and abroad in the ice-cave complex!

So absorbed was Silberhutte with these observations that for a moment he inadvertently left his mind unguarded, only realizing his danger when alien thoughts rushed in to detect his presence. Before he once more closed the shutters on his mind, he read disbelief, rage, and something akin to panic in the thoughts that crowded in upon his own; panic that he had managed to reach the lair itself. These disordered, frightened thoughts were strangely sluggish and came from close at hand—from the minds of these very figures ringed about the volcanic blowhole—but the others, whose sources he noted with alarm were also fairly close, though he could not place them exactly, were much more active and immediately purposeful.

Silberhutte again cast his glance across the space where those oddly indented stumps of ice stood up from the cave's floor, and as he did so, he spied a small motion among the ranks of silent, petrified ice-priests. Again the Warlord froze . . . then watched in morbid fascination as jerkily, one by one, the domed heads of the encased ice-priests came up and their slowly opening eyes, which seemed to have no pupils and were uniformly crimson, swiveled to stare in his direction!

And immediately it was as if chains had been thrown about the Warlord's massive shoulders, as if his feet were suddenly shackled to the ice-layered floor. He had never before met with hypnotism in any form but knew its principles, knew that what he now felt was not a physical power but the purely mental one of mind over matter—the minds of the ice-priests over the material of his being! It was not even telepathy, which he could understand and handle more than adequately, though certainly there were parallels. For while his mind now worked swiftly and lucidly to free his body from the ice-priests' hypnotic shackles, still those shackles tightened about him, denying him the use of powerful sinew, muscle, and bone. It was as much as he could do to back away from the pit, stumbling and barely managing to remain upright, holding on grimly to his great ax as those crimson eyes bored awfully into his own.

Finally, concentrating all of his mind on the breaking of his invisible bonds, the Warlord could no longer hold in place those shutters that protected his thoughts from external influences. Down crashed his mental barriers—and in rushed the concerted sendings of a dozen evil, powerful minds, the chaotic and monstrous imaginings of this nightmare Brotherhood of Ice.

But the ice-priests, too, had their limits. Now, as they concentrated on the Warlord's mind, they were obliged to relax their hypnotic hold on his body. He found himself free to move, to flee, and turned to do just that—

—Only to find himself face to face with that trio of monsters whose footprints were melted into the three ice mounds at the rim of the pit. There they stood, and while Silberhutte believed that he might handle them easily enough (for what were they but skin and bone?), he was not so sure about the *things* they had with them!

About the feet of the ice-priests, crouching like great hounds at the ends of their leads, were three fantastic creatures unlike anything the Warlord had ever thought to see. Six-legged, like huge insects—protected by black, chitinous plates which sprouted short, coarse red hairs, and with lashing forked tails whose barbs dripped a clear fluid that set the icy floor steaming poisonously—the things were the stuff of a madman's dreams!

The advancing ice-priests smiled (if such a word may rightly describe what they did with their alien faces) in hideous anticipation as they drew closer, drawn on by the straining of their awful servitors. Silberhutte, turning to left and right, could see no escape; the cave was a dead end, containing only the broken circle of ice-priests frozen about the central pit. And now, as the leashed hounds and their masters blocked his single route of egress, so the Warlord found himself backing toward that pit.

Then, quick as thought, one of the terrible creatures slipped its leash and hurled itself straight at the Warlord's throat. He cried out once—no cry of horror, though he felt great horror; not even a cry of rage, though certainly he was enraged to be trapped here like a rat at the mercy of beings whose instincts he knew to be more savage, merciless, and cruel than the instinct of any rat—no, none of these, but a battle cry. And with the echoes of that cry reverberating and setting the lair of the ice-priests to a tinkling of startled ice, he lifted his great ax, smashed the slavering cockroach thing to one side in midair, and threw himself headlong into battle. . . .

De Marigny and Moreen regained consciousness together. They had been literally whirled unconscious at the end of their subterranean flight, driven round and round in a tight circle until they had blacked out. The wonder was that the girl had not been torn from the Earthman's arms by centrifugal force, to be dashed against the blue-glistening walls of their ice prison, but she had not. Now, recovering but still filled with a whirling nausea, they clung together as before; and for some little time that was as much as they could do.

It was as de Marigny became cognizant of their immediate surroundings that the full extent of their plight was brought home to him. To begin with, the Warlord was no longer with them; whether of his own volition or at the will of some other, Silberhutte had parted company with them. Equally disconcerting to de Marigny was the fact that he no longer wore his flying cloak—but there was worse yet to come.

The girl had her face buried in the furs that covered his chest, and so she knew nothing of their whereabouts, was not aware that they lay upon a hard, cold floor of ice in a small cave. De Marigny knew, however; knew moreover that there was only one exit, and that it was guarded. . . .

But what guards!

There were two of them, two huge insect-things that crouched down for all the world like guard dogs—except that they bared no teeth but hissed warningly through jaws like those of great reptiles. De Marigny saw them and was relieved to see also the stretched chains attached to their collars and fastened to iron staples hammered into the ice of the walls. The—hounds?—were at the fullest extent of those chains, uncomfortably close to his feet.

Drawing breath in a huge gasp, he snatched back his feet and hugged the girl to him all in one movement. Shaken from her exhausted half-sleep, Moreen opened her eyes to peer into those of the two monsters that now snapped and slavered only feet away. Galvanized into action by de Marigny's movements, they hissed loudly and hauled dangerously on their chains, scrabbling at the ice floor with legs like hairy, jointed bones.

Then an astounding thing—for before de Marigny could stop her, Moreen had slipped from his arms to hold her hand out to the chained creatures, as if she were about to pet a pair of domesticated animals in a Viking settlement on Numinos!

"Moreen, no!" he cried, stark horror in his voice.

She pulled her hand back from the snapping snake jaws of the things and turned to him in seeming surprise. "But why? They will not harm me."

"Not harm you?" he cried, dragging her back bodily from the chained monsters. "Girl, they'd kill you! That's why they've been put on duty here, to keep us in. They're killers."

"You don't understand," she told him patiently. "No lesser beast would ever harm me. They sense something in me—something which I myself do not understand—and even the wildest of them are calmed when I speak to them. The great eagles of Numinos have perched on my shoulders, and the wild dogs of the hills have accepted meat from my fingers." She turned back to the hissing cave-things and shrugged. "These creatures are—different—yes, but for all that they are living creatures. Therefore I am safe with them."

Her logic baffled de Marigny. "But *look* at them!" he cried. "Do they look harmless?"

"Henri," she answered, kissing his brow, "I have trusted you—with my life. Now you must trust me. Indeed there is something very strange about these creatures—for see, they continue to snap and hiss even now that they know me. Still I say to you that they will not harm me."

Frowning, she turned from him, approaching the insect-things on all fours. They reared on their chains, jaws slavering and barbed tails lashing as, unhesitatingly, she again stretched out her hand to them.

"For God's sake!" de Marigny whispered, fighting the urge to grab her and drag her back. Ignoring him, she drew closer to the hideous creatures; and as she did so, they arched their necks and drew back their flat reptilian heads—for all the world like angry snakes about to strike.

And strike they did, so swiftly that the eye could scarcely follow their movement. Moreen had no time to snatch her hand back out of harm's way. Razor fangs opened her flesh, injecting yellow poison. Wide-eyed in disbelief, her mouth forming an "O" of surprise to match de Marigny's expression of horror, she fell back into his arms. No living creature would ever have done this to her, she knew that, and so—

"Not real!" she gasped as de Marigny feverishly took her hand and gazed at it in amazement, his jaw dropping. Then they both stared at the clean, unbroken flesh of her hand and wrist. "They are not real!"

As one they turned their heads to look again at the monstrous hounds—seeing immediately that she was right. The creatures had disappeared, vanished into thin air, and with them the chains that had seemed to tether them to the frozen walls. They had not been real, had existed only in their minds, illusions placed there by the evil genius of the ice-priests.

Suddenly de Marigny recalled what Silberhutte had said about Theem'hdra's ice-priests being greatly skilled in the arts of illusion and mass hypnotism, and at last he understood. Well, it was a lesson learned, knowledge which would doubtless prove very useful in the near future.

As for the immediate future: there were things to be done, and at once!

"Come on, Moreen," he helped the girl to her feet. "We have to find Silberhutte—and then the time-clock." And as they hurried together down the unknown ice tunnel toward whatever terrors or triumphs lay ahead, he pictured in his mind's eye an upturned hourglass in which the sands of time flowed swiftly indeed—sands which were rapidly running out. . . .

Within a very short time the pair emerged from the prison tunnel into that same great ice gallery whose many exits had so recently baffled the Warlord. For them, however, there was to be no indecision; coming to them clearly from close at hand, sounds of battle pointed the way as surely as any signpost. There was the clash of iron and the splintering of ice—but above all else, clear and resounding, came the enraged if somewhat frustrated roar of Silberhutte's bull voice! As they skirted the great hall, it was easy to discover the mouth of the tunnel which issued these furious reverberations.

All caution to the wind—ignoring the fact that his weapon had been taken from him along with the flying cloak—de Marigny rushed down the vast natural tunnel of blue, softly glowing ice toward the lair of the ice-priests; and as he came round the final bend, with Moreen hot on his heels, there opened to his eyes a scene strange and macabre. He took in the circle of frozen ice-priests at a glance, then concentrated his amazed attention on the actors and the action. As Moreen pantingly caught up with him, her gasp told him that she, too, was struck by the weirdness of the scene.

One ice-priest—tall, naked, spindly as a stick-insect—stood with his wax-white back to the pair. His arms were raised shoulder high, his hands alive with mesmeric motion, outstretched toward the Borean Warlord. But the mushroom-headed ice-priest was not the sole source of de Marigny's and Moreen's astonishment; no, that doubtful honor went to the insane activity of Silberhutte. For the Warlord had obviously gone stark, staring mad!

He crouched between the lone ice-priest and the central pit with its perimeter of frozen figures, his eyes wide and full of darting motion, his great ax held out before him. Every few seconds he would turn, leap toward a wall, and strike at it shatteringly, all the while yelling his rage. But it seemed to the astounded watchers that there was as much terror as rage in the Warlord's savage battle cries. . . .

Chapter Four

"Where is the Time-Clock?"

NOW Silberhutte embarked upon a series of dodges, feints, wild turns, and tumbles, his ax flashing in a blur to left and right, as if he fought half a dozen fleet-footed foes which only he could see; and through all of this the solitary ice-priest pivoted to follow his every movement, long-fingered hands tracing mystic passes in the air. This could only possibly be one thing—and de Marigny already had ample evidence of the mastery of the ice-priests over magic and illusion. The Warlord had become the latest victim of that power, as had been his friends so very recently. He had not seen them enter the terminal cave, saw nothing now but the illusions engendered of the lone ice-priest's mesmerism enhanced by the telepathic embellishments of that being's now wakeful, ice-encased brothers. And his plight was indeed a sore one.

Following the attack of the first creature, the other priests had deliberately released their "hounds" upon him, and since then they had called for the reinforcements with which Silberhutte now battled. And no matter how many of the insect-dogs he cut down or smashed aside, others were there to take their places, supplied from some seemingly inexhaustible source to the rear of the "three" priests who continued to bar his exit.

One thing was certain: he was losing the battle and knew he must soon fall before the concerted savagery of the pack. Constantly he tripped over their fallen, broken bodies, and only a series of miracles had sufficed so far to protect him from their slavering jaws. On more than a dozen occasions their barbed, venomous tails had come close to splashing him with their acid, and already he was beginning to feel a mental and physical weariness as his great strength was put to this most grueling test.

Finally that which he most feared occurred: stepping back from a frontal attack by one of the hounds, he tripped over a broken carcass and sprawled on his back between two of the frozen priests, his head and shoulders over the lip of the pit that went down to the glowing, sluggishly surging lava. Instantly the hounds were on him, closing from all sides. Then—

"They're not real, Hank!" came de Marigny's warning cry in the Warlord's ears, strangely hollow and echoing. "Whatever you see, none of it's real . . . not real . . . not *real!* It's an illusion . . . illusion . . . *illusion!* It can't harm you . . . can't harm you . . . *can't harm you!*"

And at once the hissing, slavering snake faces surrounding the Warlord began to fade, to dissolve away into mist, so that he instantly knew and understood de Marigny's message.

Illusions, his friend had called out to him. The mental mischief of the ice-priests. Visions called up to sap his strength and render him helpless—to kill him! Well, the warning had come in the nick of time, for struggling against the hounds, the Warlord had been at the point of falling backward into the lava pit. Now he sprang to his feet, mentally brushed aside the rapidly dispersing mist of nightmarish chitinous bodies and slavering, ethereal jaws, gazed up into the monstrous crimson eyes of the lone ice-priest whose evil skills had conjured the visions.

For a moment Silberhutte paused. . . . Then, with a grunt of exertion—even as the naked ice-priest frantically recommenced his esoteric passes—he narrowed his eyes, lifted his great ax, and drove its keen edge into the willowy giant's fragile chest. With a single, high-pitched, whistling shriek of agony and disbelief the ice-priest died, felled as a grass-blade before the scythe; and a moment later the Warlord stepped over his crumpled body, freeing his ax and almost absently cleaning its edge on the sleeve of his jacket.

Finally the red haze of battle and illusion-engendered weariness cleared from Silberhutte's eyes, and for the first time since releasing himself from the cloak in mid-flight, he saw his friends. They hurried toward him, their faces drawn and anxious, and he caught them to him crushingly. Then he drew a deep draft of the cold cavern air, released them, and said:

"Thank you, Henri, Moreen. When I cut loose from the cloak, my idea was to track you down and come on like the cavalry. But you outflanked me—thank goodness!" He turned back and gazed grimly on the broken circle of ice-priests. "Now there are one or two things these fellows are going to tell us. We already know they're telepathic, so—"

"We underestimated you, Warlord, that much we grant you," came a cold, booming voice in their heads, cutting short Silberhutte's words. *"There were none such as you three in Theem'-hdra. Strength such as yours—aye, and powers such as you possess—made men mighty in the Old World. Such men were wizards whose words were law, whose law was—"*

"Cruel and corrupt!" Silberhutte spoke out loud. "Now listen, you ice-priests. We've no time to waste, so I'll make it short. We came to Dromos to find a box, a machine stolen from us by Ithaqua. One of you is already dead. I killed him and I'm glad of it. I don't care how many more I have to kill to get the machine. We three," he indicated Moreen and de Marigny, "we're all of a like mind." Flanked by his friends, he hefted his ax in his huge fist and strode closer to the circle.

The three could not see the awful corpse faces of the four beings whose backs were to them, but the remaining five gazed at them with eyes red as the fires of hell. The veins that stood out in the domes of their mushroom heads were visibly pulsing now, and suddenly there was a tangible electric tension in the air which had not been present a moment earlier.

Moreen gasped and moved behind the Warlord, catching de Marigny's hand. He wrapped an arm about her, said: "Something's coming, Hank—I feel it!"

"No tricks," Silberhutte warned the ice-priests sharply, carrying his ax as if it were weightless and stepping closer still to the frozen figures.

"Tricks? You dare relegate the magic of the ice-priests of olden Khrissa to mere trickery? Fools—you know nothing

of us—nothing!" Now the eyes of the five were boring into theirs with increasing intensity, crimson orbs that seemed to protrude obscenely as their owners concentrated . . . concentrated.

"Mind over . . . matter!" gasped the Warlord, experiencing again that iron constriction he had known earlier. "Telekinesis—or something much . . . like it." He tried to lift his ax but froze with the great blade only half-upraised. Though the muscles of his mighty frame bulged and strained, his earlier exertions had all but sapped him, making him easy prey to the mental "magic" of these masters of weird phenomena.

Moreen, too, was held immediately helpless. Though she was young and strong, she had only a woman's physical strength; nor was her mind sufficiently sophisticated to grasp readily the nature of the forces involved. Only de Marigny, as yet untried by any real physical exertion in this frigid subterranean complex, found himself capable of the slightest movement.

Illusion, "magic," mind over matter, hypnosis—whatever powers these ice-priests possessed and however they chose to use them—there must surely be rules to the game. All actions have *counter*actions, produce *re*actions. De Marigny, unable to defend himself, knew that he must attack; but how? Then, like a glimmer of light in a maelstrom of darkness, he remembered Annahilde's dreaming powders. And that single spark rapidly fanned itself to a flame, for he knew that the dreaming powders—together with the warming powders—were still tucked away in his clothes where the ice-priests had failed to search.

"Fight fire," he told himself, *"with fire!"*

Slowly, agonizingly slowly, he forced his hand to the pocket that contained the dreaming powders, brought forth the pouch, lifted it toward his face. And all the while his eyes were held by the crimson gaze of the ice-priests, and each slightest movement of his body was slower than the one preceding it. Then, before he could even give thought to the task of disseminating the powders, the pouch was snatched from his hand and thrown down on the ice of the floor, taken from him by no visible power. Telekinesis—"magic"—the mind power of the ice-priests!

Despair filled de Marigny—despair and the mad, triumphant laughter of the ice-priests, booming and mocking in his mind—until suddenly he became conscious of a frenzied tugging at the hair of his head and the fur fringe of his jacket. Armandra's familiar winds!

In a flash he saw his salvation—his, the Warlord's, and Moreen's. "The . . . pouch," he managed to whisper. "The . . . powder!" And instantly the cave was filled with a tinkling of disturbed ice as frantic winds lifted the pouch from the floor, hovered it before the stricken Earthman's eyes, plucked at it until its contents spilled in air and formed a cloud.

"In their . . . faces," he commanded. "Blow it . . . in . . . their faces!" And the whirling cloud of powder was immediately rushed away, driven into the faces of the ice-priests by sentient winds. They breathed air, those chill, soulless beings—and now they breathed Annahilde's dreaming powders. . . .

The effect was instantaneous.

For a brief moment the three beleaguered adventurers were granted a fleeting glimpse of the terrors that threatened the ice-priests—a single glimpse that leaped to their minds telepathically and involuntarily from the minds of the ice-encased ancients—but that one glance was sufficient in itself to testify to the efficacy of Annahilde's powders. Silberhutte, had he so desired, might easily have remained in telepathic contact with the stricken ice-priests, might have probed their stunned and hag-ridden minds to witness at firsthand the monstrous illusions that now enmeshed them; but that would have meant sharing their terror of the incredible nightmare hordes which now pressed in on them from all sides. Rather than suffer that, he withdrew, shuddering at what he had so briefly glimpsed.

Masters of illusion the ice-priests were, but theirs were illusions of the mind, born of advanced development of the ESP areas of the brain. Annahilde's powders, on the other hand, produced hallucinations which were external, "artificial," as it were; and the difference was that between a disturbing dream and a drug-induced hallucination.

For the powders worked on those areas of the mind that govern an individual's capacity for fear—his capacity to suffer it as determined by his capacity to inflict it. In the olden times the ice-priests had been masters of terror, and now they paid the price. What kind of horrors would terrify a ghoul, a mass murderer, a torturer, a homicidal maniac, a soulless monster? Whatever the kind, those were the horrors—indescribably in mundane terms—which now threatened the ice-priests of primal Theem'hdra.

The reactions of the three to their sudden release from the mind chains of the ice-priests were varied. De Marigny, to say the least, was relieved and delighted that his ruse had worked so well; Moreen was mystified and frightened, stumbling and clinging to her man's arm as the numbness abruptly left her limbs; and Silberhutte: he knew only that his anger, the rage and frustration he felt at the mere thought of these vilest minions of Ithaqua, had trebled. Given another chance he doubted that they would hesitate to kill himself and his friends out of hand; or worse by far, they would hold all three and wait on the return of the Wind-Walker. Plainly they must not be given that chance.

Showing that ruthless efficiency of which he was more than capable when circumstances demanded, commencing before the effect of Annahilde's dreaming powders could wear off, the Warlord waved de Marigny and Moreen back from the broken circle of tormented figures and swung his great ax high against the upper part of the nearest column. The massive icicle shattered where the ax bit. Pausing only to gauge his aim, Silberhutte next swung at the base of the pillar, then threw his weight against the collapsing slab of ice and toppled it bodily into the pit. A moment later and, with a belching roar, a great gush of steam came up mephitically, flowing outward along the tunnel's ceiling and settling as fine snow in a matter of seconds. The dessicated prisoner of the pillar, already immersed in hideous hallucinations, had known nothing at all of his final, fatal immersion. That at least had been a mercy.

But now the remaining eight were rapidly recovering, blinking their crimson eyes, and moving their heads from side to side, groping dimly with their minds . . . and finding the mind of the Warlord open and waiting for them. He spoke to them with his mind, at the same time speaking out loud so that his friends would also hear him:

"Mercy is something of which you've no knowledge, ice-priests. You could no more understand mercy than you could show it. So be it. Your destruction here and now should come as no surprise to you; it's what you would do to us if the roles were reversed. Even so, you'll decide how many are to die; the matter is in your own hands. There are questions I will ask—to live you must supply the answers. But before we begin, just to be sure we understand each other—"

He again lifted his ax and struck mightily at the second pillar. The blow failed to completely shatter the icicle but severed the neck of the shriveled being encased within it. That dweller in the ice was not so lucky as the first, was briefly aware of the doom rushing upon him, and his mental shriek was awful to hear in the moment before the keen edge of Silberhutte's ax cut it off. One more shattering blow followed—and a further creaking of ice, a toppling of frozen flesh, a second vast puff of poisonous vapor and settling cloud of fine, blasphemous snowflakes—before the thing was done.

Now only two figures remained on the nearer rim of the pit, but the crimson eyes of the five who now twisted their necks to gaze across from the other side of that volcanic blowhole—which, through nameless centuries had sustained the evil lives of the ice-priests and now, with utter equanimity, was taking them—surely mirrored their disbelief, their fury and hatred, their fear of these strangers come across the lightyears to exact a vengeance for deeds ancient, monstrous, and without number.

"In what you have done," came the booming voice in their heads, weaker now but still full of acid hatred, *"you have signaled your own unenviable end!"*

"You take," grunted Silberhutte, again lifting his avenging ax, "a lot of convincing. Don't you understand? You're in no position to threaten. You're beaten!" And moments later yet another ice-priest screamed his last and toppled to boiling oblivion.

Now the eyes of the remaining six were bulging as before, the veins of their awful heads pulsing malignantly, and again there came that tension in the air that forewarned of a further manifestation of their power.

De Marigny, snatching up the pouch from where it had fallen, shook the dregs of Annahilde's dreaming powders into his palm and held up his hand where the ice-priests could see its contents. Then, clenching his fingers over the small heap of precious grains, he cried: "No more of your tricks—or I'll send you straight back to hell! You're not the only ones who deal in nightmares, but I fancy mine are worse than any you might dream up. . . ."

For an instant the tangible *electric* feeling went out of the air, and de Marigny believed he had convinced the ice-priests against any further use of their powers. Then—

With a roar and a crash fire licked up from the central pit, a mad gout of leaping flame that indiscriminately enveloped both ice-priests and adventurers in a moment, overwhelming all and spilling them in a blazing torrent down the length of the tunnel! Burning, feeling his skin cracking and peeling from him even as he heard Moreen's scream and saw her hair blossom into licking flames, still de Marigny thought to open his hand, thought to hoarsely utter one last command to Armandra's familiar winds—if indeed the winds themselves were not already consumed in the devouring fire.

"Go," he told them, his voice a cracked whisper in the inferno. "Again—the powder—in their faces!"

And perhaps because he felt those precious powders snatched from his palm by eager, frantic gusts of air, and so knew there was at least a chance that this was some ploy of the ice-priests and not a genuine eruption brought on by Silberhutte's feeding of the lava pit, de Marigny was the first to recover from the effects of the illusion. Even so he was awed by the power these beings commanded, that depleted as they were, still they could so readily employ man's elemental and immemorial fear of fire.

For he had actually *felt* the terrific heat of the thing, had *felt* his eyes melting and his skin being crisped and stripped from his body. He had *seen* the ice-priests themselves engulfed and had *heard* in his head their telepathic shrieks of agony. And all a great illusion, a living nightmare conjured by these sole survivors of ancient Theem'hdra.

And so de Marigny recovered first . . . to see Moreen, unburned, curled on the cold floor where she had fallen, mercifully fainted away from all shock and terror; to see the Warlord frenziedly beating at himself, at his clothes, in a final attempt to quell the "fires" that smothered him and consumed his flesh; to see the mouths of the ice-priests snap open in a concerted rictus of horror as once again the

197

even greater horrors born of Annahilde's powders gripped them; and also to see the cave of ice, unaltered, blue and luminous and bitterly cold as ever!

And it was de Marigny, too, who, as the Warlord was released from his private hell of flames to fall trembling and white as snow to the icy floor, grabbed up his friend's great ax and cut down one, two, three of the stricken ice-priests, toppling their encased figures into the pit in a passion of loathing more desperately ruthless even than that displayed so recently by Silberhutte himself. Only the choking *vapors* that rushed up from the seething pit forced him back from his task—the vapors and the hideous "snow" which they immediately formed—but then he stepped forward again to cut down a fourth and fifth ice-priest, and would have continued with the sixth and last had not Silberhutte, recovered but staggering still, stayed his hand and wrested the ax from him.

Only then did de Marigny fall back to lean panting against the glistening wall, nausea growing in him as he realized that he of all people—a truly "civilized" man—had been gripped in what could only be described as a berserker rage. He who had so recently wondered at the Warlord's—inhumanity?—now knew that he would nevermore criticize his friend's instincts, for indeed the ice-priests more than deserved each and every stroke made against them.

"Not this last one, Henri," Silberhutte was panting, shaken but sound, still astounded to find himself unblackened by fire. "Not him, my friend, for he's all we have left, and he has the answers we need. He'll supply them, too—by God he *will!* You tend to the girl—I'll see to him."

With that the Warlord lifted up his great ax before him and poised it inches in front of and level with the pulsing, bluely veined dome of the ice-priest's head. Then he lowered it until its keen, slime-spattered blade was almost resting on the forepart of that being's loathsome skull. The eyes of the ice-priest opened wide in terror, and he audibly sucked in air as Silberhutte began to speak:

"The weight of this weapon is not inconsiderable, ice-priest. If I let it fall, it would probably crack your head wide open. And if I added my own weight to it—then it would split you to your rib cage! At this very moment I am

198

tempted to do just that, and at the first hint of any further trickery I will. If you doubt me, try me. It will be the last thing you ever do. Do we understand each other?"

Slowly the obscene head nodded, crimson eyes focusing briefly, shrinkingly on the blade of the ax where it glittered dully through thin, pinkish blood and drying brain matter.

"Good," said the Warlord, his face cold as the ice that formed the walls of this inner adytum of evil. "Now then, before my arms tire as the weight of the ax numbs them—where is the time-clock? Where is it, ice-priest? And if you would live, you'd best tell me no lie!"

Chapter Five

A Mind Unlocked

"Hold your ax steady, Warlord, and believe me when I say there is much I can tell you," the ice-priest answered. He looked down from his great height, ignoring as best he could the thin edge of sudden death poised before his face; but the booming power was gone from his telepathic voice and it was more like a whisper now, running frightened through the minds of the adventurers. *"If the time-clock is your primary concern, then its secret is easily told. It is close by, not far from here—you can reach it in a very little time."*

"Where is it, exactly?" Silberhutte demanded, placing menacing emphasis on the last word.

"Do not rush me, Warlord, for I will not lie. And once more I beg you, hold well your ax. If it falls, your questions go unanswered and I simply . . . go!" Now the ice-priest seemed more in control of himself, had gauged the urgency of his enemy's need and was using it to prolong the questioning.

"He's stalling!" said de Marigny. "He's avoiding giving direct answers."

"Could it be," the Warlord spoke to the ice-priest low and dangerously, "that you believe your two brothers will return to rescue you? If they do come back before we know what we need to know, then you will surely die."

"And should I fear this?" the crimson eyes of the ice-priest went from Silberhutte's face to the blade of the great

200

ax. *"Warlord, I am already dead! If you do not kill me, Ithaqua will when he returns."*

"Why should he do that?"

"He will surely kill any that you leave alive, for we will have failed him. He has no patience with failure. However, if you and your friends are still here when he comes—then he may let us live."

"It was your task to trap us for him?"

"What profit to deny it?"

"When will he return?"

The ice-encased figure offered a mental shrug. *"You might as well ask when will the wind blow. He commands his own comings and goings."*

Listening to this conversation, de Marigny found his natural curiosity becoming piqued. Also, now that there seemed to be no further immediate danger, he felt the cold beginning to grip him, biting to his very bones. Quickly he took a pinch of Annahilde's warming powder, offering another to Moreen as, rapidly recovering from her faint, she got to her feet and began uncontrollably to shiver.

Silberhutte, too, had sensed the relaxation of danger; now he lowered his ax to the frozen floor. After all, what possible harm could this one ice-priest do them, when they had already disposed of nine such monsters?

By now de Marigny's curiosity had the better of him and he took up the questioning. "Why are you here on Dromos in the first place?" he asked.

"We were 'rescued' from olden Khrissa by Ithaqua—who may say how long ago?—when the common people turned against us. They would have overwhelmed us by sheer weight of numbers, and so we fled to Ithaqua whom we worshiped. He brought us here. I tell you this happened, indeed I know that it was so, but I personally remember little of it. My memory does not extend beyond the ice of the caves, the great snows of the upper world, the lava pit and its sulphur fumes."

"Then how do you know it was so?" asked de Marigny.

"Ithaqua has on occasion reminded us of our debt."

"Debt? He has kept you here on this great snowball of a world—encased in ice for millions of years—and you consider yourself to be in his debt?"

"Without him, we would have been dust aeons gone,"

the ice-priest reminded, and after a pause continued: *"Occasionally he provides diversions . . ."*

"Diversions?" de Marigny repeated. "Here on Dromos?"

"Of course. He brings us women from time to time, from Borea and Numinos, but they are nothing more than brief amusements. On the other hand he promises that once he has you three in his power—then that he will give us a green world of our own to rule. Perhaps Numinos, or Borea—even the Motherworld."

"Well," said the Warlord, "that's one mad dream we've put paid to."

"Three of us yet remain," the ice-priest retorted. *"With our powers, three should be sufficient—at least for any minor world."*

"Three," the Warlord mulled over the number, frowning as it set him to wondering. "Why were only three of your brothers free and wandering abroad in Dromos when the remaining nine were encased in ice?"

For answer there came another mental shrug and the ghost of a laugh. *"Ithaqua made the rules, Warlord. Perhaps he feared to have more than three of us free at any one time. Fit and well and working as one—strong and mentally alert and not drowsing in the ice—who can say what our limits would be? Such illusions as we could create might fool even the Wind-Walker himself."*

By now Moreen was almost fully recovered from her faint and already the warming powders were working in her blood. She had only half-heard the conversation between the two men and the ice-priest; her naïve mind was still staggering from the dizzy turns events had taken. But as she became more conscious of her surroundings and what was taking place, she realized that something was very wrong.

The Warlord—that massive and sometimes brutal man—as if engaged in casual conversation with an old friend, leaned on his ax and gazed up at the ice-priest with an almost bemused expression on his face. De Marigny, one arm loosely about her waist, seemed equally unconcerned. The entire atmosphere was completely unnatural—the more so because the crimson eyes of the lone ice-priest blazed hypnotically and bulged in their sockets as if at any moment to leap from their owner's monstrous head!

Moreen felt the hypnotic spell of those eyes and instantly averted her gaze. What was it the ice-priest had said? That his illusions might fool even Ithaqua himself?

"He's fooling you!" she screamed, tugging at de Marigny's arm and lashing out with her foot at the Warlord's shins. "Don't look at his eyes!"

For a moment, caught off-balance, the two men looked startled; then their eyes met and their jaws dropped in spontaneous astonishment. It had been so close, and they had been so completely hoodwinked. But now their faces hardened as they too averted their eyes from the hypnotic gaze of the ice-priest.

The awful head of that ice-encased figure had commenced to shake violently from side to side—one of the very few movements its owner could readily perform—in frustration and rage. Triumph had indeed been close, only to be snatched away by a slip of a girl. Carefully, insidiously the ice-priest had worked his hypnotic spell, drawing the Earthmen into a web of false security—but now that web was torn aside, and the evil spinner himself stood exposed to the gaze of the adventurers.

Silberhutte quickly stepped around behind the last ice pillar, out of range of the evil, powerful eyes of its prisoner. He reached around to the front of the icicle with one hand and cupped the ice-priest's small chin, trapping his head and holding it still. With his other hand the Warlord gripped his ax close to its heavy head, reached around and pressed the naked blade of his weapon to the spindly giant's trembling throat.

"Look away, Henri, Moreen," the Warlord commanded. "It's between the two of us now. *You!*" He spoke to the ice-priest in a withering telepathic blast of anger and loathing. "I want all of it, everything, and no holding back. Open up, ice-priest, and let me see what's hidden in there, in that black pit of nightmares you call a mind. Do it now, creature, while I'm still fool enough to let you live!"

And so powerful was the Warlord's command that it could no longer be denied. For a single moment only he probed at the innermost recesses of the ice-priest's thoughts, at the tightly guarded core of that being's mind—then broke through triumphant to the secrets hidden within. He looked —and he saw!

He saw all the pent-up evil of nameless aeons, the festering frustration of centuries unnumbered, the lightless horror of a million lifetimes spent in the abstract—but not *always* abstract—contemplation of hideous tortures and the endless plotting of mad dreams of conquest. He saw what the final destiny of olden Theem'hdra was to have been beneath the crushing heel of the ice-priests had they gained full control in that primal continent; and not only that but the fate of the universe itself if ever beings such as these were allowed to expand and overflow like pus into the clean and healthy worlds of space and time. These things and many others he saw and knew now why Ithaqua himself had seen fit to restrict the activity of these ice-priests whose depravity, whose lusting after all things loathsome, whose delight in the diabolical and sheer *potential* for total horror were so immeasurable.

He saw the many possible fates considered by the ice-priests for himself and his companions, the insufferable tortures and degradations plotted for them; and if he shuddered at what had been planned for himself and de Marigny, he positively shrank from the diseased diablerie of Moreen's unspeakable fate. For the ice-priests had been promised the girl when Ithaqua was done with her, and their intentions toward her were far more complex, detailed, and depraved than his. It was surely a terrible thing in itself to envisage the girl ravaged and brutalized by the Wind-Walker, yes, but then to be thrown to the ice-priests with their less mentionable anomalies and deviations—including, at the end, group anthropophagy *while yet the girl lived!*—that was to glimpse the essence of hell itself, pulsating like sentient slime in the cesspit minds of these most foul and detestable creatures.

Yet even now the ice-priest held back, refusing Silberhutte access to one final pocket of closely guarded knowledge, an almost complete set of answers to the Warlord's all-important questions. Closing his eyes and baring his teeth in a grimace of concentration against the frozen surface of the ice pillar, the massive Texan wrapped a knotted mental fist about the ice-priest's mind and squeezed . . . squeezed . . . and once more crashed through to a treasure trove of secrets.

Primarily he was seeking the time-clock; yes, and at last,

finally he knew its location. For all at once he became aware of the most intimate details of this entire subterranean labyrinth of ice caves and tunnels, became heir to a plan of the frozen underworld which was immediately and as plainly recognizable to him as the lines in his own palm; so that now, in his mind's eye, he could see the time-clock where it stood, not too far distant, with de Marigny's flying cloak thrown carelessly about its base.

But if sight of the time-clock was a glad thing, not so the other secrets pried from the ice-priest's ravaged brain; secrets which, when the Warlord knew them, drove all else from his mind in a passion of horror and fear—

Fear not for himself but for Armandra, the Woman of the Winds, wayward daughter of Ithaqua the Wind-Walker. Armandra, on her way to Dromos right now, at this very moment, *and closely pursued by her monstrous father!*

For this was what the Warlord had most feared—that Ithaqua had deliberately brought the time-clock to Dromos solely in order to trap Armandra—and now his fears seemed fully realized. He saw how the ice-priests had blocked Armandra's every telepathic attempt to contact her man, how they had insinuated their own doom-laden suggestions into her mind until she suffered continually from hideous doubts as to Silberhutte's well-being. Finally, when her spirit had been at its lowest ebb, then they had sent out a desperate cry for help, a cry cut short before Armandra could discover their deception, that this was not the Warlord who cried out in distress.

And of course the Woman of the Winds had not hesitated for a single moment but had set out at once to walk those eerie winds that constantly blow between the words. That act which Ithaqua had never once managed to persuade her to perform—despite his countless enticements, his myriad threats—she now undertook without a second thought. For she went, or so she thought, to the aid of her beloved Earthman, caught up in some nameless evil.

Silberhutte saw how well the plot had been laid and executed, and he heard the cynical, sniggeringly gleeful laughter of the ice-priest whose mind he had forced to reveal these things. He heard that laughter—heard it turn to a mental shriek, a cry of horror that went on and on, threat-

205

ening to tear his living soul from him and drag it down to hell—

—And then de Marigny was pulling him away from the pit, away from the headless ice-encased *thing* whose thin blood drenched his hands and arms and pinkly patterned the broad blade of his ax.

"Hank!" de Marigny cried, "what in all—?"

"No time, Henri," the Warlord answered, his voice a cracked whisper, his eyes suddenly deep sunken in a chalk-white face. "No time for explanations. Armandra is coming here—Ithaqua, too—and before they get here, we have to find the clock. I know where it is, and it's close. But remember: there are two more of these creatures on the loose down here. If we meet up with them . . . then we must kill them by whatever means are available to us. And be sure about one thing, Henri," he gripped the other's arm fiercely. "They *must* be killed; we daren't leave one of them alive! The universe will never be safe or sane as long as things like the ice-priests live. . . ."

Chapter Six

The Last Ice-Priest

THE TRIO of adventurers hurried from the shattered lair of the ice-priests, along the blue-glowing tunnel and out into the great gallery. As they went, the Warlord related all he had seen in the secret inner mind of the ice-priest. De Marigny immediately grasped most of what his friend had to say, but Moreen found Silberhutte's revelations much harder going.

The girl had no experience of Armandra, the Warlord's mate, and so found the idea of a mere woman walking on the winds that blow between the worlds hard to accept. And yet perhaps it really was so; indeed Moreen was not yet over the amazing way in which she herself had been transported between worlds; and had not that, too, been the work of this daughter of Ithaqua, this Armandra? But there would be time later, she told herself, for the pondering of such problems; for the moment it was an effort merely to keep pace with the two men, who seemingly raced against time itself.

Hurrying one-third of the way around the gallery's perimeter and ignoring several lesser burrows that branched off from it—including the one where the illusory insect-hounds had held Moreen and de Marigny prisoners—the Warlord unhesitatingly plunged headlong into a tunnel whose arched, icicle-festooned entrance was somewhat taller and wider than the rest. Racing along behind him, de Marigny and the girl followed the winding corridor of ice until, suddenly, they found themselves on a declining gradient down which it was as easy to slide as run. In a little while the sloping floor leveled out and then, coming around the final, gradual bend—

At first there was a reddish glow that lighted the ice walls and drowned their blue sheen in bronze tints, then a wash of heat that set the air to shimmering and caused the icicles of the high ceiling to drip as they slowly melted, and finally the bend was behind them while ahead they saw— the time-clock!

They saw it . . . *across a river of sluggishly moving lava!*

De Marigny was stunned, brought up short beside the Warlord where he had skidded to a halt on the wet ice not ten paces from the oozing flow of molten rock. The channel the lava followed entered the tunnel from a low, wide archway to the right, cut straight across the floor at right angles, and disappeared under a similar arch on the left. It was all of forty feet across, with a surface of powdery pumice that continually quivered and formed cracks, from which hissing clouds of steam emerged and an occasional tongue of red fire greedily licked.

Beyond the lava stream, leaning against a low mound of rocks and pebbles, with de Marigny's flying cloak in a heap at its base, the clock stood and seemed to waver in the heat haze rising from the lava barrier. De Marigny gazed longingly at the clock and knew it to be completely beyond his reach. He took a pace forward as if to defy the heat that already was searing his legs.

"How solid is that stuff?" he spoke over his shoulder to the Warlord. "I mean, would it take my weight if I—"

"No way," Silberhutte answered, placing a hand on the other's shoulder. "Look." He quickly shrugged out of his fur jacket and twirled it round his head, then let the heavy garment fly out over the lava to fall in the middle of the stream. It alighted, glowed instantly red at its fringed edges, burst into flame even as the scum of surface pumice quivered and parted beneath its weight.

The sight of Silberhutte's jacket sailing out across the molten rock had given de Marigny an idea, however, and now he moistened his dry lips as he turned to the Warlord. "Armandra's little winds!" he exclaimed. "If they could lift my cloak, float it across here—"

Now the Warlord was interested; a gleam of hope came into his eyes as he gripped de Marigny's shoulder. "Right!" he cried, turning to left and right, lifting his face and casting about in the sulphurous air for Armandra's familiar winds, finding—nothing.

"Not here?" de Marigny's voice echoed his disbelief, his disappointment. "Then where are they?"

Hearing his words, the Warlord started as from some sudden shock. The haggard look came back into his eyes as he turned to his friends. "I haven't contacted Armandra since we arrived on Dromos," he said. "At first I didn't want to, for if there was going to be trouble, I didn't want her following us here—better if she knew nothing of how things were. Now—well, she's coming anyway, called by those damned deceiving ice-priests. Yes, and she must be pretty close at that. Why else would her familiars leave us?"

"You think they've gone off to meet Armandra?" said de Marigny.

The Warlord nodded. "They must have. Wait—" He closed his eyes and a frown of mental effort gradually grew on his face.

De Marigny, not wanting to disturb the Warlord's concentration—knowing that he was attempting to contact Armandra telepathically, that the outcome would probably be vitally important—signaled Moreen's silence and himself kept perfectly still.

With the passing of a few more seconds the lines of effort on Silberhutte's face changed to lines of puzzlement, then of anger. Under his breath he said: "There's interference . . . those damned ice-priests . . . but I'm reaching her. . . ."

In the next moment the words, "Ithaqua—*damn his black heart!*" burst from Silberhutte's lips as, galvanized into frantic activity by what he had seen through Armandra's mind, he sped away back down the ice tunnel.

So as not to leave his friends completely in the dark as to his intentions, before passing out of sight around the curve of the frozen walls, he hoarsely called back: "Stay here, Henri. Do what you can. Armandra is almost here—but Ithaqua is closing in on her fast! I must see what I can do." Then he was gone, but echoing back to the two at the edge of the lava river came his final words: "Good luck. . . !"

"Luck, Hank!" de Marigny yelled back, frustration and a clutching sickness welling up in him that there was nothing he could do to help the situation. In desperation he turned his attention once again to the lava barrier that alone kept him from the time-clock.

For locked in that machine, built into it by Kthanid the Elder God, was a weapon whose power could stop even the awesomely powerful Great Old Ones—the Cthulhu Cycle Deities themselves, of which Ithaqua was one. If only there were some way to cross this slow-moving flood of molten rock, then the rest would be a matter of the utmost simplicity. But there was no such way across . . . was there?

Yes, there was, but it made de Marigny's mind, his soul and entire body cringe merely thinking of it. He knew if he dwelled upon it too long that he could never bring himself to face it. But face it he must, for there was too much at stake here.

He turned from the river of lava and took twenty deliberate paces up the ice corridor before halting and turning back. Moreen saw his intention and ran toward him. "You can't," she cried, "you can't! No man could leap that distance—it's too far."

"A hop, a skip, and a jump," he answered, gritting his teeth. "I could have done it once; perhaps I still can."

Trembling with horror, she stood back from him. "You'll broil your legs—the lava will strip them to the bone!—and what if you slip and fall?"

"Don't, Moreen!" he almost snarled. "I have to try." He faced the lava river, went into a half-crouch, and—

"No!" came a sharp mental command, booming and echoing in de Marigny's mind. *"No, Earthman, you are not to die here, not now. Ithaqua would not wish it so. He has his own plans for you—and for the girl."*

Maintaining his crouch and whirling into a defensive position, de Marigny's wide eyes found the crimson orbs of the ice-priest where the spindly giant had stepped from jagged shadows cast by a row of icy stalagmites. He prepared to launch himself at the gaunt creature, whose hands already were weaving strange patterns in the air; but a freezing coldness, a numbing paralysis was rapidly spreading through his limbs. In a moment the metamorphosis was complete; and with his muscles frozen into immobility, he toppled forward and crashed to the floor like a stone statue.

Now the ice-priest turned to Moreen, trapping her between himself and the molten rock river. Before he could fix her with his crimson eyes, however, or fascinate her with the mesmeric motions of his hands, she spun away from him and sped toward the lava. He swiftly followed, his eyes bright with a timeless lust, only pausing in his bony striding when the girl skidded to a halt close to the Warlord's discarded ax. She cast one terrified glance at her pursuer, then bent to grasp the great ax with both hands.

Laughing hideously in his mind, the ice-priest came on. She was a mere girl and could hardly lift the ax, much less put it to any use. Thus the incredibly ancient being believed, and possibly that was the way girls had been in olden Theem'hdra. This was why he now resorted to purely physical methods to take her, when he might easily have caught her by spinning a telepathic mind web. But he had not reckoned with Moreen's desperation, her determination.

As he came up to her, the girl straightened, turning to face him and dragging the ax with her. Such was the weapon's weight that she had to lean backward to control it as, rising up with her turning, the ax pulled her arms out straight. The great blade passed in front of the ice priest's middle and pulled the girl around with it. He moved closer, intending to throw his arms about her and put an end to this farce—until at last he saw his danger.

She had increased her rate of spin and already the blade was flashing around again, faster, inexorably, to the point where it would make a deadly connection. The ice-priest saw this and could not believe his eyes—saw, and the evil smile of triumph died on his monstrous face—died even as he was to die. The blade of the ax, still sharp for all its grisly work, came leaping around and sliced into his side, crippling him and knocking him from his feet. Before he could do more than writhe in agony on the floor, Moreen hauled the ax free and used her last ounce of strength to swing it at his mushroom-domed head, splitting it like an overripe melon. . . .

Moreen was still being sick when de Marigny limped up

211

to her, his face a mass of bruises and small cuts. He paused to touch her shoulder—then looked beyond her with eyes which could no longer credit the truth of anything they saw. For when the ice-priest had died, so too had died the illusory river of lava!

A few paces away, Silberhutte's jacket lay on the frozen floor of the tunnel untouched by fire. The clock, its four hands moving on their great dial in completely incomprehensible patterns, seemed almost to wait in silent sentience beyond. But at last its waiting was at an end.

Silberhutte had entered the great ice gallery and was on the point of plunging into that tunnel which led back to the volcano entrance to the frozen underworld. Such were his exertions that his breath came in great gasps and his legs and arms moved like massive pistons. All the time he sought mental contact with Armandra, but telepathic intrusions from some undetermined source close at hand kept interfering. Then, suddenly, his and his woman's minds locked onto each other, became as one, and he skidded and slid to a halt just within the mouth of the tunnel as Armandra herself came around a curving wall of ice toward him.

Armandra, the Woman of the Winds! And borne up by the very air, she floated into view, inches above the floor of the tunnel, her hair a golden halo that drifted above her, her face a carmine skull that glowed through her flesh, her white fur jacket and skirt alive with eerie motion. She came, and recognizing her man's presence, a shudder passed through her as she settled to the floor and the carmine light died in her eyes.

Then they were locked in each other's arms, locked physically and mentally, and their telepathic exchange was a barrage of passion and fear, of love and loathing as they told their tales in lightning-fast disorder; until at last the present loomed in on them and only one all-important fact remained uppermost in their minds. The fact that Armandra's awful father was close behind.

"How close?" Silberhutte asked out loud, taking her hand and hurrying her back along the way he had come, across the ice gallery toward the tunnel that led back to his friends, where—to his knowledge—they waited at the edge of a river of lava.

"He keeps his mind closed to me," she gasped, exhausted by her journey through the interplanetary void. "I don't know how close he is—but he's close, Hank, so close! I had the feeling he could have taken me at any moment, but that he deliberately held back. Now—"

She paused, her now green eyes opening wide as an almost electric shock of horror passed through her. They froze at the entrance to that tunnel whose sinuous folds contained the time-clock and fearfully looked back. A blast of cold air—so cold that even they could feel it—blew snow and ice particles into the gallery, setting the myriad hanging icicles to an eerie creaking, a tinkling and chiming. The temperature dropped further still, plummeted, and the white rime upon every surface visibly deepened, turning the blue glow from the ice walls to a scintillant glare of madly winking diamonds.

"He's here!" she cried, even as an awful shadow fell across the gallery, flowing like ink from the tunnel mouth where so recently they were reunited.

"Close your mind to him!" the Warlord warned. Then, the paralysis broken, he caught Armandra up and ran into the tunnel, ran to where a huge hump of ice loomed up from the floor, and carried Armandra into the temporary protection of its shadow. From that position he watched the gallery, saw the monster Ithaqua—shrunken now but still three times greater in size than any man—stride into view.

Ithaqua! Anthropomorphic, black figure of hell, cold and dark as the spaces between the stars which spawned him, inky blot of a head turning this way and that, carmine eyes gazing—but only for a moment—into the very tunnel where Silberhutte and Armandra hid from him. Then, when the monster would have passed them by—

"They're here, master, here!" came that treacherous telepathic voice in their minds, in Ithaqua's mind, too, from a source which only now made itself apparent.

It was as if the ice-priest had stepped out of thin air, or out of the walls of ice themselves; but now this sole survivor of his kind cast aside all magic and illusion to show himself, tall and gaunt—and cringing like a whipped dog before his monstrous master! One hand he used to fawningly beckon Ithaqua into the tunnel, urging him to hurry, while with the other he pointed out the hiding place of the Warlord and his woman.

And now Ithaqua came, webbed feet finding purchase on the icy floor, carmine eyes glaring suspiciously and massive fists clenched threateningly where they hung at his sides. He came, and the chill of empty space came with him, riming the walls and floor of the tunnel inches deep with frost in the space of only a few seconds. The ice-priest ran to greet him, held out spindly trembling arms to him in supplication—was paid for his services with one lightning sweep of the monster's arm that flattened him to the iron-hard ice of the wall like a swatted fly.

Thus the last of the ice-priests died.

Chapter Seven

Eruption!

AND AS IF that sole survivor of the immemorially ancient ice-priests had never existed—as if he had not been born evilly, lived evilly, and grown into the evil priesthood, finally to be snatched from the wrath of honest people and carried here by Ithaqua himself, only now to die so abruptly at the hands of that self-same storm-spawn—so the Wind-Walker ignored his shattered corpse and advanced into the tunnel.

His carmine gaze seemed to penetrate the ice-layered walls of volcanic rock, causing the tunnel to glow a dull pink, like a gateway to hell. And high though the ceiling was, still Ithaqua had to stoop to fit his monstrous manlike form into the icicle-festooned tunnel; and his vast blot of a head rocked from side to side as he advanced, step by step, toward that massive stump of ice that hid his quarry from his gaze.

Except that it seemed no longer to hide them . . .

Perhaps it was that he detected certain telepathic traces that they were unable to conceal—or that he sensed their fear—or simply that he knew instinctively where they were. Whichever, he ignored a dozen other great fangs of ice where they stuck up from the floor and made straight for their particular refuge. And as he came, so his head ceased its inquisitive side-to-side movement and he began to stretch out his fearful arms before him.

"*Run!*" Silberhutte commanded, his voice ringing in the shocked air like a pistol shot.

Taking Armandra's hand, he raced away with her down the frozen burrow toward the lava river, hidden from view by half a mile of winding, curving walls of ice. Ithaqua saw them at once and sent a blast of telepathic derision coursing after them—then came on himself, his vast strides effortlessly closing the distance between them as the two he pursued slipped and slithered in their haste, scurrying like mice before the sure tread of some demonic cat.

Looking back as Ithaqua's shadow began to overtake them, Silberhutte saw the monster pause, reach up, and snatch down from the ceiling an icicle with the girth of a barrel. In the next moment, guessing correctly the Wind-Walker's purpose, he gathered up Armandra on the run and leaped high as a ton of ice came crashing and careening down the corridor after them, bouncing and slithering like a juggernaut over the rippled floor. Another moment and the pair fell, Silberhutte cushioning Armandra's soft body with his own, amidst a chaos of shattering ice.

Half-stunned from the roaring of tortured ice—loud as an avalanche in the sounding walls of the tunnel—still the Warlord protected his woman as their bodies slowed to a halt, a tangle of arms and legs in a shivering of frozen fragments. Half-stunned he lay there as Ithaqua drew near and finally towered over them, his carmine gaze searing their very souls. Then, acting instinctively and with incredible bravado—despite the hellish ringing of mad, alien laughter in his head and the sure knowledge that this *must* be the last thing he would ever do—Silberhutte shook a mental fist in the face of the monster and charged his mind to fire one final telepathic salvo:

"Hell-Thing!" he cried. "Star-born spawn of an unholy mating between—"

But the Wind-Walker would hear no more. His eyes were sputtering pools of fiery rage as he reached down to sweep Armandra aside, sending her spinning half-conscious across the debris-littered floor. Then, deliberately, he lifted up one great webbed foot and poised it over the head of his mightiest mortal enemy—but before that awesome club could fall . . .

. . . A beam of purest white light lighted the tunnel, its needle tip searing the Snow-Thing's shoulder and sending him stumbling back, staggering away from his intended prey. Only for a single instant did that beam lick out, but in that solitary moment of time the changes wrought in Ithaqua were astounding. From a dumbly snarling, murderous beast-god he became a cringing, vaguely anthropomorphic shape that wavered like smoke, mewling telepathically as he backed away, holding his hands up before a bloated black face in which flinching carmine eyes were slitted now and full of—fear?

Fear, yes—even Ithaqua—for this was that power against which he could not stand, the power of the beneficent Gods of Eld—the cleansing beam of the time-clock's weapon!

Then Ithaqua turned and fled, bounding away down the ice tunnel, rapidly shrinking as he made of himself a smaller target, careening heedlessly from wall to wall as he sought to avoid that purifying needle of light which licked out after him again and again until he disappeared around the curve of the wall and was gone. And as de Marigny set the time-clock down on the ice-littered floor the Warlord was already helping Armandra to her feet, hugging her to him and offering her comfort as any man might comfort his woman.

Leaving the time-clock, it took de Marigny only a few seconds to convince Silberhutte and Armandra that they would suffer no harm from his fantastic machine. For all that it was a creation of the Elder Gods, it was not an extension of their power (except in the form of its single weapon) and could not cause them physical pain such as would be caused by one of the star-stones of ancient Mnar. Then it was simply a matter of bundling them in through the opening of the clock's panel, into that place where Moreen waited for them, an utterly fantastic place whose dimensions were greater—infinitely—than external appearances might ever account for.

Quickly de Marigny demonstrated the use of mental *rapport* in binding his passengers to the clock's sensory systems, and once they had the hang of it and were over their initial astonishment, then he flew that incredible vehicle of the Elder Gods out of the frozen underworld, up the massive throat of the volcano, and into the outer world of Dromos. There, stationary in the air above that mighty vent, he briefly explained his purpose in directing the clock's beam back down into it:

First, that if Ithaqua yet hid in the underworld, he might permanently be sealed in down there; and secondly, that the underworld itself was and had been a place of evil for so long that its door should not be left open on any sane or ordered universe. Then he said no more but triggered the clock's weapon to pour its ray with an ever-brightening glare into the volcano's vent.

For minutes he played the beam into the root of the volcano, continuously increasing its power until his passengers were obliged to quit the time-clock's scanners; for even though they viewed the scene outside with their minds, the sight threatened the mind's eye itself! And although he had used that awesome weapon before, even the clock's master did not know the full extent of its power, so that the great gout of flame that suddenly licked forth from the volcano's rim came as a complete surprise to him.

He lifted the clock high into the skies of Dromos then and watched that ancient cone fill with fiery life, spewing its molten heart miles into the air. A river of lava coursed down the side of the volcanic mountain, hissing and obscuring the view in clouds of steam from melting drifts of snow. In another moment a fantastic pyrotechnic display commenced—with lava bombs and flaring streamers of fire hurled in all directions—out of which, rising like a dread phoenix from the flames, came the black and once more gigantically bloated figure of the Wind-Walker, fleeing the fire and racing madly for those high-blowing currents of etherwind which only his feet knew, whose ways only he had ever wandered.

And as he cleared the rim of Dromos, so he saw the time-clock where it seemed to wait for him on the reaches of the void; and he threw up his great hands before his flinching eyes, knowing full well his vulnerability and that at any moment he must surely feel the fatal sting of de Marigny's ray. But no, the beam did not come, and slowly the Wind-Walker lowered his hands to stare in alien amazement at the time-clock where it faced him squarely across a distance of less than two hundred yards.

Now, in his expanded size, he dwarfed the clock completely, made of it the merest toy, which in his hands it had once been. But in de Marigny's hands, for all that it seemed so tiny, the clock was the most awful weapon. And still the beam did not come.

For long moments they stood thus high in the sky over Dromos—darkly looming Wind-God and coffin-shaped vehicle of unbelievable journeys and near-infinite power. Then, as at a mutual signal though none was given, they broke apart and went their separate ways; Ithaqua striding off, bemused beyond a doubt, into unknown star-spaces, and the time-clock winging ever faster inward, away from Dromos, past Numinos, down toward Borea itself. . . .

Much later Silberhutte was to ask de Marigny: "When you could have finished the monster for good, you didn't. Why?"

De Marigny was to shake his head in answer, replying: "No, something told me that that wasn't the way into Elysia. I remember that Titus Crow once told me much the same thing. And of course we don't know for sure that I could have killed him. Better to retain the threat of his extinction, I think, than to try to destroy him and fail."

But the Warlord's patience had left him. "I don't understand," he grated. "After all we've been through, couldn't you—"

"I am glad," Armandra had broken into the conversation, "that you let him go, Henri. My father always was, he is now, and he must always be. He is one of those elementary evils which *must* exist, so that we lesser sinners may be reminded where our ways may ultimately lead us."

"And I, too, am glad he lives," Moreen had added in her turn. "Once he flew with me all around Dromos, and he was gentle. Perhaps if we knew how to make him so, he would be gentle again. . . ."

"Perhaps," the Warlord had then grunted, subdued but unable to keep the cynicism out of his voice. "And perhaps not."

Epilogue

IT WAS ALL of three weeks later (Earthtime, for de Marigny still used the chronology of the Motherworld) when at last the time came around for him to take his departure from Borea. Three weeks, but it might easily have been a much shorter period had he felt able to tear himself away from the plateau and its polyglot tribes and peoples.

Now the adventurers stood together on the roof of the plateau surrounded by the many thousands of its inhabitants come to see the departure of the time-clock and its crew. The talking was all done, the farewells all said; and only the wind any longer had voice, blowing a thin rime of fine snow crystals across the flat roof and between the massed ranks of spectators, piping an eerie, far-distant tune.

Much had happened in the days since the return of the four to Borea. There had been a second visit, however brief, to Numinos to see Annahilde and carry her and her sons into the safety of the Isle of Mountains; several trips to the sunward side of Borea, where Silberhutte had discovered those tropic islands and lands so often dreamed of; one short mission of vengeance in the time-clock, undertaken solely on the insistence of the Warlord, to destroy utterly Ithaqua's totem temple out on the white waste and recruit the Children of the Winds in their thousands into the brotherhood of the plateau; yes, and banquets and tournaments and pleasurable things galore—

—Until finally de Marigny had said: "It's time," and

had gone off with Moreen to their rooms high on the plateau's rim.

And later Silberhutte had followed and the two men had talked, when for once Armandra kept out of her man's mind to let him make his own decisions. For this was the way she had known it must be sooner or later.

"Hank," de Marigny had said, when finally the conversation had led them to it, "I think your decision is the right one. If I were you, I would do the same thing."

"You don't know what I've decided," the other pointed out.

"Oh, I do," de Marigny answered. "And if ever I return to the Motherworld, I'll tell them that you're a king in Borea—that you rule all the tribes of the south, where an auroral sun always shines, however strangely—and that your queen is strange and beautiful beyond belief. I'll tell them that you walk on the wings of the wind there together, and that no man was ever so loved . . . or so lucky."

"That we walk the winds together, Henri?" the Warlord had raised his eyebrows in question. "Armandra is Itha-qua's daughter, yes—and she walks the wind when the fancy takes her, granted—but I remain earthbound, my friend."

"No more, Warlord!" the other had laughed, handing over a silken bundle which Silberhutte at once recognized as being the flying cloak.

"Henri, I couldn't accept your—"

"Why not? I've no further use for it now that the time-clock is mine again." And before the other could further protest, de Marigny had asked: "Will you tell them that Moreen and I are leaving, and that we'd like everyone to see us off from the roof?"

And now they stood together on the roof: Armandra and the Warlord, Tracy Silberhutte and Jimmy Franklin, Oontawa and Kota'na, with all of the plateau's Elders ringing them about and the tribes thronging behind. Only the sad winds spoke, until Armandra, unable to bear the silence any longer, her golden voice full of anguish, begged:

"Must you go?"

As if in answer, of its own accord, the panel in the front

of the time-clock swung open, and the four hands on its weirdly hieroglyphed dial commenced moving in a different pattern, a new and unfathomable sequence.

Then, without another word, de Marigny and Moreen passed into the clock and became part of the purple light that softly pulsed within.

Behind them, the panel clicked shut. . . .

ON SALE WHEREVER PAPERBACKS ARE SOLD
—or use this coupon to order directly from the publisher.

FANTASY / HORROR

H. P. LOVECRAFT

ON SALE WHEREVER PAPERBACKS ARE SOLD
—or use this coupon to order directly from the publisher.

SCIENCE FICTION

FROM THE MASTERS OF THE GENRE

POUL ANDERSON

☐ 12040689	INHERITORS OF EARTH	$1.25
☐ 12032744	ORBIT UNLIMITED	$1.25
☐ 12037438	A WORLD NAMED CLEOPATRA	$1.50

JOSE FARMER

☐ 12040713	MOTHER WAS A LOVELY BEAST	$1.25
☐ 12045951	TONGUES OF THE MOON	$1.50

THEODORE STURGEON

☐ 12044673	A WAY HOME	$1.50
☐ 12044590	STARSHINE	$1.50
☐ 12044772	STURGEON IN ORBIT	$1.50

A.E. VAN VOGT

☐ 12044269	AWAY AND BEYOND	$1.75
☐ 12044129	DESTINATION: UNIVERSE!	$1.50